a season of you

a season of you

Emma Douglas

St. Martin's Paperbacks

This is a work of fiction. All of the characters, organizations, and events portrayed in this novel are either products of the author's imagination or are used fictitiously.

A SEASON OF YOU

Copyright © 2017 Emma Douglas.

All rights reserved.

For information address St. Martin's Press, 175 Fifth Avenue, New York, NY 10010.

ISBN: 978-1-250-11100-5

Our books may be purchased in bulk for promotional, educational, or business use. Please contact your local bookseller or the Macmillan Corporate and Premium Sales Department at 1-800-221-7945, ext. 5442, or by e-mail at MacmillanSpecialMarkets@macmillan.com.

Printed in the United States of America

St. Martin's Paperbacks edition / October 2017

St. Martin's Paperbacks are published by St. Martin's Press, 175 Fifth Avenue, New York, NY 10010.

10 9 8 7 6 5 4 3 2 1

For my Nana, who made all kinds of art, and my Grandad, who loved a good Scotch.

acknowledgments

As always, a big thank-you to the great team at St. Martin's, including my lovely editor, Eileen. And to Miriam Kriss for continuing excellent agent-fu. Thanks to the lovely Lulus for general cheering on and awesomeness and to Sarah for never agreeing when I think my books in progress suck. Lastly, thank you to all the awesome readers out there, you rock!

Right this time of year, everybody's warm
Singing songs of merry, sheltered from
the storm
But this time of year, a ghost rides by my
side
And it sounds so much like you, love, still
whispering goodbye

From "This Time of Year"
Track 7, *Blacklights on the*
Christmas Tree, Blacklight 1998

chapter one

"Not to misquote Monty Python or anything, but that is an ex-tire." Mina Harper stared at the back of her Jeep and fought the urge to kick the offending wheel. No point making it any flatter. It was already doing an annoyingly good imitation of a squished and melted doughnut as it was.

From the rear seat, her yellow Lab, Stewie, whined, nose pressed against the window. Mina looked up and then straightened, gripping her flashlight tighter in her left hand. Stewie wasn't happy about still being inside the car while she was outside. She wasn't happy about being outside in the freezing weather.

She pulled the collar of her coat tighter around her neck as a gust of wind flattened her bangs against her face with an icy touch. She'd only been out of the car a couple of minutes and she was already chilled. And getting damp. Raindrops were hitting the ground around her with increasing frequency, the sound of them pinging on the roof of the Jeep just audible over the wind. "You're better off in there, dopey dog," she said, pressing her hand briefly against the window to reassure Stewie.

As if in agreement, thunder rumbled in the distance, setting Stewie off into a flurry of barking. Great. That was all she needed.

She stared up at the sky, trying to gauge the weather. It was nearly midnight and the sky was a mess of gray, black, and stormy blue clouds, no stars to be seen. Not a sky she'd want to paint. The kind that made it hard to judge the distance of a storm.

And not the kind of sky that Lansing Island usually got in early November. Sure it was fall, but the island was off the coast of California. Winters were cool, not freezing.

The icy wind stinging her eyes was apparently unaware it was behaving unseasonally. Really, she should have known things weren't going to go smoothly tonight when she'd turned on the car radio to discover that Lansing's local station had decided to start with the Christmas music already. "Santa Got Run Over by a Reindeer" was going to be stuck in her head for days now. She'd turned the radio off when they'd started playing "This Time of Year," an old Blacklight song. The holidays were hard enough without hearing her dead father sing about them.

"This was meant to be an easy night, Stewie," she muttered as she waited, eyes peeled for any signs of lightning. If she was going to be kneeling on wet ground next to a big metal thing and holding a tire iron, she really didn't want to do it in a lightning storm.

Flash-fried Mina was not going to be on the menu. If the storm got worse, she'd suck it up and call Nicolai who ran Cloud Bay's biggest garage and operated the island's only tow truck. He'd be cranky if she called him out to change a tire at midnight, but she'd rather deal with cranky Nicolai than massive bolts of electricity dropping from the sky onto her head.

But she didn't see any flashes, so after another watchful minute, breathing icy sea-scented air, she made her way around to the back of the Jeep and opened the rear door to dig out her jack. She knew how to change a tire. And she could do it in less time than it would take Nicolai to get to her. It was just going to be a thoroughly cold, wet, and annoying experience.

She stretched briefly, trying to ease her shoulders— sore from a long day of painting—dragged out the tarp she carried for emergencies and dumped it onto the ground behind her, and then found the set of hazard lights she also kept stashed in the back.

Her half-frozen fingers fumbled as she tried to extract the jack, but eventually she got it. Her back protested a little as she heaved the spare tire free, but she managed. Stewie whuffled nervously at her the entire time, straining his harness to look over the back seat to where she stood. "You stay in the warm, buddy," she said. She didn't want to have to wrangle an overly eager Labrador on top of everything else. Not to mention that she didn't want to have to give Stewie the bath that would be inevitable if she let him out to splash around in the puddles rapidly forming around her feet. Stewie had never met a body of water—no matter how tiny—he didn't like.

She set the lights at the front and rear of the car, then

carried the last one back to set by the flat tire. Lansing Island didn't exactly have much traffic at midnight, but better safe than sorry.

Right. She still had thirty minutes before she had to report for her shift. So she could do this. Would do this.

She spread the tarp, which would at least keep her clothes clean if not dry, but as she twisted and leaned down to switch on the hazards, her foot slipped and she fell, flashlight flying out of her hand.

"Fuck," was about all she had time to think before her head hit the side of the car.

Will Fraser frowned out the window of the office above the Salt Devil Distillery, trying to see through the rain starting to pour down. He'd seen a car pull up, leaving the headlights on, and then what he assumed was a flashlight bobbing around, and had been wondering if he should call Nicolai and tell him someone might be broken down half a mile down the road. But just now, the flashlight had moved weirdly. And now he could swear it was lying on the ground some distance from the car.

The window fogged with his breath and he rubbed a patch clear with his flannel shirtsleeve, straining to peer through the rain and darkness. The flashlight wasn't moving. Not a good sign.

Looked like he'd be going out into the rain himself. Awesome. He'd thought that sitting down to do some paperwork for the bar had been the pits on a Saturday night. Now he was going to get soaked into the bargain.

He moved quickly as he pulled on a coat and grabbed a beanie off the rack that stood near the office door.

Lansing Island had a pretty mild climate—it was California after all—but so far the fall had been cooler than usual. Add in the rain, and the weather tonight was definitely not what you wanted to be out in for long.

Five minutes later he pulled up facing the Jeep on the side of the road, his headlights illuminating Mina Harper lying beside it, not moving.

"Fuck," he breathed, heart suddenly hammering. Then he bolted out of his car, not caring about rain or wind or anything other than getting to Mina.

He reached her side and dropped to his knees, ignoring the furious barks of her dog who was still inside the Jeep.

His fingers found the pulse on the side of her neck. The steady beat made him feel suddenly weak with relief.

Alive.

Okay. Alive was good. In fact it was fantastic. And she hadn't been lying there long, assuming she'd fallen when he'd seen the flashlight go flying. Less than ten minutes.

His headlights gave him enough light to see by as he carefully felt his way down the arm she wasn't lying on and then did the same with her legs. He and his brother Stefan kept their first aid training up to date in case anything ever happened in the bar attached to the distillery. This was the first time he'd ever had to put that training into action for anything more serious than a burn or a cut finger. He focused on breathing and continued his assessment. Nothing obviously broken.

Just a limp, unconscious girl. Not good.

Her rear tire was flat as a pancake and there was a

tire iron on the tarp near it. Clearly she'd been about to change the flat. Might have been smarter to wait for help in this weather, but he could hardly go back in time and argue with her about that particular decision.

Nope, he had to work out what to do right now.

Maybe she'd slipped and banged her head. It seemed the most likely scenario as he thought about the small arc of light flying through the air that had caught his attention. A slip, then her letting go of the flashlight as she stumbled and hit her head. That would explain how she might have passed out. In an ideal world he'd stabilize her neck, but he didn't have anything to do that with and, as lightning suddenly flashed in the not-really-so-distant distance, he decided he didn't want to wait for the paramedics to arrive.

If she'd just slipped, it was doubtful she could have hurt her neck in a major way. A lightning strike would do more damage to both of them than him moving her could.

Okay. So that was the plan. Move her. Take her to the clinic in Cloud Bay. He climbed to his feet, jogged to his car, and opened the passenger door. Then he went back for Mina.

He had no doubt he could lift her. Mina was all fine lines and big eyes. Tallish but slender. Too slender lately. She'd gained back a bit of the weight she'd lost after her husband had died, but she was still thinner than she should be. He doubted she weighed more than an empty whiskey barrel, and he spent enough time lugging those around. Plus, she was a lot easier to get his arms around than a barrel. He knelt again, maneuvered his arms around her gently. She groaned, a small muffled noise, as he lifted her awkwardly and rose to his feet.

Sound was a good sign, right? Meant she was coming around. But her eyes were still closed and now that he could see all her face, he could also see that there was quite a bit of blood on it. He clamped down on the urge to do something about it. Head wounds always bled like stuck pigs. Better to get her to the doc than fuss too much with the blood. He had a small first aid kit in the car; he could find some gauze once she was safely out of the weather.

By the time he reached his car, Mina's eyelids were fluttering. He slid her into position in the passenger seat and strapped the seat belt around her. As he straightened, her eyes flew open and she started to turn her head.

"What—" She stopped, put a cautious hand to her head. "Owwww."

"It's okay. Stay still," he said.

"Will?" She sounded confused, tugged at the strap of the seat belt. "What?"

"I think you fell. I found you lying on the road. You were out cold. I'm taking you to the doc."

She blinked. Her eyes—dark in this light but a storm-tossed shade of green gray she shared with her half brother and half sister by day—looked huge in her face. She was too pale beneath the blood stains. Then she shivered.

Cold. Right. He needed to get her out of here.

"Stay still," he repeated, and came around the car to turn the heater up. Then he shut the door and went to the trunk to find his first aid kit. The blast of warm air when he got back to the passenger door was welcome. His face and hands were starting to feel numb in the wind, and despite his coat and hat, the cold was seeping into his bones.

Mina's eyes were closed again.

"You still with me, Mina?" he asked and she opened them, a little slower than he liked. Concussion, maybe. That meant he was supposed to keep her awake. He took a gauze pad out of the kit, unpeeled it from its wrapping, and pressed it gently to her forehead.

"Hold that in place." Giving her something to focus on should help keep her awake. "The doc will clean you up but that will help stop the bleeding. Don't nod," he added. "I'm guessing your head feels like crap. Just hold that gauze there and I'll have you at the clinic in no time at all."

Despite his warning, she shook her head. Carefully, but definitely. "Stewie," she said.

That damn dog. He'd forgotten all about him. A glance at the Jeep revealed Stewie had twisted around in the back seat and was glaring through the rear windscreen, barking wildly. Not happy about being parted from his mistress.

Will had never seen Stewie look anything but good-natured before. Mina hardly ever went anywhere without the big yellow Lab, and he seemed to be one of those dogs who loved everybody. Hopefully he didn't think that Will was hurting Mina and decide to show a more protective side. Because Mina was right. It wasn't fair— or safe—to leave the dog in her Jeep alone.

"Is the car unlocked or do you have the keys?"

"Pocket," she managed. "Jacket."

He hoped she meant an outer pocket. Because, God help him, he really didn't want to put his hands under her clothes and pat her down to find the keys. But as luck would have it, the keys were in the first pocket he tried.

He pulled them out, shaking them in front of her face to get her attention. "Okay. Stay awake, I'll get your beast," he said.

The rain was pounding now and he had a fleeting image of what wet and dirty Labrador feet were going to do to the leather of his back seat. But he'd restored his Mustang once. He could do it again if he had to.

Stewie was still barking his head off as Will opened the front door of the Jeep. He'd rolled up the tarp, the tire iron, and the jack into a bundle and stuffed it onto the floor in front of the passenger seat. The flashlight he'd stuck into his jacket pocket.

"Calm down, dog," Will grumbled at Stewie, keeping his voice friendly, hoping Stewie would relax a little. The barks subsided so maybe he'd found the right tone.

Mina's purse was on the passenger seat so he grabbed that and turned off the headlights before he moved to the back to get Stewie. The dog was so pleased to see him, wriggling and dancing in place on the seat, it took longer than it should have to get him free of his harness and out of the car. Mina had left his lead attached which made things a little easier, but Stewie still leapt and barked and tried to lick Will's face off as Will locked the Jeep.

By the time they got back to his car and Will had harnessed Stewie in the back seat, he was worried that Mina had fallen asleep.

But as Stewie barked at her, she opened her eyes and said "Quiet" in a voice that wasn't much more than a whisper.

To Will's surprise, Stewie obeyed, settling back down to lie on the seat though he kept his head turned toward Mina, a soft whine escaping him.

Will settled into the driver's seat and started the car. He pulled out his phone and called the clinic to let Callie, the doc there, know they were coming, and then pulled out on to the road. Mina's eyes were drifting closed again.

He needed to keep her talking. "Where were you going at this time of night in the rain?" he asked because it was the first thing he could think of.

"Work. Had a shift at search and rescue," Mina said. Her voice was still too soft, and he pushed the Mustang a little, going as fast as he dared on the wet road as they head toward Cloud Bay, the island's only town.

"Midnight shift? What are you, a glutton for punishment?" Working marine search and rescue was a weird enough thing to want to do in Will's book—he'd never liked boats or the ocean much—but working the midnight shift seemed even worse. Particularly when you considered that Mina's dad had been Grey Harper, lead singer of Blacklight—one of the biggest bands in the world in their time. He was fairly certain Mina Harper never needed to work a day in her life if she didn't want to. He liked that she chose to work anyway. It was one of the many things he liked about her.

"I don't mind. Night owl," she said.

Her voice was a little soft but she was making sense, and that was a good sign.

"Do I need to call them for you? Let them know you're not going to be in?"

"I'll be okay."

"Mina, you've banged your head up pretty good there. You were knocked out. There's no way the doc is going to let you go to work tonight."

Her expression turned mulish.

Okay, perhaps a different subject. Thing was, he didn't really know what to talk about. He knew who she was. All too well. But she seemed mostly oblivious to his existence. And they'd never exactly had a heart-to-heart.

Their paths crossed occasionally but it was Mina's older sister, Faith, who Will knew best of the three Harper siblings.

Faith at least came into Salt Devil occasionally, these days mostly with her guy, Caleb White in tow.

But Mina had never set foot in the bar since her husband had died. Not that she'd come often before then. Which was understandable. Grey Harper had been an alcoholic, even if he'd managed to be mostly sober in his later years.

Will could see why that might put you off drinking.

But he took it as a sign that the universe had a pretty evil sense of humor. Because he, Will Fraser—whiskey distiller, bar owner, and descendant of a whole bunch of hardheaded Scotsmen who'd never said no to a dram—had had a full-blown hopeless thing for Mina Harper since he'd first laid eyes on her, nearly six years ago.

Of course, the fact that he'd been smitten by Mina—who'd been only eighteen not to mention already engaged—when Will and Stefan had moved to Lansing was sign enough that the universe sucked.

"Why do you bring Stewie to work?" he asked, not

wanting to think about his oh-so-dumb-crush. He'd spent six years trying not to think about it, so he had plenty of practice. And right now there were more important things to focus on. Like getting them both safely into town through the crazy weather.

"Mostly because I can," Mina said. She shifted the position of the gauze on her head with a wince. Will risked a glance. The white cotton was stained red.

"Keep that where it is," he ordered. Then, when Mina winced again as she pressed the gauze back in place, "I guess if I had a workplace where I could bring my dog, I would too."

"Do you have a dog?" Mina said.

"No. Maybe one day. Not much room in my apartment for a pooch, and I work some crazy hours." Starting up a distillery was a lot of work. Not to mention that he and his brother Stefan had opened a bar on the property as well to bring in some cash while their first batch of whiskey aged. Bars, it turned out, were a lot of work too. Stefan handled the kitchen and Will tended bar, and they had a couple of waitresses and waiters who helped out on weekends or during summer but it was still a lot of work. They opened at five and didn't close until midnight unless things were dead. Add on prep time and clean-up and the work of the distillery and all the admin that went with running two businesses, and his work week tended to be long.

"Dogs are good," Mina said, sounding a little out of it.

"Yes," he agreed. "How's your head feeling?" Dumb question, but he needed to keep her talking.

Mina grimaced. "Like I whacked it on something. And my shoulder hurts."

"Do you remember what happened?"

"Not really. I was changing the tire. I guess I slipped. Then you were there." She turned her head slowly. "Why were you there?"

"We can see that strip of road from the office upstairs at the bar," he said. "I saw the car stop. Was going to call Nicolai to go check it out if it didn't start again in a few minutes. Then I saw your flashlight go flying and thought I'd better come down and see if whoever it was needed help." He gestured at the rain beating down on the windshield, coming almost faster than the wipers could deal with it. "Not a good night to be caught outdoors."

"That was nice of you," she said.

"That's me. Will Fraser, doer of good deeds." He tried to relax his hands where they were gripping the wheel too tightly.

They were nearly at the outer edge of Cloud Bay now. The town wasn't very large. The cluster of stores and restaurants and businesses in its center took up a couple of streets, and then there was a mix of houses and the odd small apartment building and a few other businesses that needed more space than the main streets could offer. The clinic—which wasn't big enough to be called a hospital but did offer an ER service—was a couple of streets behind Main Street.

As they pulled up in front of the clinic, the door opened and Callie Walsh, one of the two doctors in town, appeared holding a large umbrella. She dashed across to his car and knocked on the window. He wound it down.

"Can she walk? Do we need a wheelchair?" Callie asked.

"I can carry her," Will said. "Faster than a chair."

"I can walk," Mina muttered.

"You don't know that," Will retorted. "Now stay still and let the doc take care of you."

chapter two

Mina had to admit that she'd probably been wrong about the walking thing. Her head swam when Will lifted her carefully out of the car, and she had to close her eyes and swallow hard for a minute, not entirely sure she wasn't going to barf all over him. Which would be kind of mortifying.

To her relief, she didn't. "What about Stewie?" she asked as they started for the clinic.

"Mina, we can't have a dog in the clinic," Callie said. She was about five foot three, topped with red hair that curled wildly and bright blue eyes. Hardly a daunting figure, but her tone made it clear there'd be no arguments. "He's not a guide dog or a service dog, so the rules say no."

The rules were dumb. "But—"

"He'll be fine in Will's car for a little while. Let me take a look at you. Then we can figure out if we need a longer-term solution for Stewie tonight."

Her head really hurt too much to keep arguing. The clinic was very bright, and she closed her eyes against the glare and the stabs of pain it caused.

"Put her down here," Callie said. Will lowered her onto something soft. She opened her eyes again. She was lying on a hospital bed. Or an examination table. Something that looked like it was straight out of *Grey's Anatomy*. The back of it was raised, so she didn't have to lie flat. The room was warmer than Will's car but she still felt cold. Mostly, she realized, because her clothes were wet, the soggy fabric chilling her skin where the rain had soaked her jeans and trickled under the neck of her jacket.

"I'm pretty wet," Mina said.

"We can cope with that," Callie said. "Water is hardly the worst thing that gets on the sheets around here. We'll warm you up but I need to check you out first." She came around to Mina's side, studying her for a minute. Then she started poking and prodding her with ruthless efficiency. Limbs and neck checked. Pulse and blood pressure taken, questions asked about who was president and what day it was. In between questions, Mina tried to focus on Will to take her mind off the pain. He stood near the bed, worry clear in his hazel eyes.

Nice eyes, she thought vaguely. Why hadn't she noticed his eyes before? But before she had time to think anything more about Will, Callie started to peel the gauze away from the wound on Mina's head, which brought all her attention back to the present with an "Ouch!" of protest.

In reply, Callie made an unintelligible little noise. From which Mina guessed it didn't look pretty.

"Okay. Good." Callie found another dressing and pressed it into place gently. "I'll take care of that in a minute. First, I want to do a CT."

"You can do that here?" Will asked.

Callie nodded. "We're pretty well set up. Thanks to the Harpers." She nodded at Mina with a smile. Mina fought the urge to close her eyes. People on the island tended to love her dad. He'd been generous to the community, no one could deny that. But that didn't mean he'd always been a great guy. Or a great Dad. But since he'd died, there were a lot of people who seemed to be forgetting the not-so-good parts. It was weird to see someone you had known and loved and despaired of sometimes being turned into a myth.

"Mina's dad made some substantial donations over the years, so we have good toys to play with. Enough so that we can start figuring out what's wrong while the choppers are getting here from the mainland if they're needed. We don't have an MRI—we'd need a bigger building for that—but X-ray and CT we can do."

"I've only come here for checkups or shots," Will said.

"And let's hope it stays that way," Callie said. "I like it when my patients have nice normal medical issues." She smiled again at Mina. "Not that you have something abnormal but I just want to make sure. Now, before I get you into a gown and take you next door for the scan, does anywhere else hurt? Other than your head?"

"My shoulder," Mina said. She'd been focused mostly on her headache but the shoulder was making a play to be noticed as well, aching and throbbing in concert with her head.

Callie frowned. "Right or left?"

"Right."

"She was lying on that side when I found her," Will said.

"Okay." Callie pressed her fingers gently into Mina's shoulder. The resultant jab of pain made her gasp, but Callie just frowned and continued feeling her way around the joint. Finally she stepped back. "It's not dislocated. Hopefully just bruised. We'll check it out in the CT scan too. Anything else?"

"No."

"All right. So let's get you out of these wet clothes. Will can wait in the waiting room. There's a coffee machine there, Will. And a vending machine. Maybe you can take Stewie a cookie."

Will looked like he wanted to argue, but Callie gave him another of her "I'm the doctor here and I make the rules" looks and he just nodded.

"I'll call the S and R station for you," Will said. "Anyone else you want me to call?"

Mina shook her head. "No."

"No? What about Faith?"

"She and Caleb are off-island. Spending a week in New York." Which was a good thing. Faith had been glowingly happy in the six months since she'd met Caleb White, happier than Mina could remember seeing her since . . . well, probably since before Grey died.

That earned her a frown from both Callie and Will.

"Well then, how about Lou?" Will asked.

Did he know that Lou wasn't actually her mom? He'd only moved to the island a few years ago. After Grey had died. She didn't think he could have ever met Emmy. But

Lou had raised her, and that was what counted. She was the one that Mina would have turned to if not for one small problem. "She's gone too. Danny's in LA and she went to see him play. I think she gets back tomorrow."

She couldn't quite remember through the headache. She resisted the urge to rub her forehead. She'd already discovered that didn't help. "It's fine. It's just a bump on the head. Tell the station. And Stewie might need to— you know." She bit her lip. It was weird to be asking Will, who she didn't really know, to take care of her dog.

Will nodded, suddenly looking determined to get out of there. She couldn't blame him. His Mustang was gorgeous. She knew from Faith he'd restored it himself. If she loved a car like Will loved that Mustang, then she wouldn't be keen on the idea of a dog peeing in it either.

As Will left, she forced herself to relax, carefully lowering her head back against the pillow. Callie produced a towel and then a gown and helped Mina change, which was a slow process. But at least a hospital gown— as hideous as they were—was easy to slide up her arm so her shoulder didn't have to move too far. Between it and the headache, she was starting to look forward to the part where she got the good drugs. Was she allowed to have the good stuff? She couldn't remember what you were supposed to do for a concussion. Given that she had regular first aid training as part of her search and rescue work, that couldn't be a good sign. But trying to remember just made her head feel worse, so she gave up and let Callie ease her back onto the bed and pile warmed blankets over her.

Whoever had invented blanket warmers should be given a medal. The warmth surrounded her, driving the chill from her bones. If it hadn't been for the aching head and the throbbing shoulder, she might have even relaxed.

"I'll be back in one sec," Callie said. "Let me get Rafe to help me wheel you next door."

Mina wasn't exactly in a hurry to go anywhere. Not while the evil little gremlins who were currently tap dancing in spiked boots over her head were still there. Before long Callie came back with Rafe, one of the nurses who worked at the clinic.

"Hey, Mina," he said, brown eyes smiling as the two of them started to wheel her out of the room. He was about a foot taller than Callie, all long brown limbs. "How's that big dog of yours?"

"He's good." Rafe and his boyfriend, Kent, had acquired their cocker spaniel puppy at the same time Mina had bought Stewie. They'd done puppy training together. Though Rafe's Loki tended to live up to his namesake and be the naughtiest dog in the class, he and Stewie had always been friendly. They were always happy to see each other when their paths crossed on one of the dog beaches.

They reached their destination and Rafe and Callie helped her onto the narrow table of the CT machine. It jolted a little. She winced.

Rafe leaned over her, adjusting the position of her head. His smile was sympathetic. "Just a little longer. Then Callie will be able to give you something for the pain."

Painkillers. That sounded like an awesome plan. Best damn plan she'd heard anyone mention all day in fact.

Will blew on his hands as he walked back through the clinic doors into the waiting room. It had been nearly

an hour since Callie had shooed him out and he'd been
alternating sitting out in his car with Stewie and hanging around the waiting room watching ESPN, which
was about the only thing he could find on the TV that
was bearable at this time of night. Though replays of old
baseball games were not exactly a distraction from the
fact that he was tired and nervous about how badly Mina
was hurt. Which was kind of stupid.

She wasn't any business of his.

At least, not after tonight.

Despite Will's best efforts to keep him company,
Stewie had managed to chew up the back seat of the
Mustang pretty well in the stretches of time he'd been
left alone. He apparently didn't like being kept away
from Mina either.

Will couldn't blame him for that. And he was too
tired to be too annoyed about the seat. It could be replaced. He just hoped Stewie hadn't actually swallowed
much of it—though from what he could see the leather
was mostly shredded rather than eaten—because he
didn't want to have to find a vet in the middle of the
night if the damn fool dog had made himself sick.

He tried to stop himself yawning as he sat back in
the chair with the best view of the TV. The coffee machine's little red light winked temptation at him. He resisted. He'd already had one cup. If he had another he'd
probably be awake all night.

Before he could decide if death by caffeine was the
way to go, Callie came through the door. His heart
started to pound. "Is Mina okay?"

Callie nodded, her smile reassuring, though that didn't
calm his pulse down any. "Yes. You can come on back."

He followed her as she turned on her heel and headed back the way she'd come.

"She had a mild concussion," Callie said. They reached the door of the examination room and he held it open for her. "Which is what I want to talk to you about."

Mina was lying on the same bed, covered by pale green cotton hospital blankets. Her head wound had been properly dressed and her face cleaned up. She turned her head slowly as they came into the room. She still looked too pale but not as bad as she had when they'd arrived, her short dark hair not quite so stark a contrast to her skin.

"Okay," Callie said. "So here's the deal. Like I said, Mina has a mild concussion. There's no fracture in her shoulder and no tear that I can see—we send the scans off-island to get a specialist to look at them too for confirmation—so I'm chalking that one up as bad bruising or a sprain for now. She could go home, but she needs someone to be with her. I need someone to check on her during the night a couple of times. If not, I'll keep her here overnight."

"I want to go home," Mina said.

"I could stay with her, " Will said without thinking.

Mina frowned. "No, I've caused you enough trouble. Ivy or Leah will come if we call them."

"Why wake them up?" he said. "I'm already here and in the time it would take one of them to get organized and come get you, I could already have you—and Stewie—back home."

"But—"

"I know you and I don't know each other very well,

but you know that Faith and Caleb hang out with me, right? I'm sure they'd vouch I'm not a serial killer. And unlike, Leah or Ivy, I can catch up on my sleep during the day because I don't have to open the bar until five. You said Lou would be back tomorrow—" He checked his watch. It was nearly one thirty. "Well, later today. She can take over then."

Callie was nodding encouragingly. "That sounds like a sensible plan to me," she said. "You'll sleep better if you're home and not worrying about Stewie. I'm just a phone call away."

"I—"

"Just give in," Will said. "There's no reason to refuse." He watched her for a minute, wondering if she really had something against him or whether she was just trying to be polite. He didn't know. But either way, he wanted to help. Hell, if he was honest, he was happy just to spend some time with her. Which was lame and pathetic. He knew that. But it didn't change the fact she needed help and he was happy to give it, just as he would for anyone who wound up in her position.

"Okay," Mina said. She closed her eyes briefly. "Thank you."

"Great," Callie said, smiling at Will. She looked down at the chart in her hand briefly. "She's had some Tylenol. Next dose in three hours or so. Can't give her anything stronger than that for the first few days until we're sure there's nothing worse going on with her head. So her shoulder might still hurt. She can ice it, if that helps. Ice for the first few days then heat. She needs to come back in tomorrow afternoon so I can check on her. She should rest, keep things quiet for a few days. No exercise. No lifting anything heavy." She reeled off a list of other things Mina could or couldn't do. "I'll print you the list so Lou knows too."

Will nodded. "Stefan had a concussion a few years ago. He came off his surfboard and it whacked him on the head. So I know the drill."

Mina was quiet all the way home, other than answering the questions he asked her at intervals to make sure she was staying awake. She spent most of the journey with her eyes closed. Which was fine. If she kept them closed, she hopefully wouldn't notice the holes that Stewie had chewed in his back seat. Holes he had no intention of bringing to her attention.

"Not long now," he said and got a nod in reply.

He knew his way to her house, given it was on the same property as her sister's. He'd jogged past the lighthouse and the cottage that hugged its base often enough when he did beach runs. Technically the beach around the Harper's place, and the properties owned by the other members of Blacklight that sat to either side of it, were private, but none of them seemed to care too much about that rule when it came to locals. As long as they didn't try to do anything too crazy. Apparently his infrequent runs along the beach didn't count as crazy.

So he was familiar with Mina's cottage, which stood nestled at the foot of the island's lighthouse. Even glimpsed her a time or two. But he'd never been inside and he was kind of curious to see what it looked like.

It was a cool place to live. Right on the edge of the land, nothing blocking the view to the horizon. As far as he was concerned, dry land was definitely the best place to view the ocean from.

When they reached the outer gate to the Harper property he rolled the car to a stop. "Mina, I need the gate code."

Her eyelids fluttered open. "Huh?"

"Code for the gate," Will repeated. "We're almost there but I don't think your security guys would like me ramming through the gate."

She blinked sleepily. He sympathized. Callie's waiting room coffee was wearing off. Hopefully Mina had coffee at her place, because if he was going to stay awake all night and keep tabs on her, more caffeine would definitely be needed.

"Zero nine one six five four," Mina said.

"Guess your brain can't be too rattled if you remembered that," Will said, reaching through the open window to type in the code. "Luckily it's not fingerprint or something. You'd have to go out in the cold again." The rain had stopped but the night air was still doing a good impression of having been imported from Antarctica. Mild California climate, his ass.

"Ivy wanted to do something like that," Mina said. "Faith said it was too complicated with so many people coming and going."

Ivy Morito was one of Faith's friends, and a genius with computers. She did security for most of the people on the island who had security systems and ran a web design business on the side. She'd done both the website and the security for the bar. She'd wanted to give them all sorts of fancy features as well, but Will and

Stefan had kept it simple. Nice to know they weren't the only ones.

Poor Ivy. She could probably make three times what she earned if she went back to L.A. or somewhere with lots more rich people than Lansing had to buy her services. But she wasn't going anywhere any time soon, being hooked up with Matt Hanlon, one of the island's deputies. A guy who was, like Mina, Lansing born and bred.

The gates finished opening and he wound the window up gratefully, heading up the long drive.

"Take the left fork," Mina said. It didn't take long to reach the cottage.

"Stay here and I'll open the front door. I still have your keys."

Mina ignored him and undid her seat belt. "Sadly, we couldn't convince Ivy to stick with keys for our front doors. You need my hand for that."

Huh. Well, that was a good reminder that Mina Harper wasn't just another Lansing girl. She had money. Serious money. And courtesy of being the daughter of Grey Harper, had to worry about things like a fingerprint recognition panel on her front door even though Grey had been dead for over six years now. The Blacklight legend wasn't going anywhere it seemed. Nor were the faithful fans.

"Then wait there and I'll come and help you. Doc said you might get dizzy, and the last thing you need is another fall."

She pulled a face at him but didn't try to get out of the car. Will came around to her side, opened the door, and offered her a hand. She stood up carefully, managing to stay steady on her feet, and they headed for the cottage.

In the dark, it looked tinier than ever, the white walls pale gray in the storm light. The light was on, revolving slowly.

"Is it hard to sleep with the light?" he asked.

Mina put her hand on a glass panel next to her door. "You get used to it. And I have very good blackout blinds. Besides, I work nights a lot so I miss it a lot of the time. I like it actually. Kind of comforting. It's why I wanted to live here."

He couldn't remember if she'd lived here with her husband, Adam, or if she'd moved to the lighthouse cottage after he'd died. He wasn't going to ask.

The door panel flashed green and Mina opened the door. She waved at him to go in. "I'll get Stewie," she said.

"Oh no." He didn't move. "You go inside and I'll get the dog. You need to rest, remember."

He figured it was another sign that she was in pain that she didn't argue. Stewie didn't need any encouragement to jump out of the back seat when Will opened the door. He bolted for the house and Will stood there a moment, contemplating shredded leather before shrugging and following the dog.

Mina had turned on the lights and left the front door ajar. He closed it behind him and sighed happily as the warm air registered. Mina's heating was either speedy or she'd left it on.

"Mina?" he called, not sure where she'd gone.

"Kitchen," came the answer. "Straight ahead."

The hall wasn't very long. The whole place was kind

of tiny. There were two doors on each side of the hall and one at the far end. Plus a staircase to the left of that door, leading up to the next floor.

The whole place probably wasn't that much bigger than his apartment, depending on how much space there was upstairs. It definitely would have fit in just the massive living room of the Harper house that Faith still lived in. Apparently Mina liked things cozy.

He found her bending down to fill a steel dog bowl with food. He lifted the scoop of kibble out of her hand. "You're meant to be taking it easy, right? And bending down when you have a concussion can make you puke. Learned that one from Stefan. He barfed all over my shoes the night I looked after him. You're a lot prettier than he is, but barf is barf."

She blinked at him and then, to his surprise, her cheeks went pink. Embarrassed at the thought of barfing on him or pleased at the compliment? His heart did a hopeful bounce at the thought it might be the latter, and he squelched it thoroughly. He took the scoop full of kibble from her hand and dumped it in the bowl. "Is this all he gets?"

Mina instructed him how much kibble, and then he filled the water bowl.

"How about you?" Will asked. "Hungry? Thirsty? Or do you just want to go to bed?"

chapter three

Do you just want to go to bed?

Mina blinked, confused for a moment. Her head hurt and she was tired, but for an instant she'd thought he'd meant . . . no. Why would he? Don't be ridiculous. "I am tired," she said, trying to cover her hesitation.

She knew Will hadn't meant anything other than was she tired. Will Fraser was a good guy. Tonight had proved that. But still . . . how long had it been since a man had said those words to her? Years.

Since Adam died.

And even though she knew Will didn't intend them that way, his words still hit home with a little jolt that was like a wasp sting. A faint zing of something along nerves that hadn't zinged in a long time.

She'd had sex exactly twice since Adam had died. Both one-night stands, when she'd been looking for a way to dull the pain. She'd taken herself to L.A., found a hotel, and swiped right. The sex had been okay, but

two times was enough to learn that it didn't help with
the grief. There'd been no oblivion or fresh start or whatever the hell it was she'd gone looking for. She hadn't
tried since. And she'd never told anyone what she'd done.
It wasn't what grieving widows were supposed to want
after all. And neither time had involved anything approaching the sensation she'd just felt with Will.

Blame the concussion for that. No other explanation.

Concussion, fatigue, adrenaline. Those were the only
reasons to react this way.

Will Fraser was a good-looking guy, there was no de-
nying that. Tall and tanned, with brown hair that was
usually too long and streaked by the sun and the salt air.
Hazel eyes that smiled easily.

She knew that much from the few times she'd talked
to him at one of Faith's parties or when they ran across
each other in Cloud Bay. But she'd never really noticed
that there was a very nice voice that went with the
face.

And obviously a kind heart.

Despite what he did for a living.

But he wasn't Adam. No one was.

Her head throbbed again under the dressing. Tylenol
hadn't really done much more than dull the pain a little,
but Callie had refused to give her anything stronger. So
sleep seemed like the best option. But first, Will. He was
staying the night.

There was a man in her house staying the night.

"On the couch," she said firmly.

Will's eyes widened. "Pardon?"

"I mean, the couch, it pulls out," she said, flustered.
"The living room is the first door on the right. The sofa

in there pulls out. And there're blankets and stuff. I'll get you some."

"How about you tell me where they are and I'll get them?"

"They're in my room." What state had she left her bedroom in? Probably messy enough that she didn't want Will rummaging through her closets and possibly tripping over her underwear trying to find the blankets.

"O-kay," Will said, one side of his mouth curling up. "Maybe you should get them."

Good mouth. She blinked. Damn it. Her brain must really be rattled. "Good idea."

"Maybe I can make coffee while you do. You have coffee, right?"

"Yes. Though I mostly drink tea."

"Then I guess we just can't be friends," Will said with a grin that gave her another little wasp-sting jolt. "Go. Fetch blankets. I'll pull out the sofa."

Mina retreated to her bedroom, moving carefully. Located the blankets and sheets and a spare pillow. Then took a moment to catch her breath. So not how she'd expected this night to go. Not at all. She should be at the station, with Netflix on her laptop and Stewie snoring at her feet, listening for the radio call that would mean someone needed help. Instead she was here, feeling pretty helpless herself.

Helpless and off-balance. That was all it was. She kicked the clothes that lay on the floor under the bed, winced again as the move jolted her head, and then stared at the closet. She couldn't offer Will a change of clothes. No way those shoulders would fit into anything she owned. She'd finally managed to give away most of Adam's things last Thanksgiving apart from a couple of well-worn shirts and sweatshirts that were hidden up on a top shelf where she rarely ever looked. But she knew they were there.

Not the kind of thing she could loan out. Not even to knights in battered flannel-and-denim armor who rescued her in a storm.

The night was long and slightly confusing. Will woke her up twice to ask her what her name was and where she was. Once he gave her more pills. Her cranky responses made him laugh, and the sound of it was oddly comforting. The third time she came gasping out of a dream of cars and storms and tumbling over in darkness and then his voice was there again, soothing her with soft-spoken nonsense until her heart stopped pounding and she slipped back toward sleep. As she let the dark take her, she thought for a moment she felt his hand brush her hair gently, but didn't have time to figure out if it was real or not.

The fourth time she woke, the sun was shining for the first time in several days, the light dazzling through her window, making her squint and wish she'd remembered to close the blinds before she slept. Her head still ached but not as badly as it had last night. Time for more Tylenol. Stewie lifted his head from his spot in his basket in the corner of the room—Will had said she needed to sleep without a seventy-pound dog draped over her sore shoulder—and whined when she rolled over before heaving himself up to come over and sniff her face gently. She stroked his head for a minute and then pushed up slowly,

putting on a robe and the silly Minion slippers Faith had
bought her so she could let him out.

The house seemed quiet at first. Had Will left? She
didn't know if she felt relieved or disappointed if he had.
But then she heard a clatter from the kitchen. Good, she
could say thank you before shooing him away.

But when she'd let Stewie out the front door and wandered back down to the kitchen, she found not Will, but
Lou, putting away dishes from the dishwasher.

"Will called me," Lou said in answer to Mina's en-
quiring look. "Sounds like you had an interesting night."

Three days later, Mina left the clinic with clearance to
go back to work, though Callie had told her to take
things slowly for another week or so. Callie had stressed
the "slowly" part and had given Mina another lecture
on things she wasn't allowed to do yet. No screen time,
as far as possible. Nothing that took too much focus. No
late nights. No air travel, though that was easy enough
as she wasn't planning any trips.

The headache from hell had mostly gone, and while
her shoulder was still all sorts of impressive shades of
purple and green, it didn't hurt nearly as much as it had
for the first two days.

Though she still had to rest it. Callie had been clear
on that part too when Mina had admitted it was still sore.
That and the "nothing that takes too much focus" added
up to "no painting." The thought gnawed at her. She
hadn't told anyone yet but she had an invitation to show at
a small gallery in L.A. just after New Year's. Not that
there were many people to tell. Only Lou and Faith knew
Mina had converted the upper floor of the lighthouse

from the office it had been when Adam was alive—to an art studio. Or that she'd taken up painting again.

She'd been good at art at school, had always thought she'd go to college and study more but then Grey had gotten ill and she hadn't wanted to leave him. She and Adam had gotten married, and he'd taken over his family's boat-building business when his dad had passed away not long after Grey. There'd been no time for painting and no way she'd have left the island to go to school without Adam coming with her.

Faith had suggested she think about college again a year or so after Adam had died, but Mina hadn't been ready to leave the place where she and Adam had been happy.

But she had taken up her paints again, finding a place to lose herself where she didn't have to think. At first it was just for her but then, slowly, she'd gotten her confidence back. And when she started sharing a little of her art online—using a different name—she'd gotten a good response. Including the invitation a month or so ago.

Which she was keeping strictly secret. If she was going to be a success at this, then it would be in her own right. No mention of the Harper name, which would inevitably bring attention she didn't want until she'd earned it in her own right. She'd been using Emmy's surname—Logan—for her dealings with the gallery. She knew she wouldn't be able to keep the fact that she was Grey Harper's daughter secret forever, but for now she wanted to try. The gallery thought she lived in L.A. She'd rented a P.O. box there and kept any hints of Lansing Island off the social media accounts she used for her art.

She painted the ocean. A lot. The ocean and the

beach. But she never named the place that inspired her. And after all, water was water. So far no one had made any connection between her pictures and Lansing.

So for now she was safely anonymous.

She just couldn't freaking paint. She'd lost a week already. She had to have everything ready to ship to her framer—who had agreed to work during the holiday season—on Christmas Eve for all the pieces to be ready for the opening.

Just thinking about it had her stomach in knots. Her head wasn't aching quite so much anymore but it was full of a steady refrain of "*running out of time, running out of time, running out of time.*"

But it would be stupid to lose still more time if she pushed it instead of letting herself heal.

Knowing that didn't make it any less freaking frustrating.

To distract herself from the frustration, she needed to do something to fill the hours when she couldn't be painting.

A quick phone call let Bill know she was back on deck. He sounded happy to hear from her but said he'd call her to let her know which shifts she had later that day. Probably going to call Callie himself and find out what she could or couldn't do. She suspected she'd wind up with day shifts for a while. There were usually other people around the station during the day, and she doubted he'd leave her to do a shift alone until he was sure she was completely recovered.

The only argument she could use on him would be that she needed the daylight to paint. But that would require telling him about her painting in the first place.

Lansing was a small island. Cloud Bay was an even smaller town. Bill didn't gossip, but it would only take one slip of the tongue and before she knew it everyone would know her secret.

So she was just going to suck it up and figure out how to catch up on her art. It didn't sound exactly like something that Callie would think of as "resting," but it was going to have to do.

If Bill let her go in tomorrow, she could ease herself into it. Saturdays were always busy at the S&R headquarters. The volunteers did team training and equipment maintenance plus there were always more people on the island on weekends. More people equaled more chances of someone getting into trouble.

In some ways, that was how the team had grown over the years.

Lansing Search and Rescue was, like the clinic, an organization that had been a beneficiary of the Blacklight guys realizing that if they or one of their friends got into trouble on their boats or jet skis then they'd have to wait for the Coast Guard to save them.

So what had existed as a small volunteer lifesaving association for the wilder beaches at the time Grey and the guys had bought houses on the island received a cash injection big enough to let them expand to search and rescue as well. They mostly did marine stuff, but got called out by the sheriff's department to help on the odd occasion someone went missing on the island, or managed to fall off a cliff, or somehow created another problem that needed more hands on deck than the police and fire departments could provide. They'd even, much to the delight of the local residents, once rescued a very cranky giant ginger tomcat who seemed determined not to ever climb down the tree he'd been chased up. That one had even made the local paper.

So yes, weekends were their busiest times. Which was why she often took the night shift. Night shift was still pretty solitary. Just manning the radio. The volunteers all slept at their own houses. If a situation came up, whoever was manning the station sent out the alert and everyone scrambled. Other than that, it was usually just one person—or in her case, one person and one goofy Lab—keeping watch.

But she could see why Bill might not want her working alone. And to be honest, as she fought back another yawn as she pulled up in front of her cottage, she had to admit he and Callie had a point. Even though her head was recovering, she still felt about eighty percent steamrolled. The kind of tired she hadn't felt since the first few blurry months after Adam had died. The kind of tired where you just want to fall into bed and disappear.

Lou had been fussing over her, staying each night and cooking and making Mina rest. Spending so much time with her, it made Mina feel vaguely guilty. It wasn't exactly a quiet time of year for Lou. The high school had Thanksgiving and Christmas activities looming as did all the other places Lou volunteered.

But she couldn't quite bring herself to chase Lou off just yet. Unlike Faith and Zach, Mina was more than happy to spend large chunks of her days alone. Grey definitely hadn't passed on his extrovert genes to his youngest child, but sometimes it was nice to be fussed over.

Lou, curled up on the sofa working on her laptop, looked up, blue eyes smiling when Mina walked into the living room. "What's the verdict?"

"All clear," Mina said. "I can go back to work tomorrow."

"So soon?" Lou pushed her black-framed glasses back up her nose. "Are you sure?"

"Callie said it was fine," Mina said, bending to kiss the top of Lou's silver-cropped head. "I'm sure Bill will put me on day shift for a week, maybe a little longer. So other people will be there to continue Mina-watch." Bill Morrison was a worse mother hen than Lou when it came to the well-being of his team.

That didn't seem to mollify Lou. "You need more rest. We need you well for the holidays."

No need to remind Mina of that. They were less than a week out from Thanksgiving, and Thanksgiving celebrations rolled right on into Christmas preparation and then Christmas itself in Lou's house.

And maybe Mina was a grinch, but if she could use recuperating as an excuse to avoid some of the relentless holiday season cheer, then that could only be a good thing. She didn't drink, but there'd been times over the last few Christmases when she'd wanted to. Times when pasting a smile on her face and pretending to enjoy herself so as not to be the weeping widow and ruin things for everyone else had made her want to run screaming from the house.

"Mom, I'm fine. It was just a bump on the head."

Mina sat next to Lou. "It's been lovely having you here fussing over me."

"Is that code for 'but you can go home and leave me alone now'?" Lou asked with a smile.

"Something like that. You know me, I'm the weird introvert daughter."

"You're not weird," Lou said. "Well, no more than any one else in the family, at least." Her smile widened. "I will get out of your hair, though. You're not the only one who likes some time to herself. Plus I need to finish my lesson plans."

"Gotta whip those kids into shape with their Shakespeare," Mina said with a smile. Lou had taught English at the small high school in Lansing since Mina had been old enough to remember. In fact, Lou and Grey had met when he'd been looking for a tutor to teach Zach and some of the other Blacklight kids during a tour. Lou had applied on a whim, and the rest was, well, somewhat messy history.

"First semester we do contemporary authors, not classics," Lou said. "I leave the Bard until they're well and truly tamed."

Lou's students tended to adore her. Lou was tough but fair and went out of her way to help kids who needed it. Half the island had probably passed through her classroom at some point in time. She managed to instill them all with enough love for books and stories that the small bookstore in Cloud Bay did a booming trade even off-season.

"Well, you can plot your world domination more easily without having to run around after me," Mina said.

"I will," Lou said. "I'll head home after lunch. I put lasagna in the oven earlier."

"I know," Mina said, inhaling appreciatively. "It smells delicious. I'll set the table." She stood, waiting to see if Lou was going to object to her doing even that much but nope, apparently she was allowed to handle silverware as she only received a wave of Lou's hand in the direction of the kitchen. Her stomach rumbled a little. Another good sign. She hadn't had much of an appetite for the last few days.

"Oh and there's a message on your landline. The light's blinking," Lou said.

Mina paused. "Who from?" Most people she knew would call her cell, not the landline. She only kept the landline because occasionally Lansing got a storm bad enough to knock out cell service.

"I didn't play it. Whoever it was called while I was out back throwing a ball for Stewie."

Curious, Mina headed for the phone. "Probably just a telemarketer," she said. But when she hit the replay button, it was Will Fraser's voice, calling to ask how she was feeling.

Mina listened to the message, which was perfectly polite and friendly and felt herself start to blush. She hung up hastily and headed to the kitchen, busying herself with digging out silverware so as not to think about why she might blush at the sound of Will's voice.

"That was nice of him," Lou said behind her.

Mina dropped the knives she was holding with a noisy clatter. "Don't sneak up on me," she said reflexively, scooping up the silverware.

"I didn't sneak," Lou said, shaking her head as she

came to stand next to Mina, reaching up to the cabinet where Mina kept her plates. "He's got good manners that one. What are you going to do to thank him?"

"Thank him?" Mina's mind was blank for a moment.

"For rescuing you." Lou shivered. "I hate to think what might have happened if he hadn't seen you." She put the plates on the counter and squeezed Mina's hand briefly.

Mina didn't really want to think about that either. Or about Will. In fact, the few times he'd crossed her mind since the accident, she'd deliberately turned her attention to something else. Because each thought had brought a little jolt that she didn't want to think about. Just like now when she'd heard his voice.

"I hadn't really thought about it," she said. "But you're right, I should do something." She frowned, trying to think of something appropriate. She was out of practice with how one might thank a man. Especially when that man was barely a friend. She didn't want to send the wrong message.

"What's the frown for?" Lou asked.

"It's just—"

"It's a thank you, not an invitation. Not that an invitation would be the worst thing in the world." Lou hesitated. "It's been a long time, Mina." Her blue eyes were kind.

"Mom. I don't care how long it's been. I don't—"

"Okay." Lou held up her hands. "It's your life. I'm just saying Will Fraser seems to be a good, smart, hardworking guy. Faith likes him."

"He owns a bar. He makes whiskey." Mina says flatly.

"Oh, sweetie," Lou said. "That's—"

"Mom, I don't want to talk about it. I'm not looking to date and if I was, then I wouldn't be dating someone who makes booze for a living."

Lou bit her lip, clearly wanting to argue. But then, she just sighed. "Then just make the man some cookies or something. Men are easy enough to please if you feed them."

"What kind of cookies do guys like?" Mina asked Faith as they headed to the beach early the next morning. The weather was still cool, but Faith had turned up at Mina's front door as she did a few times each week anyway. Her concession to Mina's still recuperating head was to propose that they walk not jog.

Itching for some movement, Mina had accepted. With Callie's warnings in mind, she'd donned sunglasses and a cap to shield her eyes. At least the gray morning meant there was little glare. Between that and the cap, her head was happy but cold. Still, cold was better than another bout of concussion headache. But even the cold couldn't completely drive away the thought of Will and how she was going to say thank you that had been bugging her since yesterday. So here she was, asking her big sister. Who had always known how to charm anyone she chose. Not that Mina was trying to charm Will, of course.

Trying to act casual—there was a small chance that Faith would think the question was no big deal if Mina acted normal—she kept her eyes on Stewie who had bolted ahead of them as he usually did on their morning walks. In the early morning sun, the new red collar Faith had brought for him gleamed around his pale fur. It looked good from a distance when you couldn't see the cartoon turkeys printed on it. Apparently Faith thought everyone should be dressing up for the holidays this year. She probably had a Christmas-themed collar ready for Stewie too. Knowing her sister's sense of humor, it would be humping reindeers or something. Mina threw the ball she was carrying in Stewie's direction and started to move down to where the sand was damp and it was easier going.

Faith's hand on her arm stopped her. "Oh no, I think this is a conversation we need to have standing still, little sis."

Mina stopped and turned to face her sister. Faith's eyes were shielded behind her hi-tech sunglasses. Their mirrored surface showed only Mina's own reflection, but Mina was pretty sure if she could see her big sister's eyes, they'd be looking way too interested. Damn. She'd thought she might be able to get away with the question without getting the third degree.

Do not blush. "Why?"

"Because you just uttered the word 'guy' in a sentence in conjunction with something that suggests there's a guy you want to please with cookies. This is news."

"It's not news, it's a reasonable question."

"A question that requires context. So, spill."

"How much context can a question about cookies possibly require?"

"Well, for a start, who's the guy and what's the purpose of the cookies?"

"Purpose?"

"What are you trying to achieve? Like, are these seduction cookies?"

Mina smiled, though her stomach tightened. "Seduction cookies?"

"Seduction cookies are totally a thing," Faith said. She pulled down the sunglasses and looked sternly at Mina over the rims. "A thing you should know about at your age."

"Adam didn't have a sweet tooth," Mina said. She waited for the familiar pang that using his name always brought. Still sharp. Though lately, perhaps there was a little ease to it too. A touch of sweet to the salt that made speaking his name not quite so hard. "For him, it would be seduction pretzels. Or seduction potato chips." She left off the rest of the sentence. The part explaining that she'd never been serious enough with anyone other than Adam to have to try and seduce them with food. Faith knew that part well enough.

"Does this guy have a sweet tooth?"

Mina shrugged. "I don't really know."

Faith waved her hand, as if brushing this problem away. "Most guys do. Let's assume he does. Which brings us back to the purpose of the cookies."

"I'm just trying to say thank you. So these are non-seduction cookies."

"Thank you?" Faith sounded puzzled. "Wait, you're making cookies for Will?"

Mina didn't like the look of the smile blooming across her sister's face. "He did rescue me. Saying thank you is only polite." She sounded like Lou now. Well, there were worse things in life than being as nice as Lou.

"Cookies for Will Fraser," Faith said. "Are you sure you don't want them to be seduction cookies?"

Mina's stomach went from tight to rock hard. "Why would I want to seduce Will?"

"Have you seen Will? The man is not exactly ugly."

"I didn't see you snapping him up when you were single," Mina pointed out.

"Not my type. But he could be yours. A bona fide knight in shining armor. A *hot* knight."

Mina decided to ignore that last comment. "Not sure a coat and beanie constitutes shining armor. He does have a cool steed though." Grey had quite the collection of cool and expensive cars most of their lives. Mina had never admitted how much she liked them. Adam had been into boats not cars. And it wasn't like she needed a fancy car on the island. Her Jeep was enough. But Will's pretty blue Mustang made part of her itch for something a little more exciting.

Faith rolled her eyes. "I think if you're fixating on the car rather than the man than your priorities are wrong."

"Maybe but I'm the one who gets to decide my priorities. And dating isn't one of them."

"Will's a good guy. And he's . . ." Faith trailed off, biting her lip.

Alive. Mina's gut tightened. That was probably what her sister had just stopped herself from saying. Unlike Adam.

"Lou already tried this speech. Will owns a bar."

"Oh, Mina." Faith's voice was equal parts exasperation and sympathy. "That doesn't make him a bad person."

"I don't care."

"He's not like Grey. He's not an alcoholic. He doesn't even drink a lot."

"He and his brother make whiskey."

"That doesn't mean he's downing bottles of the stuff every night."

"It doesn't matter. I don't drink." She'd never been a big drinker. And since Adam's accident, the thought of alcohol turned her stomach.

"And I respect that. But that doesn't mean you can avoid everyone who does. I mean, you don't avoid me. Or Lou. Or you know, just about everyone else who lives on this island."

"I don't date them though. And it doesn't matter if you don't understand. It's my life. So I get to pick. Anyway, you spent years not dating anyone on the island and avoiding a relationship because of Dad. You had your hang-up and I get to have mine." She folded her arms.

"I changed my mind when I met the right guy." Faith said gently.

"Yeah, well, that's the difference between you and me," Mina said.

"What is?"

"I've already had the right guy. And now he's gone." Not waiting for Faith's answer, Mina turned and ran down the beach toward Stewie.

chapter four

"Will, someone here to see you."

Will looked up to see his brother Stefan standing in the rear door of Salt Devil, apron around his waist and an amused look on his bearded face. He straightened from where he'd been unscrewing the rear seat of his Mustang.

"Who?" he asked, kind of irritable. He was freezing his butt off out in the small back lot of the bar but needed to get the seat out to assess the damage. It was proving harder than he remembered from when he'd originally replaced the seat. Probably should have done it the day after Stewie had decided the Mustang was his new favorite chew toy, but they'd been busy at the bar all week and the weather had been wet. Today being Saturday, it was also going to be busy, but he'd stolen time he didn't really have to work on the car. So he didn't really need the interruption.

"Her," Stefan said, nodding his head to the right.

Will turned and saw who was standing at the end
of the alley that led from the customer lot out the front
of the bar to the back of the building.

Mina Harper. *Jesus*. Just as well that he'd moved
away from the car or he would have probably banged
his head on the door or dropped the socket wrench in
his hand. Way to make an impression.

He flicked his eyes back to Stefan and bit back the
'Thanks for the heads-up, bro' on the tip of his tongue.
He'd never outright told Stefan about his crush, but his
brother wasn't dumb and Will was fairly sure Stefan
knew which way Will's affection lay. Stefan nodded
once then disappeared back into the kitchen, closing the
door with a not-so-subtle thud.

Leaving Will alone with Mina.

"Mina, hi," he said, trying to sound unsurprised she
was there.

She nodded, smiled tentatively, and held up a square
Tupperware container. "I wanted to say thank you. For
the other night. I made you cookies. Chocolate chip. I
hope you like chocolate?"

"Um, yes." She'd made him cookies? That was . . .
kind of adorable. "I mean, thanks, I love cookies." That
much was true. He did. Stefan made a mean oatmeal
raisin that they sold in the bar during the day, and they
flew out the door. Will always tried to steal a few before they went out for the customers, much to Stefan's
exasperation. But chocolate chip was his favorite.

He smiled at Mina. She looked a lot better than when
he'd left her house the morning after her accident. There
was some color back in her face, so she was just pale
rather than ghostly white. She'd brushed her dark bangs

over her forehead but the wind blew them up briefly and revealed a neat pink line covered with a couple of small butterfly strips, which was a definite improvement over the bloody cut he remembered. A starting-to-fade bruise marred the skin around the cut and bled down to the top of her razor-blade cheekbones, but otherwise she looked healthy, her gray green eyes clear, not foggy with pain.

Granted her faded jeans looked about a size too big and, combined with well-worn Doc Martens and a navy blue sweater that looked hand-knitted, the overall impression was of an urchin being somewhat swallowed by her clothes. A gorgeous urchin, all big eyes and cheekbones and . . . that mouth that he was suddenly finding very hard to look away from, but an urchin all the same.

An urchin who was still holding out the container of cookies while he stood there like an idiot staring at her. Smooth.

He cleared his throat, closed the distance between them with a couple of steps, and reached for the Tupperware. "I can get Stefan to put these in a—" But Mina wasn't paying attention to him, she was looking past him. At the Mustang. At the open rear passenger door and the seat. Which even from her distance about ten feet away was clearly more than a little worse for wear. Stewie had chewed quite the hole near the top on the passenger side and torn a series of strips off the back of the seat on the driver's side to top things off. The dog hadn't done as much to the base of the seat, presumably because it was hard to chew on something when you were lying on it.

"What happened to your car?" Mina asked, eyes narrowing as she continued to stare at the damage.

"It, um . . ." He tried to think of a plausible excuse.

"Did Stewie do that?" she demanded.

"Kind of."

She glared. "Damn it, Will. You should have said something."

"It's not a big deal."

She shoved the cookies into his hands, marched over to the car, leaned down, and stuck her head inside. "He ate half your seat." She sounded horrified.

"He was bored. It was cold." He wasn't entirely sure why he was defending her dog, but he was.

Mina withdrew from the car. "That seat is leather and given how old your car is, I'm assuming it's custom. I'll pay for the damage."

"No. Thanks for the offer but it's not necessary."

"My dog destroyed half your car," Mina said. "I'm paying." She walked back to him, looking determined.

"Mina, I said it's not necessary."

She frowned, dark brows drawing together. "Is this some weird guy thing?"

"Define 'weird guy thing.' "

"A thing where your male ego can't handle a girl paying for something." She stuck out her chin, eyes more green than gray now, anger brightening them.

Something to remember. Not that he intended to make a habit of pissing her off. Quite the opposite, in fact. "Nope. Not that."

"Then what?"

"It sounds a bit . . . strange." And someone who'd grown up with the kind of money her family had probably wouldn't understand.

"I'm used to strange. Try me."

He shrugged. "It took me a long time to restore this car. And I've paid for every last part of it myself. I'd like to keep it that way."

She rolled her eyes. "Okay, that's a little strange. But look at it this way. You've already paid for the restoration. This is just maintenance." She watched him a moment, must have read the "no" in his expression. "How about you pay the bill and I give you the money?"

"Nope, it would be the same thing." He doubted Mina had ever had to scrimp and save to pay for anything in her life. It wasn't her fault. But he'd worked for this car, squirreling away money here and there between trying to pay off his student loans and save to pay for the additional studies he'd taken in brewing and distilling.

Her face twisted in frustration. "I can't just let you be out hundreds of dollars because of your weird car fetish."

"I don't have a weird car fetish. I'm just very fond of this particular car. And she's definitely not weird." He grinned at Mina, then reached out to pat the roof of the Mustang. "Don't listen to the mean lady, Lulu."

Mina snorted. "You named your car Lulu?"

"Your Jeep doesn't have a name?"

"Um, no."

"Well, no wonder it broke down and stranded you in a storm."

"I'm not sure that's how flat tires happen, Will." She smiled though. "But you're trying to distract me from the subject on hand."

"Which is?"

"I want to pay you back for the damage to your car. My dog did that. And that's not okay."

She really wasn't going to let this drop. Which meant Mina Harper thought she owed him a favor. For a moment, he kind of wished he was a douchebag who could leverage this opportunity into asking her for a date. But Mina had been through a lot. If he ever got a shot at her, he wanted it to be because she was into him, not because he'd guilted her into going out with him. Damn scruples. He held up the container. "You could pay me in cookies."

She shook her head at him, bangs flying. When they settled, she pushed them out of her eyes and pinned him with a "no dice" look. "I'd have to bake you cookies every week for a year."

"I am okay with that plan. I love cookies." He cracked the lid of the container, inhaling the aroma of chocolate and sugar and butter that wafted out with pleasure. As his stomach threatened to rumble, he took out a cookie and bit into it.

It tasted even better than it smelled.

God. She gave good cookie. A batch of these every week, not to mention a chance to see Mina every week, would be one hundred percent okay in his book. He finished his mouthful, and then took another bite, tempted to stuff the whole thing into his mouth. *Classy, Fraser.* He swallowed and smiled at her instead. "Yep, I'm definitely okay with a cookie payment plan."

"My dog ate half your car, Will."

"Nah, it was more like a sixteenth. Less, probably."

"Still, cookies aren't enough." She bit her lip and for just a second he felt exactly what it would be like to close his teeth gently over that plump curve of her mouth and taste her.

Fire flooded his brain and made him forget how to breathe for a second.

Damn. He really needed to get it together. "Seriously, it's fine."

Mina felt her teeth clench. Will might be shrugging it off but there was no way repairing the damage Stewie had inflicted on the Mustang could be cheap. But he was going to be all male about it. That much was clear. She had the money but he wasn't going to accept it. Which meant she was going to have to figure out another way to make it up to him.

"How about dinner?" she blurted before her mind fully engaged.

Will almost choked on the cookie he was eating. Coughed. Swallowed. "Excuse me?"

Shit. What had she just done? Ask a man out for dinner and there was only one way he was going to interpret it. Damn. Stupid mouth. She tried to think of a way to backpedal. "I mean, um, Thanksgiving. What are you doing? Is the bar open?"

Will shook his head, still looking kind of stunned. "No. We close for Thanksgiving."

"Then come to ours. Faith's, I guess. At the big house."

For a second she saw disappointment in his hazel eyes. Crap. She didn't want to hurt his feelings. But better to be clear about things up front. "Unless you're going home for Thanksgiving, of course," she offered to fill the silence that seemed to be stretching too long.

Will shook his head. "No, we only close for the day. Stefan and I were just going to hang out."

Stefan. She hadn't thought about Stefan. The brothers

weren't from Lansing, so they had no family here. So it wasn't really fair to leave Stefan stranded. "He could come too. Faith and Caleb won't mind." And, added bonus, inviting both the Fraser brothers made the whole thing less date-ish.

She couldn't quite interpret the expression on Will's face. But then he nodded. "Okay. Thanks. I'm sure Stefan would love to come."

What did that mean? That Will wasn't happy about it? Or wasn't happy about Stefan coming along? God. She needed to stop over-analyzing. Or she was going to start babbling. "Great." She paused. "Come any time in the afternoon. We do this late lunch/dinner thing. We eat about two. Musician's hours, I guess. Lou makes a great turkey. Takes days by the time she brines it and—" She stopped herself. Definitely veering into babbling territory.

Will's face eased. "Lou's cooking? That should make Stefan happy. He bought one of her apple pies at one of the school bake sales a year or so ago and I think he's been trying to recreate it ever since."

"No one beats Lou's pie," Mina agreed. Right. Time to make a graceful exit. "I should go. I have to get to work."

"You're back at work already?"

"Callie signed off yesterday," she said. "And it's just for the afternoon. Not a night shift."

"How many shifts do you work a week?" Will asked.

"Four or five."

"Isn't that a lot? I mean, people on the island aren't that accident prone are they, that the search and rescue is busy every day?"

"No, but someone still needs to man the phones in case something does happen. Most of the other volunteers have day jobs. I don't. So it's easy for me to cover nights."

"Four or five shifts a week sounds a lot like a job to me."

She looked down at her shoes. "You know what I mean." She didn't need to work to earn a living.

"So you spend four or five nights a week down in the S&R alone? Can't they just redirect the phone to someone else's line or something?"

"Sometimes they do that. But if there's an emergency, then having someone on the premises means they can start getting everything ready while the team is gathering. Saves time. And time is kind of important in those situations. A few minutes can make a difference."

"Yes," he agreed. "I guess I hadn't thought about it."

"Besides, I'm not alone, I have Stewie."

"Guess I can't argue with that. The dog has strong teeth, we know that much." He smiled at her, a lopsided sort of grin that made Mina's stomach tense. Not unhappily. And that made her nervous.

"Okay. So, I'll see you on Thursday?"

"Definitely," Will said, smile widening.

"Great." She swallowed, mouth suddenly dry. "Enjoy the cookies." She turned and fled back up the alley toward her Jeep. Oh, God. She'd just asked Will to her family's Thanksgiving dinner. Why on earth had she done that? And how on earth was she going to explain it to Faith?

By the time Mina made it to Search and Rescue headquarters, everyone else on the team had already arrived.

She said her hellos, answered the inevitable questions about her recovery, and then retreated to watch from the sidelines as the rest of the team did fitness drills to kick things off. Bill had banned her from doing anything too strenuous. So she was stuck timing drills and making notes. Still, she was glad of the distraction. If she'd been sitting at home, she'd just be obsessing about the fact she'd invited Will to Thanksgiving dinner. And about the fact that she was going to have to tell Faith what she'd done.

"Bored senseless yet?" Bill said as he came to sit by her side, watching the team as they formed up for another round of suicide sprints.

He knew her too well. "Not quite senseless." She tried not to sound too grumpy about it. He was, after all, only following Callie's orders. And it wasn't as if she actually enjoyed fitness drills.

But she didn't enjoy sitting around either.

Really, concussions sucked. Callie still had her avoiding anything that might strain her eyes. No painting. No drawing. Limited screen time. No reading even. There was only so much napping and listening to quiet music and podcasts a girl could do. She'd reached her limit at least a day ago.

"It's not forever," Bill said. "As long as you learn not to keep banging that head of yours."

"Lesson learned," she said. She couldn't remember the actual fall but the aftermath was still fresh in her mind. Maybe because it wasn't over yet. If it had been, she wouldn't be having this conversation. "Next time I get a flat tire in a thunderstorm, I'm calling Nikolai."

Bill chuckled. "Smart choice." He stared down at the

milling figures. "You know, if you want to be really use-
ful, there's one thing you could do for me."

"Oh?" she said. She clicked the stopwatch into motion again as the team started their next set. "What's
that?"

"Well, I need to go to San Francisco next week for a
couple of days. Actually we're leaving tomorrow. Marla
has her checkup and some tests on Monday and we
thought we'd make the most of it and have a break before the holiday crazy really hits."

"Tests?" Mina tried to keep her voice calm. Worry
squirmed in her stomach. Marla was a breast cancer
survivor. Was something wrong?

Bill held up a hand, making an "all good" gesture.
"Just routine follow-up. Nothing to worry about."

Mina let out her breath and hit stop on the watch,
writing down the time while she let her pulse slow down
a bit. "That's good."

"Yes, but the mayor sucked me into this Christmas
Festival committee of hers."

"She did?" Mina twisted to look at him. Bill, who ran
Cloud Bay's only garden center with Marla, when he
wasn't whipping the Search and Rescue team into shape,
wasn't much of a joiner. Didn't have much time to be
between the two. "How did that happen?"

"Marla said it would be good for me." He looked
sheepish. "Marla loves Christmas."

"Ah," Mina said. Bill would bend over backward
to make sure Marla got whatever made her happy after
almost losing her. She understood. "But what do you
need me for?"

"They have a meeting on Tuesday afternoon. It would

be nice if someone from the team could fill in for me. Make sure we don't get signed up for anything crazy."

She'd really rather stick a fork in her eye. A dull and rusty fork. Cloud Bay liked to pack its calendar full of various corny events designed to keep the tourists coming to the island all year round. None of them pulled the enormous crowds that CloudFest, the music festival her dad had started twenty odd years ago, did every summer, but they all helped the local economy. But a Christmas Festival was new. They'd always had a tree in the small town square near the docks at Cloud Bay and carol singing on Christmas Eve with presents for the kids who lived on the island, but not a full-on festival designed to attract tourists. It seemed like a reach. There'd have to be something seriously wrong with the weather before Lansing ever had a white Christmas. Surely people who went away for Christmas went to places where the weather was actually, well, Christmassy?

Even if she still loved Christmastime, she would have thought it was a bit lame. But Bill didn't often ask for favors, and filling in at a meeting was something concrete she could do rather than twiddling her thumbs. And, after all, how bad could one meeting possibly be?

chapter five

On Monday morning, Mina found Faith in the kitchen, sitting at the piano, idly picking out a melody. The song wasn't anything Mina recognized but it had been a long time since she'd seen Faith go near the piano. So she paused to listen, not wanting to disturb Faith's train of thought if she was possibly writing a song. And because she wasn't looking forward to the conversation she was about to have. She should have told Faith about inviting Will and Stefan on Saturday, but she'd stuck her head in the sand. But now it was Monday and Thanksgiving was Thursday and, well, here she was.

Ready to spill the beans. Kind of. But if she could delay it a few more minutes, then that was just fine with her.

But apparently she wasn't quite quiet enough because Faith swiveled around on the piano stool and wriggled her fingers in greeting. "Hey sis."

"Hey yourself. That sounded good. Working on something?"

Faith shook her head. "Just noodling."

"Slow day at the office?"

"Kind of. Leah's busy at the studio and Theo's off-island for a couple of days, doing some meetings in L.A. So I'm slacking off for the morning."

Mina doubted that. Faith had never really been one for lazing around. "Where's Caleb?"

"Lou roped him into doing a talk at the high school."

"Another one?" Lou had been shamelessly using Caleb White for school events since he'd moved to the island to live with Faith.

"Well, I guess the kids don't get the chance to meet too many professional athletes here. Makes a nice change from rock stars." Faith smiled. "Besides, he's thinking of running a tennis camp this summer, so it will help if the kids here get to know him."

"A camp for island kids?" That was a good idea. Lansing was small. Summers could get long for kids stuck here while their parents made the most of peak tourist season. At least for the ones who didn't have jobs.

"A mix, I think. Local kids, definitely, but maybe some others. He's still figuring it out."

"Won't that be kind of super busy with CloudFest?"

"The plan would be to have it early summer. Before it gets too hot and yes, before, the CloudFest madness starts. There's enough summer to go around." Faith stood and came over to kiss Mina's cheek hello.

"I actually called the office first, to see if you were there. When they said you'd gone, I wondered if you'd been dragged into the Christmas Festival planning."

Faith snorted. "Unless our esteemed Mayor Rigger has had a total personality transplant, I think that's one committee I'm safe from being invited to."

"Angie's okay. She's doing a good job as mayor."

"She's doing a good job at being a pain in the ass," Faith said. "She came up with a new noise ordinance for summer. Or she tried to. Lou got wind of it and we managed to get the town council to shut it down."

"Yikes," Mina said.

"Yikes is right. So don't get me started on the Christmas Festival. I mean, we're an island off the coast of California. Our winters aren't exactly snowy-wonderland-postcard-Christmas territory. How many tourists does she think we're going to get?"

Nice to see someone else felt the same way about the festival as she did. But Faith usually loved Christmas. "Is it the festival you don't like or the fact it's Angie running it?" Mina asked.

"I'm thinking of the islanders," Faith said. "People need some time off to enjoy the holidays with their families. They shouldn't have to be putting on a show for tourists all year."

"People also need to earn a living," Mina said gently. "CloudFest brings plenty of summer money, but it's not easy for everyone to make it through the rest of the year." Faith, as much as she would deny it, still spent a lot of time in the music world. Between that and running the business side of Harper Inc., she tended to run with people who weren't exactly worried about where their next paycheck was coming from. "Angie's just trying to do her best for Lansing."

"Why are you defending her?" Faith's eyes narrowed. "You don't even like Christmas."

Mina hid a wince. She'd liked Christmas just fine before Adam had died. It had been one of their favorite times of year. It was just Christmas without him she'd struggled with for the last three years. "I just think you need to try and get along with Angie. After all, your mom and her dad are kind of dating." Which was the root of the problem. Mina had always thought Angie was fairly rational—she was closer to Faith's age than Mina's, so she didn't actually know her terribly well—but when it came to Seth Rigger moving on after his wife's death, well, Angie seemed to hold Faith personally responsible. Then again, the two of them had never really been close even before Lou and Seth got together.

"Which is why I haven't yet pushed her off the pier," Faith said. "I like Seth."

"Plus Lou would definitely ground you," Mina said with a laugh.

"Probably," Faith agreed. "But at least it would definitely get me out of anything to do with the Christmas Festival."

"I'm going to start calling you Scrooge," Mina said. "Scrooge Harper has a nice ring to it."

"You won't find it so funny if Angie tries to drag you into it."

"Aren't I tarred with the Harper brush? That should keep me safe." Maybe she shouldn't mention she was going to the committee meeting tomorrow.

"Don't count on it," Faith grumbled. "I'm sure she'd love to turn one of us into a good little Angie-is-awesome-bot, and she knows it's not going to be me. So don't be surprised if you get tapped on the shoulder. After all, the search and rescue is bound to be involved. And of all the people who work there, you're the one—"

"Without a day job," Mina finished. "I know." She hadn't thought about that part. That as far as most people on Lansing were concerned, Mina didn't work. They didn't know about the painting. They knew about the search and rescue hours she put in, but that was volunteer work. Nighttime volunteer work, at that.

So she could see exactly why everyone might think she was free as a bird to pitch in. Possibly only her concussion had saved her from being asked any earlier. Organizing a Christmas Festival sounded like hell. She'd witnessed the stress that went with running CloudFest her entire life, and while a Christmas Festival would be nothing like the scale of a world-famous rock festival, if you threw small town politics into the mix, it had the potential to be truly horrible. She'd agreed to tomorrow to help Bill out, but Faith was right, Angie was likely to pounce and try and talk Mina into pitching in with the whole thing. The committee weren't the only ones who were going to have to roll up their sleeves and dig in to get the festival up and running. She frowned.

"I thought you said Angie was okay?" Faith grinned evilly.

"Let's talk about something else," Mina said. She'd worry about Angie tomorrow. That gave her plenty of time to come up with reasons why she couldn't be involved if Angie tried to rope her in. Like the pile of work she had waiting for her in her studio. Not that Angie knew about the studio, of course.

"Sure," Faith said. But her grin stayed in place. "How about you tell me how the cookie delivery went?"

"It went fine," Mina said, cautiously. "Seems like he likes chocolate chip. So thanks for the recipe."

"Most guys do." Faith studied her a moment. "Why do I feel like there's more to this story?"

"Coffee?" Mina asked brightly. She wasn't quite ready to confess yet.

"Lou said you're meant to be avoiding caffeine," Faith replied. She pointed at one of the stools lining the long granite counter. "Sit. I'll make you a decaf. But only if you tell me the rest of the story."

"Withholding caffeine is an unfair negotiation tactic." But she sat anyway.

"I go with what works," Faith said as she pulled out coffee and cups and milk and arranged it all in front of her gleaming coffee machine.

"Do I get a cookie if I tell you?"

"That depends if the story is cookie-worthy. Is it?" Faith tilted her head at Mina.

"Well, it turns out that Stewie-ate-half-Will's-backseat-and-he-wouldn't-let-me-pay-so-I-invited-him-to-Thanksgiving," Mina said in a rush. If she talked fast enough, maybe Faith wouldn't really take in the information.

"What?" Faith said, freezing where she stood, one hand holding the coffee canister in midair.

"I said Stewie ate half Will's backseat and—"

"You asked *Will* out on a date?" Faith interrupted.

"It's Thanksgiving, that's hardly a date." Mina tried to sound casual.

"It's you interacting with a man socially," Faith retorted. "That's at least a step in the right direction. And it's a definite step up from non-seduction cookies."

"He got the cookies. But Stewie ate half of Lulu's back seat," Mina buried her face in her hands, remembering the mess of shredded leather. "Cookies didn't seem like enough."

Faith grinned. "Whatever you say. But asking a guy to a family dinner sounds date-ish to me."

Darn. She wasn't the only one who thought that. She remembered the grin on Will's face as he'd said yes. "Gah! I asked Stefan too."

"Two men. Well, in for a penny, I guess," Faith said. Her eyes were dancing. "Brothers. Kinky."

"Stefan—" Mina paused. Then stopped. She'd been about to say "Stefan doesn't interest me," which carried the implication that Will did. She didn't want to think about that. "I don't think Stefan even dates."

She pictured Will's older brother a moment. The man was even taller than Will. They shared the same hazel eyes but Stefan was darker, his hair closer to black, his skin more tanned than Will's. And he had one of those big beards that were so popular right now. Something she didn't understand. Not her type even though, like his brother, he was not hard on the eyes. Not that Will was her type either. "I've never heard about him hooking up with anyone on the island, have you?" Maybe the question would distract Faith from the subject of Will and whether or not Thanksgiving dinner was a date. An accidental date.

Faith frowned. "You know, I have no idea. Which probably means no. Unless he's unusually sneaky about it."

"Maybe he keeps to your old system. You know, only off-island."

"I'm not even sure he leaves the island that often." Faith hitched one shoulder then started making coffee.

Mina had no idea if this was true or not. She didn't exactly track the movements of the Fraser brothers. She contemplated Stefan again. Big but quiet. Focused. Private somehow. Which meant she shouldn't be standing here with Faith speculating about his love life. "Whatever it is, I've invited him and Will. So I hope that's okay."

"Well, Lou always cooks for an army and you know there's plenty of room at the house." Faith didn't look at all concerned about two extra guests being added to her Thanksgiving quota. So that was a relief.

It would have been awkward to uninvite them. And then she would have had to think up another way to thank Will. Judging by Faith's reaction to the news she'd invited him to Thanksgiving, if she'd actually asked him out to dinner, the Cloud Bay rumor mill might have actually caught fire.

But she'd been fairly sure that Faith wouldn't bat an eyelid about two more mouths to feed. Grey had practically made bringing home miscellaneous friends and hangers-on at any time of the year a hobby. And given his girlfriends were usually not the homemaker type, Faith had learned to work with caterers at a young age. And Lou had helped them out when they needed it, not that Grey ever knew that part.

"Thanks, I appreciate it," she said. "Are we still helping Lou with pie prep on Wednesday?"

"Yup. And decorating tomorrow, if you feel up to it.

Caleb is apparently big into decorations. He says Christmas starts at Thanksgiving. I'm letting him run with it. But you can give us a hand if you're free." Faith grinned at Mina. "Maybe Caleb can scare up some mistletoe."

Mina pointed at Faith. "I doubt Caleb will appreciate you kissing random people under the mistletoe."

Faith's grin widened. "I have no intention of kissing anyone but Caleb. But I think it's a thoughtful touch for my single guests. Who knows, maybe Leah will feel like kissing somebody. And anyone who wants to avoid being kissed will just have to avoid the mistletoe."

Knowing Faith, that probably wouldn't be easy. She'd probably deck the whole house out in mistletoe. In fact, she definitely would if she thought it might make Mina kiss someone.

Well, she was just going to be disappointed.

Mina's eyes sprang open at twelve minutes past three Tuesday morning. She didn't have to turn her head to check the time on her phone. She knew this particular sensation clicking like the turn of a key in a lock in her brain.

Hello, insomnia.

She tried to stay still, staring into the darkness. Sometimes, for a value of sometimes meaning once in a blue moon, she could trick her brain into remembering it was tired and fall back asleep if she didn't move, if she stayed still, breathed slow, listened to the waves outside her window and let them carry her back down to unconsciousness.

But tonight it didn't work.

She felt wired. Stupidly alert.

Crap.

She hadn't had insomnia in months now. Once upon her time, in her family, she'd been considered the morning person. Which, by normal standards, made her merely a late sleeper. Grey had been an up-until-four-a.m., sleep-past-noon kind of guy. But apparently Mina had enough of her mother in her to not mind occasionally seeing a time closer to sunrise. In Emmy's case, she'd been chasing the morning light that was a photographer's holy grail. In Mina's, it was that she'd never really liked feeling as though she'd missed half the day.

Adam had been a big fan of mornings. Up early to try and steal some time out on the water before he had to start his day whenever he could.

But after Grey had died, Mina had had trouble sleeping for months. She used to lie next to Adam in bed, listening to him breathe, not wanting to wake him, a thousand what-ifs running through her head.

Denial was supposed to be part of grief but she wasn't in denial. She knew Grey was dead. It was just her brain's way of coping with that seemed to be coming up with a Technicolor movie reel of every possible way it might have worked out differently.

What if Grey had gone to a doctor a few months earlier?

What if he'd never started drinking?

What if Mina or Faith or Zach had been a match for a liver donation?

What if the second rehab had been the one that had stuck instead of the fourth?

What if Grey had been crap at music?

All the ways it might have worked out that her father would still be alive.

She'd let the list run and then she'd slide out of bed and vanish to the living room where she could cry silently or stare out the window until her brain finally shut down again.

That had been her first experience of just how much of a mind fuck what-ifs could be.

The second had been after Adam had died. The list had been longer then.

A thousand ways the night of his death might have gone differently so he wasn't on the bend in the road at exactly the wrong moment.

A million ways his life might have been different.

A million ways hers might have been.

She'd beat that eventually too. Mostly because she started working nights. Insomnia never seemed to bother her when she slept while the sun was in the sky.

But now, here she was again. And she could feel the what-ifs lining up in her head. She tried to beat them off by thinking about why she had woken. Had she heard something? But no, Stewie was still snoring in his bed in the corner of her bedroom and he'd be awake if there'd been anything or anyone worth worrying about near the cottage.

Maybe it was the remnants of the concussion then. A concussion was a brain injury, after all. Callie had made that clear to her. Brains were weird. They could be weirder when they were healing.

So maybe it was that and the fact that she was working days again. The perfect storm combining to bring her old enemy back to life.

Fucking what-ifs.

She threw back the quilt and swung her legs around, the shock of cool air enough to wake her fully if she hadn't been before. The movement brought Stewie snuffling awake, and he padded behind her as she walked to the kitchen as the first of the what-ifs popped into her brain.

What if Adam hadn't died?

That was an old one. A thought so familiar she could almost ignore it these days. A thought she had multiple times a day, though sometimes now it was hours and hours apart. It had been barely minutes in the beginning. A never-ending parade of questions driving her mad.

What if he was still here?

What would her life be like?

What would they be planning?

No. No thinking about that one. She filled a glass with water. Sliced an apple slowly, laying the pieces onto a plate in precise lines. Cut cheese to have with it and found a handful of spiced nuts to round out her snack.

She carried the plate and glass into the living room, as she tried to avoid thinking. Pulled the afghan around her and ate apples and cheese while her eyes prickled as she fought back the memories and the goddamn questions with Stewie by her feet, whining softly at her. She wasn't sure if it was just Labrador angst at missing out on food or whether he picked up her mood.

But not even Stewie could stop the what-ifs. And if she wasn't going to think about what her future might have been like, apparently her brain was going to go backward.

Twist the knife a little.

What if Grey hadn't died? Would she have married

Adam at eighteen if she hadn't been dealing with Grey's death?

What if they'd waited longer?

What if they'd broken up?

What if she could just be happy?

What if no grief rose unexpectedly to claw at her throat and make her weep in the shower when she thought she was having a good day?

She curled onto her side, pulling the rug around her. Pushed her head into the sofa cushions as though she could hide from the mess inside her head. Tried to think of something else. Breathed deep.

And smelled something unexpected. Something warm and almost smoky clinging to the wool of the afghan. The smell of Will Fraser. The smell of a man. Left over from the night he'd spent on her couch.

She wasn't used to that anymore. To the reminder of a man in her house.

Adam had always liked aftershave that was kind of woodsy. Fresh and green. But Will's was different. Thank God. She didn't need scent memory complicating everything else when her brain was trying its best to fuck with her.

But it seemed she had a scent memory of Will regardless. It wasn't all that clear. Just the sensation of arms around her and the same smell she smelled now floating into her nose and distracting her for a moment from the pain in her head and the cold seeping into her bones. Darkness and warmth and that smell. A sensation of . . . safe haven, almost.

From the night of the accident. It couldn't be anything else.

And as she leaned into the memory and breathed into the scent, another what-if floated into her head, with a sudden clarity.

What if she kissed Will Fraser?

The shock of it brought her to her feet, heart suddenly pounding like she'd run half a mile. Or, indeed, been well and truly kissed by a man who knew what the hell he was doing.

And in the wake of the thought, came a flash of . . . heat mixed with longing that was worse than the thought itself. Something she hadn't felt in a long time.

A sensation she was utterly unready for.

And in sudden desperation, she knew she wouldn't be sleeping again tonight. And that meant, if she didn't want to let the what-ifs drive her insane by morning, she needed to do something.

Something that would blank her brain.

She almost fled up the stairs to her studio, slapping at light switches and reaching for the first piece of paper she could find, then scrabbling for a pencil. Only to stop after the first minute of hand moving across paper when she realized that, for the first time since Adam had died, she was sketching a face.

Will's face.

Fuck.

She dropped the pencil like it was a hot coal and crumpled the paper. Then found watercolor paper and an easel and the biggest brush she owned. Focus. That was what she needed. Paint the sea. Paint and water. She knew how to do that. She'd been doing it relentlessly for three years, painting the sea like it held the answers to all the questions she didn't know she had.

Tonight it was just going to have to work its magic again. Save her from herself.

Because she sure as hell wasn't ready to think about why she wanted to draw Will's face.

chapter six

When Mina walked into the meeting room at the mayor's office just after lunch on Tuesday, she was regretting her promise to Bill. She'd managed to fall asleep again around five, after forcing herself away from the easel then woken late, with her shoulder aching.

She'd beaten back the pain with a long hot shower and a hefty dose of ibuprofen but by the time she'd done that and walked Stewie and gotten herself organized for the day, she'd lost the morning. Apparently Callie had been on the money when she'd said Mina needed to rest her shoulder for another week or so before doing anything too strenuous, but too late now. She'd given into the urge to draw, and her fingers still itched for a pencil. She should be back in her studio, painting.

If she hadn't promised Bill she'd do this, she'd still be there. Spending a few hours locked up with Cloud Bay's mayor and whomever else Angie had roped into her festival plans—and in hindsight she should have asked Bill who else was on the committee—wasn't exactly appealing.

The first person she spotted was Angie herself. Dressed in one of her usual slick power suits—today's deep green could only be a nod to the season given the color didn't really suit her—blonde hair tamed into a low bun, Cloud Bay's mayor was surveying the people assembled in the meeting room with an expression of satisfaction—until she spotted Mina. At which point, the Mayor narrowed her eyes as if to say "What the hell are you doing here?" before her expression relaxed.

"Mina. I remember now. Bill rang and said you'd be coming today. Nice of you to help out." The smile she directed at Mina was tight and hardly welcoming, but it was better than being run out of the room, so Mina would take it.

She smiled back then nodded at Ryan Beck, Angie's assistant who was hovering, as usual, by Angie's side. He was dressed equally impeccably in a dark gray suit with a tie that wasn't far off the shade of Angie's suit. Mina hoped they hadn't actually coordinated their wardrobes. That would be taking the festive spirit way too far. But their coordinated slickness made her feel that maybe she'd underdressed. She'd put on black jeans, a chunky knit sweater, and boots, even slicked on mascara and lip gloss. Cloud Bay wasn't really a business suit kind of town. But if she'd thought it through, she would have remembered that Angie—and her shadow, Ryan—were the exceptions. But too late now. To avoid thinking about outfit choices, she turned her attention to the rest of the room to see who else had been roped into this nonsense.

She didn't get very far. Standing on the opposite side of the long black conference table, wearing dark pants and a red plaid shirt that made her feel slightly better about her own clothing choices, was Will. Unlike Angie, Will looked perfectly delighted to see her.

Her stomach swooped a little. Damn it. She wasn't going to be flustered by Will. There was nothing to be flustered about. She'd only had that mad thought about kissing him because she'd been sleep deprived and not thinking clearly. There would be no kissing Will Fraser.

Resurrecting her smile, which she suspected had slipped a little, she nodded at Will. Then she turned her back on him and started saying hello to the rest of the committee members.

Matt Hanlon, one of the town's deputies, at least was a friendly face. He was engaged to Ivy Morito, one of Faith's best friends. He stood next to Patty Bleecker, who ran the town bookstore with her wife Evie, and Sam Unger, who owned the largest grocery store on the island, the three of them talking quietly. Patty smiled at Mina but before she could join in the conversation, Angie clapped her hands briskly.

"Okay everyone, let's get started and then everyone who needs to can get back to work." Her eyes flicked to Mina as she spoke, and Mina bristled. Was that a dig about her not having a job? Maybe she'd been too quick to defend Angie to Faith yesterday.

But she was determined to play nice. After all, as far as Mina could tell, Seth made Lou happy. That was a good thing. One she hoped would continue. So she was probably going to have to see Angie at family gatherings for the foreseeable future. Easier to keep things civil.

Angie wasn't likely to be at Thanksgiving at least. Not with Faith hosting. Mina hadn't asked Lou how she and Seth were going to spend the holidays, but Faith would've been a lot blunter about Angie if Lou wasn't going to be at the Harper house for Thanksgiving, so maybe they were spending the day apart. Or doing one meal with Seth's family and the other with the Harpers.

Though how anyone could eat two Thanksgiving meals in one day—particularly if Lou was cooking one of them—was beyond her. But that was up to Lou. And as much as she liked Seth, Mina wasn't going to cry if Angie wasn't there.

She wouldn't be the only one missing. Zach was on tour, so he wasn't coming home. Nothing new. Since Grey had died, Zach seemed to regard Lansing as radioactive. His visits were short and the gaps between them seemed to stretch longer and longer. She'd probably seen him more off-island than on in the last three years. But even though it would only be Faith, Mina, and Lou as far as family was concerned, she was sure Faith had invited a horde of other guests as usual.

"Mina? Are you joining us?" Angie asked, her tone overly polite.

Mina blinked and realized that while she'd been pondering family politics, everybody else in the room had taken a seat at the conference table. The only chair left unoccupied was the one to Will's right.

Crap. Just where she didn't want to sit.

"Sorry," she said and walked around the table, trying not to look like she was scurrying.

"Hey," Will said softly as she took her seat.

"Hey," she said back, shooting a glance up the table

at Angie. The mayor was fussing with a laptop, so she was probably safe. "What are you doing here?" Was he the joining in type? Civic responsibility wasn't what she associated with a guy who owned a bar and brewed whiskey for kicks, but maybe that was unfair.

Will folded his arms as Angie took her place at the head of the table, the movement tightening his shirt around his biceps. For a moment the pure curve of muscle highlighted by the sun coming through the windows behind them caught Mina's attention, and her fingers flexed instinctively, itching for a pencil all over again.

Weird. She hadn't drawn figures for years. She'd spent the last three years painting the ocean. She drew Stewie and other dogs and cats or plants that grabbed her attention if she was out with her sketchbook, but mostly she'd painted the ocean that sprawled beyond the lighthouse windows. Over and over and over again. As if capturing its many moods might someday reveal a secret. What secret she had no idea. She just knew that all she'd wanted to capture since she'd picked up a paintbrush after Adam's death was the sea.

Definitely not people. Absolutely not a man.

Definitely not the man she was staring at now. Who was gazing back with something she didn't want to think about lurking in the hazel depths of his eyes. The same scent she'd breathed in from her sofa last night drifted across to her, and her breath hitched.

Idiot.

She broke the gaze and dug in her purse for a notebook and pen. She was here to take notes for Bill. Not to think about Will Fraser.

"Pen and paper. Old school," Will said.

"I'm here instead of Bill. He's in San Francisco."

"I know," Will said.

"You do?" How did Will know Bill?

"Yes. Bill's garden center isn't that far from Salt Devil. He and Marla come in now and then."

"Oh." She opened the notebook. Which turned out to be one of her smaller sketchbooks, not the notebook she used as a planner. Damn it. She turned the book over. Start with a blank page at the back. Easier to tear out once she was back home.

"I have lived here for five years," Will continued, sounding amused. "I have managed to meet people in that time. Being a business owner and all. Which is why I'm here."

"Very civic minded of you," she managed.

He hitched a shoulder, making another nice ripple in his shirt. "I like Christmas."

"People who like Christmas should want to spend it with their families."

"Well, my family lives a long way away and my mom is in France with her sister. They're doing the European Christmas thing this year. So that option's out. Besides, I like customers too, and the festival will bring tourists."

"Tourists who'll inevitably get into trouble."

"I think the kinds of people who come to the island for a Christmas Festival are going to be a bit tamer than your sister's CloudFest crowds."

Most people were tamer than the thousands of ardent music fans who swelled onto Lansing for CloudFest every year. But that didn't mean they still wouldn't manage to fall off a cliff or out of a boat or get caught in a tide. That meant what was usually a relatively quiet time of year for Search and Rescue wasn't likely to be if the festival proved popular. Just what she didn't need this year, when she was already behind on her deadline for the gallery show.

"Tourists are tourists," she said. "They get into trouble."

"I never pegged you for a pessimist," Will said. But before Mina could answer, Angie clapped her hands again to get everyone's attention.

"Welcome everyone. Thanks for coming along today. We're going to come back to a couple of the items we talked about last week, but first Ryan is going to give us a progress report on what's happened this week."

As Ryan started to speak, Mina started taking notes.

"You know," Will said, leaning slightly so he was practically whispering in her ear. "You could take notes on your phone. Then just e-mail them to Bill."

"Shh." She shot him a warning glance, trying to ignore the lingering patch of warmth on her neck where his breath had touched her skin. "Concussion, remember. I'm not supposed to use anything with a screen much."

Will winced. "Sorry. I forgot. Are you okay?"

"I'm fine. Just following doctor's orders." She turned her attention back to Ryan. Only to find several minutes later that she was no longer taking notes but instead sketching Will's hands with rapid strokes of her ballpoint. Crap. She hastily turned the page, smoothing it down hard as though she could smooth away the image underneath with each stroke.

She didn't dare look at Will. What if he had seen it? As she focused again on what Ryan was saying, she saw Angie, at the far end of the table, watching her with narrowed eyes. Caught. Double crap. Pasting an innocent expression on her face, she picked up her pen and turned her attention back to writing, not drawing. This time she lasted about ten minutes before she realized that she couldn't remember a single thing Ryan had said after "twelve inflatable snowmen" and that her pen was now sketching the curving line of Will's eyebrow.

Holy crap.

She slammed the book shut just as Ryan finished speaking. The thump echoed across the room.

"Something wrong, Mina?" Angie asked.

"No, sorry," Mina muttered. "Ignore me." Why was this room so hot? Her cheeks felt like they were glowing. Damn pale skin. It gave far too much away. Doing her best to ignore the blush, she pulled the notebook back toward her. But she didn't open it again. She knew exactly what would happen if her pen got another shot at blank paper. Whenever she got something stuck in her head that she really wanted to draw, she couldn't shake it. Her fingers had a mind of their own.

What seemed to be on their mind right now was the man seated next to her. Suddenly too big and too male. Too damn real.

Worse, she was starting to think that thoughts of Will Fraser weren't just a three-a.m.-can't-sleep blip on the radar. Not when sitting next to him was making her so edgy. And even if she'd had the vaguest inclination to write a Christmas wish list, she was damn certain that an out-of-the blue inexplicable teensy crush on Will Fraser wouldn't be on it.

"Going somewhere?" Stefan drawled as Will walked into Salt Devil's kitchen carrying Mina's Tupperware.

"Thought I should return this," Will said, holding out the plastic container. Perfectly reasonable excuse. Nothing to see here. If it worked on Stefan, hopefully it would work on Mina too. Though, in her case, he had a backup plan. He'd seen the drawing forming on the page of her notebook before she'd slammed it shut. He knew his own face well enough. What Mina was doing drawing it was another matter. One he really wanted to investigate.

Besides, after she'd closed the book, she hadn't taken another note. He'd only just managed to keep half of his attention on the meeting too. Christmas tree decorations and raffles and candy cane treasure hunts were nowhere near as interesting as the information that Mina had drawn him. Maybe she was one of those people who just doodled. But maybe not. His face had been clear in the lines she'd been drawing.

He hadn't even known she could draw. But clearly she could. Her long fingers had moved the pen over the page in an easy rhythm. Almost a dance. Lucky notebook, was all he'd been able to think after the fact that she was drawing him had registered. After that she'd slammed the book shut. Had she caught him watching her?

Hopefully not. And what was she doing wasting her time manning the radio for search and rescue if she could draw like that? He didn't remember anyone ever mentioning that Mina Harper was an artist. Couldn't think if he'd ever seen her with a sketchbook in her hand anywhere. But the Harpers owned a big chunk of land and a long stretch of beach where she could hide away. And Mina didn't often cross his path.

When her husband had been alive, he'd seen her around town and the island far more often. But she'd retreated—understandably—after his death. He shook off the thought. He didn't want to think about Adam. The guy was dead. Sad—Will had liked him a lot—but there was nothing to be done about it. He'd been in the wrong place at the wrong time—which just sucked— and died way too young. But Mina was alive.

Alive and drawing him in her notebook, when she was meant to be doing something else entirely. He needed to think about that. And what it might mean.

Plus he had his notes and Mina, if she was supposed to be reporting back to Bill about what the committee had decided, was going to need a copy of them. So that gave him two excuses to turn up on her doorstep. He'd seen her Jeep head out on the road that led to the Harper end of the island rather than take the left turn that would have taken her back to the neat white cement block building down by the waterfront where the search and rescue team were based when the meeting had ended.

"Mina tell you she has a Tupperware shortage?" Stefan asked, one brow lifting.

"It's rude to keep people's stuff," Will retorted. "Don't worry, I'll be back before things pick up." On a Tuesday in late November, Salt Devil wasn't doing a roaring trade. Things would pick up after five thirty when people decided they needed a beer after work or that they couldn't be bothered cooking dinner. But Stefan could handle the three people currently in the bar by himself for an hour or so.

Stefan, who was, as usual, standing near the big stove stirring something—chili by the smell of it—simmering in a large pot, frowned. He moved away from the stove, coming to stand by Will. "Nice shirt."

Will shrugged. "Thanks, thought I might as well change early." While he never really dressed up to tend bar—Salt Devil wasn't that kind of place—he did make a point of changing out of whatever clothes he'd been wearing during the day to work at the distillery or in the office before he started a shift. This time of year, that usually meant a flannel shirt and a T-shirt with jeans and boots. Which was what he was wearing now. Okay, well, apart from the fact the shirt was somewhat nicer than usual. Green wool rather than flannel. A shirt he wouldn't usually wear to the bar. One more suitable for a date. But no way in hell was he admitting that to Stefan.

"You sure you know what you're doing?" Stefan asked.

Will hitched the container under his arm. "Pretty sure I can handle returning Tupperware."

Stefan's gaze didn't budge. "Which would be fine if that was all you were doing."

"You got something to say?" Will asked.

Stefan smoothed a hand over his beard. "She's been through a lot."

"I'm aware of that," Will said. "I'm not an asshole."

"And you like her a lot."

Damn. He and Stefan had never actually discussed Mina before now. The uncomfortable truth. Better left unconfronted when previously there hadn't seemed as though there was much chance of him ever being able to do anything about his crush. But that was then and this was now, and apparently his big brother felt the urge to interfere. Or second-guess. Or whatever the hell he was doing. "So what if I do?"

"What happens if she shoots you down, is all. You've liked her for a long time, yeah?"

"I've hardly been pining for Mina Harper," Will said, giving Stefan a "drop it" look. "I've dated. Unlike some people I could mention." Stefan hadn't dated anyone since his last girlfriend had dumped him via Skype from Afghanistan. Three years ago.

"You pick women who are short-termers," Stefan said, ignoring Will's attempt to change the subject. "Like Ali. Nice gal but you knew from the outset she was only here for a year."

"There was always the chance she'd stay."

Stefan snorted, shaking his head. "No there wasn't."

Well, that was true. Ali had come to Lansing to teach at the elementary school on a year's contract. Not many of the people who came to the island on short-term gigs—not that there were many of those—stuck. "People surprise you. We've stayed," Will pointed out.

"We sunk our life savings and then some into a distillery. That has a way of focusing your attention."

"And whose idea was that again?" Will inched toward the door.

Stefan stepped in front of it, arms folded. Apparently he'd decided that now was the time for "Stop trying to change the subject."

"I'm not entirely sure what the subject is."

"You and Mina Harper. You sure that's a good idea?"

Will shrugged. "Hard to be sure about anything. But I figure it's time I found out."

"She might not be ready. She might never be ready. Some people don't get over a loss like that."

Their own mother being a case in point. She'd never remarried after their dad had died. But she'd been in her forties. Hardly old, but not as young as Mina either. "If that's so, then I guess it's better if I find out," Will said. "Then I can get on with things."

"You in a sudden hurry to settle down?"

"No. But I'd like to eventually. Of course, I'm not as old as you yet."

Stefan grunted and turned back to his chili. Standard response for Will making any mention of his brother's love life. Stefan was in danger of turning into a monk. Though monks probably didn't run bars and make whiskey for a living. Fancy herbal liqueurs maybe, but not whiskey. But right now he had more important things on his mind than Stefan. Like Mina Harper. And whether or not he was about to make a complete fool of himself.

chapter seven

It was dumb to be nervous about knocking on a door, right? A simple knock. Then, "Hi, Mina, I brought your Tupperware back, thanks for the cookies." That was a completely normal and reasonable thing for him to do. Add in the offer of meeting notes, and there was no reason for her to think he was odd for turning up here.

So why did he feel like he was back in junior high trying to figure out how to ask Hannah Shapiro out on his very first date?

He wiped his palm on his jeans.

Knock. Smile. Give her the Tupperware. See what happened next.

Man up.

Suddenly he'd forgotten how to breathe, but he managed to raise his hand and knock. The sound seemed to echo. Then, silence.

Shit. Was she even home?

But before he could work out what his Plan B was,

there was the skittering sound of dog claws on floor-boards, followed by a happy bark and Mina's somewhat muffled voice saying, "Sit." Then the door opened.

Mina.

Wearing an old white shirt and tight black jeans that showed off her long legs and looking somewhat surprised to see him. "Will?"

"Er, hi," he said. God. *Gorgeous.* Every time he saw her, that was all he could think. She'd worn some sort of dark green complicated sweater wrap thing at the meeting that had hidden her shape. But her white shirt hung open and beneath it she wore a tight black tank that followed the lines of her body with devotion. He wrestled his reptile brain back into submission and lifted the Tupperware container. "I brought this back for you."

"Oh." She looked at the container, but before she could say anything else, Stewie lunged past her and stuck his nose at Will's crotch. Or maybe he was after the spiced apple muffins Will had grabbed from the bar's kitchen before he'd left that were currently in the paper bag he had in his free hand.

"Crap. Stop," Mina snapped, grabbing for his collar. "Sorry," she said as she hauled Stewie back.

"No problem," Will said. "Dogs will be dogs." He looked at her hopefully, willing her to invite him in. He held up the bag with the muffins. "I brought you a couple of Stefan's muffins. They're pretty good. Not as good as your cookies. But don't tell him I said that or he'll cut off my supply."

"You brought me muffins?"

"Anyone who sat through that meeting deserves a reward." He held out the bag. "Apple spice. They're good."

Stewie whined a little, straining his nose toward the bag. Apparently he agreed with Will's assessment of the muffins.

"Oh," Mina said again. "That's . . . nice of you." She stepped back, keeping hold of Stewie. "Do you want to come in?"

He wasn't going to wait to be asked twice. "Sure," he said. Keeping the muffins out of Stewie's reach, he followed her into the house and down the hall to the kitchen.

Last time he'd been here, the place had been closed up, blinds down, not many lights on, and he'd been too focused on Mina to pay much attention to his surroundings. Now the light seemed to come from all around him, making the room almost dazzling. He squinted a little, taking in the view of endless ocean beyond the headland that seemed to fill the windows forming half the wall on the far side of the room. The effect was slightly disconcerting, like the house was actually surrounded by the waves.

Too much water.

Turning, he put the Tupperware down on the counter along with the muffins. "You better keep these out of Stewie's reach," he said, pushing the bag toward Mina. "We had a Lab when I was a kid. He was huge. And good at stealing food off counters." Stewie was now sitting by Mina's feet, gazing intently up at the exact place on the counter where the bag sat, doing a good impression of a dog who hadn't been fed in days.

Mina smiled down at the dog. "Stewie's mostly well behaved." She opened the bag to inspect the contents. "Would you like one of these? Or coffee?"

He wasn't going to say no to that invitation. "Both." He nodded toward the small coffee machine. "I can do coffee if you do the muffins."

Mina hesitated. "That kind of feels like asking you to do your job in my house."

"I like making coffee," he said. "That's why I do it at the bar and not Stefan." He moved over to Mina's small espresso machine. If he was remembering correctly from the night he'd stayed over, the coffee beans were in the farthest of the set of bright blue canisters that sat on the counter next to it.

"In that case, sure," she said. "Though if you can't be bothered, I have one of those pod gizmos as well."

"Perish the thought," he said.

She laughed. "I guess I shouldn't confess to you that half the time I use that instead of bothering with the machine?"

"I'm going to pretend I didn't hear that."

"Will Fraser. Coffee snob."

"Not a snob. I'll drink most forms of caffeine. But I like espresso best." He reached for the coffee. "By the way, if you want notes from the meeting for Bill, I have mine."

"Notes?"

"I noticed you stopped taking notes. Thought maybe your head was hurting." Angie's meetings were enough to give anyone a headache. "How is your head by the way?"

Mina flushed. "Practically good as new." She stared up at him, expression . . . nervous.

Had he said something wrong? He searched his memory. Muffins. Coffee. Meeting notes. Nothing controversial.

"Can I draw you?" Mina blurted.

That wasn't exactly what he'd been expecting. Not your average conversational opener. "Draw me?"

"You know. Paper. Drawing stuff. Pictures." Her hand made a fluttering gesture in the air. He wasn't sure if she was picturing the moves she'd make with a pen or trying to wave off the fact she'd made the request at all.

"No, I don't know," he said. "I can just about draw stick figures. I saw you . . ." Wait. She might not want to know he'd realized what she was drawing. ". . . doodling in the meeting. You draw seriously?"

A shoulder hitch. "I paint, mostly."

She painted. How had he lived on Lansing for over five years and didn't know that Mina Harper painted? Secrets were hard to keep in a place this small. "What kind of paintings?"

"Watercolors, mostly. Landscapes. Seascapes. That kind of thing."

"And you want to draw me?" He couldn't quite get his head around the idea. Or what it might mean.

"Sometimes I like to sketch too." Her cheeks had turned pink, as though she was regretting she'd brought up the subject at all. "If it's a problem, then don't worry—"

He moved, caught her hand before she could wave him off. "It's not a problem." Hell, if it meant spending more time with Mina, he'd probably do any damn thing she wanted. Which meant he was a fool, but not fool enough to give up the opportunity. He let go of her hand before she could get uncomfortable with the contact. Tried to pretend his hand wasn't tingling where he'd touched her.

Drawing. He'd think about that instead. "Here?" He looked around the kitchen and the cozy living room beyond it. No sign of any art supplies. You needed easels and whatever to paint, didn't you?

"No. Upstairs."

Ah. Right. The mysterious staircase. It made sense, now he was thinking about it. The upper floor of the cottage, which only took about two thirds of the space of the lower, judging by the outside, had windows on all sides. Big windows. Lots of glass. He'd always assumed—not that he'd ever thought too hard about it— that it was to take advantage of the views from the headland. But maybe it was about light. Painters liked light, didn't they? He'd suffered through art classes in elementary school and a few compulsory ones in junior high, but none of his teachers had ever suggested he explore any further.

Fine by him. He'd always been more interested in the sciences. The chemistry that his grandfather had told him about. So he knew jack shit about painting. Only that Mina liked it apparently, so he was going to have to try and not sound like a dumbass. "Now?"

She nodded. "Good light right now."

Light. Right. He'd been correct about that then. He folded the top of the muffin bag back down.

"Ready?" she asked, practically bouncing on her toes.

He nodded at the staircase. "Sure. Lead the way."

The staircase was dark. There was a door at the top of the flight of stairs as well as the bottom, closing off any view of what lay beyond. He followed Mina up the stairs, trying not to stare at the sway of her hips. When she opened the door and light poured down, dazzling him.

He emerged into the room beyond the doorway, blinking, unable to see anything for a minute. When his vision cleared, the first impression was that he was floating somehow. Everything that wasn't glass was painted white, and everything that was glass was flooding light into the room, so the ocean visible out of the windows on two sides of the room and the land on the other one seemed oddly close. The wall with the door was more solid, the only windows running along the top foot or so of it. But even looking there didn't give much relief as nearly every inch of the plaster was covered with paintings.

The ocean, he realized as they came into focus. A thousand moods of blue and gray and green. Not just the view out of the windows—though that was there in multiple versions—but other beaches and seas and oceans. Some of them had to be other parts of the island, but some of them, he thought, might be other places. Or maybe imaginary.

He moved closer as Mina bustled around the room, dragging a wooden chair from against one of the walls to the center of the room, studying the images. Mina's seas were gorgeous. But restless. No calm waters. No, these had waves and eddies and sprays of white crashing into sand. Some were outright stormy.

And what exactly did that say about her?

Not to mention the fact that there wasn't a person to be seen in any of them. Not so even as much as a boat. Just miles and miles of endless ocean. He turned back to Mina. Those eyes, a shade that would fit right in with the stormier of her seascapes, were fixed on him.

"Come sit over here."

She stood by an old wooden chair set before an empty easel almost as tall as she was.

He would have liked to study the paintings a little longer, to see if there was any secret to be found in the images she'd made, but the sound of her voice drew him toward her as surely as she had him on a line. His heartbeat seemed loud in his ears, pounding as she watched him. The expression on her face was . . . well, the closest he could come was sexual. The last time a woman had seemed quite so fascinated by his face had ended with both of them naked.

So he sat, feeling those eyes on his skin and trying not to think about how much he wanted to touch her.

That was pretty much a lost cause. Near impossible to think about anything else with her watching him that way, pupils flared despite the bright light. He didn't dare move. Didn't want to risk shattering the moment.

The sun warmed the left side of his face, the light stronger from that direction. But he stayed still, breathing in the smell of her. He wanted to taste the scent of her, like he would breathe in a great whiskey. Letting the separate parts that made up the whole sink into him until he had her memorized. She wore perfume, something spicy and warm. That was the strongest note. There was ginger in that scent and something smoky. But not the earthiness of wood smoke, something more exotic. Like incense or the smell you might get if you burned some exotic flower. But there was more to it than that. The salt of the sea, perhaps, and a tiny thread of something herbal from shampoo or body lotion. And then the note that wove through it all. The smell that was purely Mina.

But just when he thought he might have gotten all of it,

she moved away, breaking the spell. The floorboards protested with a screech as she dragged the easel away and replaced it with another battered wooden chair. After she'd placed that to her satisfaction, she moved again, movements almost a prowl, lowering sheer blinds over several of the windows, including the one facing him.

When she had the light corralled to her satisfaction, she pulled a big black sketchbook out of a drawer in an old cabinet standing in one corner of the room and a handful of pencils out of another drawer and finally, finally came back to him, sinking onto the chair facing him.

"Am I meant to pose?" he asked, as her gaze settled on him again.

"No. I need to look for a little while."

"Look all you want." The words came out a little more fervently than he intended.

God, he was going to make an idiot out of himself.

Mina was here, focused on him. Interested in his face. Drawing him. He had no idea what it meant, but it was several steps past vaguely knowing who he was. Or inviting him to Thanksgiving. Him and his brother. That was politeness, he suspected. Possibly prompted by Lou. Sympathy for the outsiders combined with Mina wanting a way to make it up to him for Stewie damaging the car.

But this? This was just Mina and him. She'd asked him to pose for her. She wanted to draw him. Him. And he wasn't willing to give up a single second of it. Even if the closest he ever got to her was her pencil tracing the lines of his face on paper. "I'm good," he said, moving his hand.

"Sorry," she said. "I get kind of lost in it. So yell if you get a cramp."

Lost in it. He knew how that felt. He could get lost in her face. He didn't think he'd ever really had a chance to just sit and look at her for quite this long. It wasn't cool to stare at women and it was downright creepy when they were clearly involved with someone else, so he'd kept his eyes to himself.

He'd tried to forget everything he knew about Mina's face. To erase the sharp chin and big eyes and the hair that was dark but threw reddish highlights like sun glinting off whiskey when she was in the light now that she'd stopped dyeing it black. He'd locked it away. Dated other women. Which hadn't worked out.

And now here he was, alone with her. Able to watch her. To count the smattering of freckles across her nose. To see how her mouth curved as she focused on the paper, apparently pleased with whatever it was she was getting down. And just now, to envy the fact that she was able to get something down on paper to keep her memory alive. It was enough to make a man want to take up art. Unfortunately he knew his artistic limitations. Like he'd told Mina, stick figures were about it. He left the artistic side of the business to Stefan.

"I'll try and hold your attention," he said.

"Probably won't have to try too hard," Mina said, almost absently.

If he hadn't already been sitting still, he would have frozen in place.

What could he possibly say to that? Mina found him attention-worthy? Not what he'd expected to hear. And maybe she'd given away more than she'd intended—in fact, watching as pink stole over her cheeks and her teeth caught her bottom lip just for a second he was certain she had—but that little slip of her tongue had made his day. Though, watching the exact spot where her teeth dented the soft curve of her mouth, he wanted to make it even better.

He fought to keep still, to not rise out of his seat and pull her close and find out just what that lip tasted like. That way lay disaster. His fingers dug into his thigh, his gut tightening with the same force.

Mina Harper was dangerous up close it seemed.

If she could do this to him with just her gaze, then what might the rest be like?

Incendiary, if he had to guess. The kind of heat that left scorch marks and a hunger for more.

But he'd never know if he did something stupid and spooked her. She was a widow. She'd been wrecked by life once—twice when you counted losing her father—and had survived. He wasn't going to be the one who wrecked her a third time. So he would tread cautiously. Treat her with the care she deserved. Wait and see what happened. Let her set the pace, if there was any pace to be set.

Even if it killed him.

Which judging by how fiercely he wanted to touch her when this was only the third time he'd been in any sort of close proximity to her, it was likely to do.

But he'd rather die frustrated than regretting having hurt her.

So he would sit here and burn.

Or think of a distraction.

Like conversation. There was an idea. He wasn't sure he remembered how to string two words together, but sounding like an idiot had to be better than sitting here hoping she couldn't read everything he was feeling in his face. Or his body. He'd hadn't been this glad of the tail of a shirt lying over his lap since he'd been in the grip of teenage hormones.

Talk, idiot.

Right. Move mouth. Make sound.

Distract the hard on.

He cleared a throat that felt suddenly like he'd swallowed a mouthful of Lansing Island sand.

"So, you're an artist," he said. "Why didn't I know that?"

Gray-green eyes lifted their focus from the sketchbook to him. Then lowered again. "Not many people do."

"Why not?"

She lifted her head again, expression suddenly wary.

"I mean, I'm no art critic but those paintings are amazing." He waved at the wall behind her.

She twisted to look in the direction of his gesture. When she turned back her cheeks had pinked up again. He was beginning to be very fond of that flush of color over her skin. It warmed her eyes. Made her look a little disheveled. He'd like to see what she looked like if he ever got to muss her up properly. Find out what other parts of her body might flush and warm like sunrise pouring over all that creamy skin. He swallowed. Art. They were supposed to be talking about art.

"It's kind of new," she said. "So it's not something I wanted to share until I knew what I wanted to do with it."

"You didn't paint before? When you were—" He cut himself off before he finished the sentence. This wasn't the best time to bring up Adam. "Younger," he said instead. Lame save, but better than blurting the word "married" into the middle of whatever this thing that might be starting between them might be.

"I did art in high school." She looked back down at her sketchbook. "But then life got . . . busy." Her pencil was moving steadily over the paper, the rasp of it like a whisper.

He couldn't see what her drawing looked like—the sketchbook was tilted back toward her. But then, he was more interested in the woman than the picture.

Busy. She'd married at eighteen. He knew that much. The first time he'd ever seen her, she'd been standing on the dock down in Cloud Bay, waiting for the ferry. He'd been minding his own business, waiting for Stefan who'd gone to L.A. for the day. They'd only been on the island a month or so. Finding their feet. And then he'd seen Mina, standing in the sunlight, wearing a simple red tank top and tattered denim shorts, dark hair piled up on her head, and looking so goddamn carelessly beautiful that for a moment he'd lost his breath entirely as the world shifted beneath his feet.

He'd never believed in love at first sight.

Now he knew better. And he knew that love at first sight didn't mean rainbows and unicorns and happy endings. Because while he'd been standing there on the dock, trying to muster up the courage to walk over to her and introduce himself, the ferry had arrived. And he'd watched her grow even more beautiful as a grin spread over her face at the sight of a dark-haired guy walking down the gangway before she'd run toward whoever the lucky bastard was and the pair of them had practically set the dock on fire with the kiss they'd exchanged.

He still wasn't sure he'd recovered from that moment. The moment he realized that his mystery girl was well and truly in love with someone else. And then he'd found out she was married—and that she was a Harper—and he'd decided he was shit out of luck.

If he could have figured out a way to convince Stefan that they'd made the wrong decision coming to Lansing and that they should get the hell out of town and back to Oregon, he would have. But they'd sunk almost every penny they had into Salt Devil, and he'd been stuck.

Luckily it turned out that starting a business—two businesses really—took up a hell of a lot of time and apart from the odd time their paths crossed either at the bar or in town, he'd been able to mostly put Mina out of his mind. Not to change his useless, doomed crush to any real degree but he'd managed to box that up somehow and keep it locked away in a back corner of his brain where it didn't bother him too often.

But then Adam had died. Driving home from a friend's birthday party. A party held at Salt Devil. He hadn't been drunk. Will was a master at separating anyone who got messy at his bar from their car keys and, besides, he'd never known Adam Clark to drink more than a couple of beers in a night. But it had been late and the tourist who hit his car had been drinking, and that had been all. Mina, who'd stayed home, was a widow at twenty.

He'd stopped seeing her around the island much at all after that. She'd never set foot in the bar again. Making her feelings on the matter of how she felt about the Fraser brothers fairly clear. He couldn't blame her for that.

Yet three years later, here they were. And he knew that if she gave him any sort of opening, he wasn't going to waste a second chance.

"So do you know what you want to do with it now?" he asked.

"It?" she said absently, still drawing.

"Your art. You said you hadn't told anyone because you didn't know what you wanted to do with it."

She looked up again, squinting slightly against the light shining into her face. "Maybe. Trouble is, when it comes to art, wanting to do a thing and being able to do a thing aren't necessarily the same."

"Isn't that true of any job?"

"Maybe."

"Well, my mom always told us that you could never go wrong doing something you love. Following a passion is a good thing."

"Sometimes you can go down a wrong path, though. Or your passion can turn selfish. Consume you. Music was like that for my dad, I think. I mean, he loved us but the music was always first. Same thing for my mom. She left him because she couldn't give up her photography. And he—well, you've probably heard all the Grey Harper stories."

"A few," he admitted. Rock star. Legendary party guy. Alcoholic. Absent father. Sex god. The mythology surrounding Mina's father was exactly that. Mythic. Epic. But Mina had been dealing with the real man, not the legend. "Doesn't mean any of them are true."

One side of her mouth quirked. "Knowing my dad, a lot of them probably are."

"Doesn't mean that you would be that way if you took

the art world by storm. After all, you'd know what to watch out for. Plus, if you have to be cooped up in your studio arting a lot of the time, how much trouble could you get into anyway?"

She smiled. "Arting?"

"Whatever the technical term is. I wouldn't know a watercolor from an oil painting."

She twisted back toward the wall of paintings. "I can help you with that. Those"—she pointed at the paintings—"are watercolors."

"Good to know. So watercolor. If that's what your passion is, then my advice would be to just go for it. That's true about most things in life actually."

chapter eight

"Just go for it? Is that the reasoning behind you and Stefan starting your business?" Just go for it. She'd had that attitude once. Leap before you look. She'd done it when she'd married Adam. But that had been a different Mina.

"Something like that." Will said.

In the bright light of her studio, his eyes were more green than hazel. A deep cool shade, brighter than the sludgy green of the shirt he wore. It would be hard to find the color if she painted him. She didn't keep many greens in her palette, preferring to mix them, but she had a few. Malachite might get there, if she darkened it. Or apatite maybe. That was a little closer. But neither was quite right.

The green was an unsettling shade. Perhaps that made sense when she was starting to realize that Will was an unsettling man. His face was forming on the page beneath her hand effortlessly. As though she'd known its planes and contours all her life. When exactly had her brain memorized his face? She didn't want to know. She drew another line, smudged it with her finger, trying to deepen the shadow beneath his bottom lip. His mouth made her nervous. She wasn't ready to think too hard about why just yet. She twirled the pencil for a moment, wondering if it was worse to stare at him or the drawing.

Trying to remember how to act normal when sitting three feet away from him was making her . . . well, that was another thing she wasn't ready to think about.

"Why whiskey?" she asked, glancing up. "Not exactly a common thing to want to do. Not unless you grew up in Kentucky, maybe."

"That's bourbon," he said. "We're trying to do Scotch. Though you can't call it that if it's not made in Scotland."

She didn't want a lecture on the different types of whiskey. Though to be fair to Will, she'd asked the question. Maybe to remind herself exactly why he was a bad idea. Her fingers tightened around the pencil, and she saw his gaze drop to her hand.

"And I'll shut up about that part now. Sorry. Habit." He looked guarded, but when she made a little "go on" gesture with her pencil, he did.

"As to why, I guess it's kind of in my blood. My grandfather was Scottish. His family owned a small distillery. But they closed it during the Second World War. Grandda always wanted to start it up again, but in the end things were too hard after the war and he decided to come to America. He was trained as a mechanic in the army, so those are the skills he used to get a job when he came to the U.S. Worked at garages and factories, fixing cars and trucks. He always wanted to start a distillery. He and Dad were supposed to do it together but then Dad died and Grandda stepped in to help Mom out. No money for pipe dreams."

No money for pipe dreams. At least she was lucky enough that money was never going to be a problem. Grey and the other members of Blacklight had been ordinary suburban kids. Maybe that was why they'd all enjoyed the perks of the wealth they'd found so much. But even their extreme partying hadn't managed to dent the money they'd made with their talent.

Unless Mina and her siblings and the other Blacklight kids were really stupid, there was money to last a few generations. Sometimes she wished there wasn't, stupid as that was. And she tried to do good with her share. Adam had been stubborn about her money—and she hadn't been old enough to get her full share of the trust when they'd married—so they'd lived fairly simply. But knowing the money was there if they ever needed it had definitely made things easier.

They hadn't struggled. She hadn't struggled. Maybe that was why she had been so reluctant to take the next step with her art.

"So you wanted to do what he couldn't?" she asked. Maybe she had the opposite problem. Fear that she could never succeed the way Grey had.

"Not exactly," Will said. "But Grandda always drank the best single malt he could afford and he used to tell Stefan and me stories about whiskey making and Scotland. I guess his brainwashing stuck."

She knew a little bit about family brainwashing. Or

expectations. Being the child who hadn't met her father's.

"He must be proud of the two of you," Mina offered.

"He died before we bought the property here," Will said. "But he got to see Stefan get his first job at a distillery. And he knew what we wanted to do. So yeah, I guess he was happy."

There was a note of loss in Will's voice that she understood far too well. And she knew words didn't always help, but she wanted to ease that loss for him somehow. It might not be fresh, but that didn't make it any less painful. "He would have been. Following in his footsteps. My dad . . . I don't think he ever really understood me. Not being musical like Faith and Zach. We never had that thing in common, you know?"

Will shook his head, slowly. Trying not to mess with the pose, if she had to guess.

"I bet he was proud no matter what you did. Did he draw?"

Mina frowned at the sketchbook and deepened another shadow. "No. Not unless you count stick figures."

"Then your mom? Is that where you get it from?"

Had Will ever met Emmy? She tried to think. Probably not. Emmy had come back to the island for Adam's funeral but the Fraser brothers hadn't been there. She would have remembered that. Since then, Mina had only seen Emmy a couple of times, all off-island. "Tammy's a photographer. Who knows where these things come from?" She looked back up at Will and caught him rubbing his thigh.

Was he getting a cramp? Or tired? She had no idea how long they'd been sitting there. The drawing was three quarters done. "Do you need a break?" she asked, with a little shake of her head.

He looked like he was going to be manly about it and refuse. But she'd posed for her high school art class once and remembered how quickly muscles could get painfully stiff. "Take a break. I told you, I get lost in it." Lost in his face flowing onto the paper. She had him mostly captured now but wasn't quite ready to let the picture go.

Will stood, and the relieved noise that escaped him as he started to lift his arms in a stretch told her she'd been right. He'd been uncomfortable. She started to put her sketchbook to the side so he wouldn't feel compelled to sit down again straight away but then froze as he completed the movement, his arms and body forming a line of such unadulterated male beauty that her mind went blank for a moment.

But then everything focused in on Will like a spotlight following a lead man. "Stay right there," she ordered, flipping the page over on her sketchbook—the unfinished face forgotten. She didn't know exactly what it was. The light. The angle of muscle and bone. Or maybe, just maybe, the man himself. But she didn't care. She couldn't have stopped her fingers sending the pencil rushing over the paper if she tried. She propped the sketchbook between her arm and her torso and started to draw, not even stopping to sit.

Will looked startled but stayed mercifully still. She made a grateful noise, not wanting to waste time talking. He wouldn't be able to stay like that for long. She needed to work fast. So she forgot about who it was she was drawing in such a frenzy and just gave herself up to it.

Stopped thinking and just chased the light and shadow

over the page, trying to capture the curve of skin over muscle and the way the light wrapped around him. For a second she wished she had her paints, to try and get the late afternoon sun and the color it gilded his skin and eyes and hair onto the page, but she could always add that later.

She had a feeling the image he made was going to be stuck in her head for a very long time.

But no. Stop thinking. Just draw. Ride the rush of it. The adrenaline of something just working. It didn't happen often. But it was like a small moment of perfect when it did. She'd wondered sometimes if that was the feeling Grey had felt out there on stage, standing under the lights soaking up the adoration of all those fans. Only she didn't want the fans, just the feeling.

It bubbled through her.

Sheer delight. An emotion she wasn't that familiar with anymore. Intoxication. The good kind. The safe kind. Though whether from the art or the man, she didn't know. Hopefully the former, as the latter would be a long way from safe.

But she wasn't going to let that spoil the moment. No, for now she was just going to enjoy the sensation. Remember how it felt. Hope that it wouldn't take so long for it to visit her again.

She made one last sweeping gesture with her pencil and then nodded to herself, satisfied. It was good. Better than good.

Will on the page—arms reaching for the ceiling, head thrown back—looked loose and somehow wild. Wild in a way that made you want to move closer even though you knew it would be foolish. Like the urge to reach through the bars and pet the fur of a caged tiger.

An urge she had no intention of giving into. The last man she'd been irresistibly drawn to had been Adam. That kind of fascination led to the kind of feelings she couldn't risk having again. But as she looked up and Will started to lower his arms, she couldn't help herself. She rose up on her toes and kissed him. Just a brief press of her lips against him but it was enough that she felt him jolt and felt the answering zing of something deep in her gut. "Thank you," she murmured, feeling slightly untethered.

"You are more than welcome," Will said, voice rumbling softly. The sound vibrated through her, chasing the aftershock of the kiss and skimming over her nerves and bringing all of them suddenly, shockingly, awake. *She wanted.*

And that particular sensation, as unfamiliar as happiness, was simply shocking. As though she'd doused herself in a bucket of the icy seawater pounding the beach outside her window.

She'd kissed him. Will Fraser.

God.

The sketchbook fell to the floor as she stepped back, stomach clenching. "Sorry," she said, her face heating even as a chill shivered down her back. "I'm sorry." The words came too fast. "That was a mistake."

"Fresh mistletoe?" Mina asked, staring up at the decorations draping the ceiling inside Faith's front door. Where had Faith even found fresh mistletoe? "It's not even Christmas yet."

Not that you'd know it from looking at the house. Nope. Sometime in the last two days, someone had come and dropped a Christmas bomb on the place. She'd painted instead of helping Faith and Caleb decorate. Tried to drive Will's face out of her head with wild seas. It had worked for a while until she'd realized there was a boat on one of those seas and a man on the boat. A man who looked an awful lot like Will. She'd given in then, and let herself sketch him again, even added a little to the portrait she'd started earlier. That hadn't really helped either and she'd gone back to the seas. Still, she'd gotten another painting—maybe two—that she was happy with out of the work.

And while she'd been painting, apparently Christmas had exploded over Faith's house.

Where there was a surface that could hold tinsel or candles or decorations or greenery, it did. It all somehow worked but in a completely over-the-top way. Growing up, they'd often spent Christmas away from Lansing—if Blacklight were touring or recording. But when they'd been home, Grey—or Lou or Emmy or whoever Grey's latest girlfriend was—had spared no expense decorating, but their efforts seemed tame next to this. She blinked, kind of dazzled.

"Caleb likes Christmas," Faith said. The smile that spread over her face as she patted the belly of the nearly life-size Santa standing by the door was indulgently goofy. "It's our first Christmas together."

"Right now it's still Thanksgiving."

"Close enough according to Mr. White."

"That much is clear," Mina said, still trying to adjust to all the red, white, green, and silver. It could be worse. Caleb could have done everything in pumpkin orange for Thanksgiving. And a Santa statue was better than a giant turkey. Just.

"You just need to get into the festive spirit. Come on, Lou made cookies."

"Lou's here already?" Mina started following Faith toward the kitchen.

"Been and gone." Faith said. "She brought approximately elleventy billion cookies, left a bunch of instructions for things we could start doing, and said she'd be back when school gets out."

"Am I right in assuming, that list includes peeling all the apples and pumpkins?" Lou was in charge of pastry, but she was happy to let Mina and Faith do a lot of the grunt work when it came to filling prep.

"Got it in one."

"Well, at least there are cookies."

"Many many cookies. She brought a whole batch of rejects she claims have botched icing and said we could eat as many of those today as we wanted."

"Just trying to stop us wanting to eat one of the pies later." Zach had always tried to steal one of Lou's pies the day before Thanksgiving. Often he'd succeeded. But Mina had learned from a young age that stuffing one's face with pie the day before meant that one couldn't completely enjoy the total food orgy that was one of Lou's Thanksgiving dinners.

Faith grinned as they entered the kitchen and grabbed a bright red apron off the counter. "Here." She tossed it to Mina before picking up a second for herself. Mina tied hers on, expecting the worst. but instead of some bad Christmas pun, the words printed across the chest simply read KEEP CALM AND COOK ON. "I was expecting naked Santa or something."

"Gotta save something for Christmas," Faith said,

donning her own apron which proclaimed Mmmm, GRAVY.

"Definitely," Mina said. She glanced around the kitchen. A binder lay in the middle of the counter, neatly labeled THANKSGIVING. That would be Lou's work. It was a little scary just how organized her stepmom could be. And Faith had apparently already started following instructions, as rows of ingredients and utensils were laid out on either side of the binder.

"So, do I get a cookie before we begin or do I have to earn them?" The air was scented with sugar and butter and spice and other good things. Which meant the cookies were close even though she couldn't see any from where she stood. Her mouth watered. A cookie or three wasn't the same as eating a whole pie after all.

"Seeing as Mom isn't here, knock yourself out. They're in the pantry."

"How will I know which ones I'm allowed to eat?" Mina asked, pivoting on her heel to make a beeline for the pantry.

"Lou stashed the good ones somewhere else. I don't even know where they are. So you're safe."

Faith sounded amused. Often the case. The lights in the big walk-in pantry came on as Mina opened the door. They illuminated the shelves like spotlights, making it easy to spot the big plastic container filled with cookies sitting smack-bang in the middle of one of the shelves. "Anything else you need from in here?" she called back to Faith as she snagged a small pile of cookies.

"Nope, I ticked everything off my list earlier."

Typical. Everyone thought Faith was the easygoing

wild child, but she was an inveterate list maker. Of course, she was the one who'd stepped up to run the business side of Harper Inc. when Grey had gotten ill. Stepped up or rather been dumped with it. Zach had avoided in his usual fashion—having ditched his musical partnership with Faith to play with another band—and Mina had still been in school when Grey had been diagnosed. In Faith's position, she'd be making lists too.

Lou was also a big fan of lists. Though she took it to a whole other level—as evidenced by the binder waiting for her and Faith back in the kitchen. Maybe it was hereditary to a degree?

Emmy had never really stuck around long enough for Mina to find out what her views on lists were. These days their relationship was mostly fond distance. And didn't involve Emmy passing on any maternal information, like her favorite organizational systems.

Thank God for Lou. Without her, the three of them—Zach, Faith, and Mina—would have grown up wild. Left to the tender care of whatever nanny or tutor or random caretaker Grey managed to put in place when he was between wives or girlfriends. He loved them, but they'd only ever held part of his attention.

"Are you eating all the cookies at once?" Faith yelled from beyond the pantry and Mina started, almost dropping the pile of cookies in her hand. Enough pondering the weirdness that was her family and how she'd been raised. Time to be more like the one person who'd held it all together—Lou—and make a serious dent in the preparation for tomorrow.

She backed out of the pantry and returned to Faith, passing her half the cookies. "Here. Pre-pie sustenance."

"Thanks. Do you want coffee?"

"No. Still meant to be limiting the caffeine." Though it was tempting to pour half a gallon of coffee down her throat. Kissing Will, it seemed, hadn't improved her insomnia. No, she'd just added another layer to her three a.m. angst. Eventually she'd given in and risen from her bed to go and work on Will's portrait some more. She'd taken the sketch and reworked it on fresh paper, adding color with her paints. Somehow, despite the fact she was painting the man who had turned her into a crazy person, she'd managed to lose herself in the familiar rhythm of the art for a couple of hours until she'd emerged blinking to see the first hint of dawn lightening the black sky over the ocean. She'd crawled back to bed for an hour or two—taking one of Callie's stronger painkillers to help bomb her brain and the renewed ache in her shoulder into submission—but she was still feeling worse for wear.

But no coffee. Instead, she was turning to sugar. She bit into a cookie with a snap, taking a moment to appreciate Lou's genius, closing her eyes to let the flavors roll over her tongue before she devoured it and another in a few more bites, all without opening her eyes.

When she opened them again, Faith was watching her, expression somewhat quizzical.

"What?" Mina asked.

"Nothing," Faith said.

"I know that expression."

"It's just"—Faith hesitated—"it's nice to see you eat. Are you feeling better?"

"My head is okay," Mina said. Though she knew that wasn't exactly what her sister was asking. But today wasn't a day she wanted to talk about Adam. Not when she'd kissed Will last night. Not when she suspected that not even Lou's cookies were going to drive the feel of that kiss out her memory. "Don't fuss."

She said the words by rote. She'd said them so often after the darkness of the first six months or so after Adam's death, when suddenly Faith and Lou's near constant checking in on her had felt smothering rather than necessary, that she wasn't even sure she knew what she meant by them anymore. She'd said them regularly, though less often, in the years since then. And really, Faith and Lou had been remarkably restrained. She knew they worried about her. Knew she'd lost too much weight and that all they wanted was to feed her and love her and take all the pain away. But nobody could. So they'd bitten their tongues and sat on their hands and given her space.

And she'd felt awkward and guilty about chasing them away.

Really, grief sucked. Which was hardly news to anyone but also one of the things that you never really understood until you were in the middle of it. It sucked and it made you half crazy, and now when she was starting to feel like she was emerging from the crazy, here was Will, which was a whole different level of crazy. But not one that she could talk about with Faith. Faith would be all for the idea of Mina dating anyone, let alone Will.

Both as a sign of Mina coming back to life and because she was still in that goofy ridiculously happy stage of her relationship with Caleb and wanted to spread the love cooties around.

"I'm fine," she said a little more gently. "Really. Now, where do you want to start?"

"I thought you could do apples and I'll do pumpkin?" Faith said. "Pumpkin skins are tough. You might mess up your shoulder again."

Doubtful that she'd do anything worse to it than she had by drawing for hours yesterday and earlier that morning. But she was happy to leave the pumpkins to Faith. As much as she liked pumpkin pie, she'd never liked scooping the mushy seedy guts of them out. Not for Halloween as a kid and not now for Lou's pies. Lou, who refused to use pumpkin from a can since they'd spent a Thanksgiving in Australia and their hostess had made pumpkin pie completely from scratch, even though it was clear she thought Americans were odd for eating pumpkin for dessert.

"Apple duty is fine with me," Mina said. Though, eyeing the two big bowls of apples sitting on the counter, the peeler set neatly beside them, she wasn't sure peeling all of them would be any easier on her shoulder than wrangling pumpkins. But so far the painkiller was holding, so she'd worry about that later.

She pulled out a stool and took a seat near the apples, pulling the first bowl closer to her. Faith pushed over a second, empty, bowl.

"Peels in there. Slices go in this one," she said as she pushed yet another bowl across the counter.

Mina nodded and reached for the first apple.

"So how did the meeting go yesterday?" Faith asked as she settled to her own task, picking up a wickedly sharp-looking knife and studying the pumpkin as though seeking the best place to make the first cut.

The meeting. Will. *No. Don't think about Will.* "It was okay," Mina said carefully. She wasn't going to blush. No blushing allowed. She focused on the apple, trying to peel it in one unbroken strip. Someone had once told her that if you could do that and then toss it on the ground, it would form the initial of the man you'd marry. It had never worked. She'd yet to see an apple peel that formed an A. "Seems like they're putting a lot of effort into the festival."

The peel coiled onto the cutting board and for a moment the swoops looked vaguely like a cursive *W*. She scooped it up and tossed them into the waiting bowl with perhaps a little more force than was strictly necessary and picked up a knife to start slicing the apple.

"Who was there?" Faith asked curiously.

"The usual types," Mina said. She reeled off a list of names.

"Not Will?" Faith said.

Mina's hand jerked, and she barely missed chopping off her finger. She heard Faith snort. Damn.

"How did you know Will was going to be there?"

"He mentioned it," Faith said. "I notice you didn't."

"I didn't think you were all that interested in what Will Fraser does," Mina said, eyes locked on her apple.

"No, but I'm at least slightly interested in what you do when Will is around," Faith said. There was a meaty *thunk* as she apparently sliced through the pumpkin successfully. "You were pretty cagey when I asked if he liked the cookies."

"I told you, he liked them," Mina said, focusing on slicing the apple as though her life depended on it.

"You know, if you want me to believe that you aren't even a teeny bit interested in Will Fraser, then you probably should look me in the eye when you talk about him instead of staring at that apple like it's the most fascinating thing you've ever seen."

Mina lifted her head reluctantly. "Will was at the meeting. He's an interested business owner. Happy now?"

Faith pointed the knife at her. "No. I know you, lil' sis. And you're being weird about Will."

"I am not 'weird' about him. I'm not anything about him." At least, she was trying her best not to be.

"Yes, you are. And that's what's weird."

"I think I've told you how I feel about Will Fraser before."

"I know. He owns the bar that Adam was at before his accident. I get it. You don't like booze. He does. But that doesn't make him a terrible person."

"We've had this conversation already." Mina tipped apple slices into the third bowl and reached for another apple. She knew somewhere deep down it wasn't just Will's job that was the problem. But it was a reasonable excuse to give Faith.

"And we'll keep having it."

"Why? Why can't you leave it alone?"

"Because if you were truly indifferent to him, you wouldn't get annoyed with me for talking about him."

"Maybe you're just annoying," Mina muttered. "Big sisters often are."

Faith stuck her tongue out but then her expression softened. "I don't want to see you miss a chance because you've made some weird association between Will and Adam in your head. You're only twenty-three. You can't spend the rest of your life alone."

"Why not?" Mina said. "Wasn't that your grand plan until you met Caleb? Footloose and fancy free?"

"Yes. But I changed my mind."

"Which is fine for you. Doesn't mean I have to change mine. Like you said, I'm twenty-three. Pretty sure that means I'm old enough to make my own decisions about my love life."

Faith held up her hands. "Fine. Okay. I'll drop it." The "for now" she didn't say at the end of that sentence hung unspoken in the air. "I don't want to fight during the holidays."

"Good," Mina said. "So let's make pie.

chapter nine

Maybe this was a terrible idea. Will eased his Mustang through the gate to the Harper estate and rolled onto the start of the drive, hands too tight on the steering wheel as he thought about seeing Mina. Maybe he should just turn Lulu around and head back to the bar. Sure, he'd have to explain to Stefan why he was acting like a complete lunatic, but he was used to his brother thinking he was weird.

He wasn't used to having to see Mina again for the first time after she'd kissed him and then practically kicked him out of her house. He hadn't heard from her since Tuesday night. Radio silence. Which maybe was better than an actual message un-inviting him to Thanksgiving, but he couldn't help thinking that basic politeness might prevent Mina from doing that. So he had no freaking idea about what sort of welcome he could expect when he walked through Faith's big-ass front door.

And he was pretty sure that he wasn't going to take

it well if Mina gave him the cold shoulder. Not after he'd finally gotten to kiss her. Nope. He knew the taste of her now. Or, rather, had a hint of it. There'd been no tongues involved in the quick kiss that had shocked him, but it had still been hot as hell. And he wanted more.

He couldn't get the picture of her out of his head. Mina all wild eyes, pupils dark and cheeks flushed, pushing her mouth against his with a quick hunger that had taken him completely by surprise. But then he'd seen realization crash over her face like someone had switched the lights off.

She'd been embarrassed. And he'd been too taken by surprise to do anything sensible like try to reassure her or talk to her and had let her kick him out. After all, hanging around after a woman asked you to leave wasn't a good idea.

But he wished he'd said something—anything—to . . . well, he didn't know what exactly. He had no idea what she was feeling. She was a widow for chrissakes. Was he the first man she'd kissed since her husband?

The stupid-ass, too-much-testosterone, Neanderthal part of his brain wanted that to be true. Then again that part of his brain was the part that wished there'd never been a husband to begin with.

It wasn't helpful in working out what the hell was going on with Mina. So here he was, driving way more slowly down Faith Harper's long drive than was necessary and trying to figure out what the hell he was going to say to Mina when he saw her.

"Any reason you're driving slower than a ninety-year-old who's lost his bifocals?" Stefan drawled from beside him.

"It's wet. And cold," Will said.

"Dude. This is California. It's not like there's any risk of ice on the road. And your precious car has survived more than fifty years. I don't think it's going to melt if it gets some mud on the paintwork."

"Someone might be coming in the other direction."

"This drive could happily fit two cars and then some," Stefan said, sounding exasperated. "Speed it up. I'm starving."

Will obeyed the instruction, grateful that Stefan hadn't made any connection between their traveling speed and Mina. Not that he had any reason to. As far as his brother was concerned, Will had gone to see Mina and taken her Tupperware back and that was it. The bar had been too busy when Will had returned for Stefan to have time to notice that Will was acting weirdly—and he'd tried his best not to act weirdly. And on Wednesday, Will had avoided Stefan by disappearing down to the distillery for a few hours during the day and then locking himself up in the office to do paperwork for the rest of the afternoon before Salt Devil opened. As Stefan regarded doing paperwork as about as pleasant as having his eyeballs poked out, Will's ploy had worked and there'd been no brotherly grilling about Mina or anything else.

Today, hopefully Stefan would be distracted by Lou's cooking and be too polite to make fun of Will in front of the girl in question.

"Any idea who's going to be here?" Stefan asked as Will finally pulled Lulu in beside a row of cars lined up outside the Harper house. Will recognized a few of them but not all.

"Didn't ask," he admitted. He'd been to a couple of

parties that Caleb and Faith had thrown since Caleb had moved to Lansing, and there was no telling who might be there. He'd met a couple of rock stars and actors. And a couple of Caleb's tennis buddies. Not to mention a poet, a married couple who taught yoga for half the year and ran a cooking school in Tuscany for the other half, and a retired Broadway singer. But the celebrities had mingled happily with the people who worked for Faith and the other Lansing residents who'd been invited. He'd also been to parties where it had been only locals. So he had no idea who might be sharing turkey and pie with them today. Really, he didn't much care as long as Mina was there. Not that he was going to admit *that* to Stefan.

Nerves rolled through his stomach as they walked up to the door to ring the bell. The massive wreath decorating the equally broad front door gave him something to study while they waited. Made from what looked like driftwood, fir branches, and silver and red glass balls all held together with silver ribbon, it sparkled in the weak winter sun that was attempting to break through the clouds. The whole house sparkled in fact. There were fairy lights draped across the walls and around the windows, blinking red and green and as he looked up, he spotted practically a whole herd of disturbingly real-looking reindeer and a sleigh sitting on the lowest part of the roof immediately above the door.

Apparently Faith and Caleb were getting into the Christmas spirit early.

He wondered why there wasn't anyone from Harper Inc. on the festival committee. Seemed like they'd fit right in. Unlike Mina, who clearly hadn't been into the whole thing.

Well, Christmas was hard sometimes. Fraser family Christmases had been pretty quiet and subdued the first couple of years after their dad had died. Full of ghosts. Maybe Mina felt the same way.

As the last chimes of the doorbell rang away, the door opened, revealing Faith. "The Fraser boys as I live and breathe," she said with a grin and a flutter of her eyelashes. "Come on in." She flung the door wider and stood there for a moment, spotlighted. Dressed in a little black dress and a tiny cardigan covered in gold sequins, she literally sparkled, looking like she was made of glowing gold from the blonde lights running through her brown hair to the tanned skin and the tiny gold chains running across the leather of her black boots.

Will blinked, reminded for a moment just how pretty Faith was. Nearly as pretty as Mina, though Faith's was a more obviously rock-chick kind-of-out-there pretty. One that he'd gotten used to through years of proximity and barely noticed anymore. But every now and then she turned it on and could command a whole room just by smiling.

"Looking good, Faith," he said, stepping forward to kiss her cheek quickly. "Thanks for inviting us."

"I believe you can thank Mina for that," Faith said, grin widening. She stepped back to let him pass and he almost stumbled after the first step, coming to a halt as he caught sight of Mina standing almost in the middle of the entry hall. She didn't sparkle like her sister, but he forgot about Faith in an instant. Mina wore skinny jeans in an inky blue and a top made of some sort of sheer lacy stuff that floated enticingly around her body. It was the deep, rich, nearly-red pink of the heart of a raspberry and she'd painted her mouth the exact same shade. Which meant he could see each curve of those gorgeous lips clear as day.

Would she taste of raspberries if he grabbed her and kissed the lipstick off her mouth?

He was vaguely aware of Stefan rumbling a hello to Faith from behind him. He didn't care, all his attention fixed on Mina. She didn't sparkle but she definitely shone. She might as well have been spotlit, everything else fading into a blur around her.

"Hello, Will." Her eyes flicked up briefly, and he followed the direction of her gaze. About five feet above her head dangled a bunch of what he assumed was real mistletoe. Mistletoe? At Thanksgiving? Wasn't that a Christmas thing? Then again, there had been all those decorations. A glance around the room told him the inside of the house was as Christmas-ready as the outside. Which brought him back to the mistletoe. And Mina.

Was she standing there on purpose? Under the mistletoe? Hell. He didn't want to do the wrong thing.

"Hello, Mina," he said, not knowing whether to stay where he was or move closer.

Stefan solved his dilemma for him by drawling, "You're blocking the door, Will," from behind. The words seemed to break the spell holding him and Mina there and she stepped back, moving out of what could reasonably be called the mistletoe zone.

"Hey, Stefan," she said, looking over Will's shoulder. "Happy Thanksgiving."

"Happy Thanksgiving," Stefan replied, moving up next to Will. He held up the covered tray he was carrying. "We brought some cookies."

Mina's brows rose briefly but she reached for the plate. "Thanks."

"Pumpkin snickerdoodles," Stefan said. "I was going to bring pie but I figured Lou had that part covered."

"She does," Mina agreed. "But cookies are good."

"Very good," Faith said, nodding. "You didn't have to bring anything."

Will shrugged. "Our mom would disagree with you on that point." His grandda would have too. Only his standard offering would have been a bottle of great whiskey. That had been Stefan's first idea too, but Will had nixed it. When it came to alcohol, given the Harper's family history, safer to let them set the tone.

"Sounds like your mom and Lou would get along," Faith said with a smile. "Come on inside." She headed back into the house and, after a backward glance at Will, Mina followed her.

"Dude, too slow." Stefan said in a pitying voice and followed the girls.

Mina managed to avoid talking to Will while everyone mingled before the meal. Between introductions—Faith and Caleb had managed to assemble nearly twenty guests—and helping Lou with preparations, she successfully managed to be wherever he wasn't. Once or twice she caught his eye across the room but had made herself turn away before eye contact could turn into something more.

Truth was, she didn't know how she felt. Why she'd stood under the damn mistletoe when she'd seen his car pull up. Granted, it was hard to avoid the mistletoe given the size of the bunch Caleb had acquired, but she could have just waited inside with everyone else while Faith got the door. Only that seemed kind of rude when she'd been the one who'd invited Will and Stefan.

Or was that just her coming up with a justification for wanting to see Will? She had no idea. About any of it. She rarely had moments where she wished she drank but right now, the thought of a shot of something to ease her nerves was appealing. Cranberry and soda just didn't cut it. Which made it hard to even think about talking about it with Will. And he deserved the conversation at least. After all, she'd kissed him.

She'd liked kissing him. He'd liked kissing her too unless she'd completely read him wrong.

But liking kissing him came with a whole other bag of emotions that she didn't even want to open let alone sort through. Which was why the kissing had been followed by the freaking out. So he definitely deserved an explanation.

Maybe it would all be better after lunch. Lou's pie, if nothing else, usually improved any bad situation. So she could avoid Will until they were both in a carbohydrate-fueled daze perhaps.

But, as they sat down to eat, she realized that she hadn't figured Faith's sneakiness into the equation. Because she found herself seated almost directly across from Will. Not next to him . . . that would have been too blatant even for Faith. Nope, instead her sister had put Will squarely where Mina was going to have to look at him for the next two hours or so while they ate.

She leaned forward turning to look at where Faith sat at one end of the long table. Her sister picked up her glass of champagne and lifted it in a toast as she noticed

Mina, sending her a smile that said she'd known exactly what she was doing.

Mina returned the toast with her own glass and plotted revenge. Maybe she could hide all the Christmas cookies where Faith couldn't find them. Or get Ivy to reprogram the house's sound system to only play disco.

Ivy, who was one of Faith's oldest friends, was seated next to Mina and interrupted her train of thought by asking her about Stewie. She and her fiancé Matt were getting a Lab puppy for Christmas and Mina accepted the distraction of answering dog questions with relief. Though, even as she talked about teething and house training and puppy brains, she couldn't completely ignore Will. Not unless she wanted to eat facing sideways. So she watched him while she ate and talked to Ivy and to one of Lou's friends who sat on her other side.

Will watched her right back. Each time those green eyes caught hers, her pulse bumped a little. He made small talk with his neighbors too, laughing and smiling. But she knew exactly where his focus was. She could feel his attention even when she wasn't looking, the weight of it warming her skin.

She was sure the food was excellent but she didn't really taste any of it.

Not even the pie.

After everyone had finally left the table, leaving behind the rubble of a truly epic meal, Mina found Will in the living room, looking out of the long window toward the ocean.

She still didn't quite know what she wanted to say to him but their silent conversation during dinner had at least made it clear enough that there was something to say.

The pleased smile that spread across his face when he saw her only confirmed it.

"I'm going to walk off some pie before it gets dark," she said. "Would you like to join me?"

"Yes."

She'd barely finished her sentence before his answer came. Which made nerves light up along her skin. She took a breath. "Okay. I need to change my shoes. And grab a jacket." She studied him a moment. "Do you have a coat?" It wasn't freezing outside, but it was definitely too cool for Will to just wear the checked cotton dress shirt he wore.

He nodded. "In Lulu."

"Meet you outside then?" Mina said.

Will nodded. "Is Stewie coming with us?"

She shook her head. "Stewie is in the kitchen scavenging and working the puppy dog eyes. Lou will be feeding him leftovers, so no chance he'll move."

"Well, for a chance at more of Lou's pie, I might stake out the kitchen as well," Will said with a grin.

"That's why we need to walk. Make room for second dessert."

"Second dessert?"

"Also known as pie two point oh."

"Even better."

She ran up to her old room to get her coat and put on the sensible boots she'd worn to walk over from the cottage earlier. Through the window she caught a glimpse of Will walking to his Mustang, stride easy, and felt her nerves twist again. He looked like he didn't have a care in the world. Maybe he didn't. Maybe women kissed him out of the blue all the time and he could take it or leave it.

She thought back to the warmth of his eyes watching her across the dining table.

Maybe not.

So maybe she needed to be brave and go down there and see what happened.

Will was waiting by Lulu when she slipped out the front door. He'd donned a battered navy coat, which made him seem more . . . Will somehow. She couldn't deny he'd looked good in his dress shirt today but it had made her nervous. Her mental image of him fit better with the guy in the coat with the cool wind ruffling his hair.

"So, which way do you want to go?" she asked, joining him.

He shrugged. "This is your end of the island," he said. "You choose."

She considered. After being around so many people for a few hours, she had the faintest edge of a headache. Or maybe that was too much sugar. Either way, she wanted to chase it away with sea air.

"Well, we could walk down to the boathouse." She stared down past the main house to the Harpers' private jetty and the small boat shed there that held the smallest of Grey's powerboats and the small two-person skiff that she and Faith and Zach had used after graduating from the tiny Hobie they'd learned to sail in. And a couple of jet skis, but it wasn't really jet ski weather. Grey had owned a few boats. There was still a big yacht moored in the marina near the ferry dock in Cloud Bay, but they'd sold the rest. And of course, there was Adam's sailboat. That was in dry dock. He'd only just finished working on it before he'd died. It was a beautiful thing, but she'd never had the heart to put it in the water.

"If you like boats, I could take you out." She had no idea if Will sailed. For Adam, boats had been like oxygen. In his blood. She'd offered his yacht to his mom, but Lilah Clark had been set on moving to the mainland to be closer to Adam's sister who lived in Boulder now and hadn't wanted anything more to do with boats after playing second fiddle to her husband's and son's mutual passion for them all those years. Mina could understand, but she couldn't understand wanting to give up the ocean that surrounded Lansing. How could you even tell the mood of the day without the song of wind and water telling you what to expect?

"Do you want to?" Will said, drawing her wandering thoughts back to him.

He didn't exactly sound filled with joy at the prospect.

"Just an idea. I'm happy to walk if you want to walk. We can walk around to Shane's place. Or at least in that direction." That was the wilder end of the island. Her lighthouse sat on the headland that faced the open ocean. To the left of her, a series of bays wriggled their way around the island, creating curls of sheltered beaches that stretched all the way to Cloud Bay harbor. But the land that Shane and Billy had bought was to the right of the Harpers', and while there were two tiny coves sheltered enough for paddling if you made the journey down the rocks to them—one for each of the houses— the coastline was rocky and wilder on that side. Just what the doctor ordered to blow the cobwebs away.

"Sure," Will agreed, and they set off, walking in

silence at first as they settled into a rhythm. It was cold out, but Mina started to warm up as she moved, sick of taking it easy all of a sudden. She loosened the zipper on her coat as they made it to the point where the garden surrounding the house turned into fields and coastline, and stepped onto the gravel path that ran along the edge of the beach.

"So do you think Stefan will be able to bribe Lou into giving him pie-making lessons?" Will asked.

"Lessons, maybe. Her exact recipe, probably not." Mina shaded her eyes to look up at him. "Has he always liked to cook?" Stefan Fraser, tall, broad-shouldered, and bearded did not look like your typical chef.

"Well, at first it was self-defense but then he discovered he liked it."

"Self-defense?"

"Our mom worked a lot at one point. Our grandda lived with us but his idea of cooking was heating up tinned chili or baked beans and maybe boiling an egg. Stefan never liked baked beans much, so he took over."

After his dad died, she assumed this was. He hadn't told her what had happened. Should she ask? Maybe not. She knew all too well the pain an unthinking question could bring up. And all about dead fathers. "Just as well. He turned out to be good at it."

Will grinned. "Yes. We wouldn't have starved, but teenage boys stink enough without feeding them extra beans. Mom would have been in danger of asphyxiation."

She snorted. Having grown up with a brother and a house that was often stuffed with male musicians who weren't shy about belching and farting around each other, she could appreciate the problem.

a season of you   133

"I'm sure your mom appreciated the help. But he didn't want to be a chef?"

"No, he went out and got some experience when we decided to open the bar while our first batch of whiskey is doing its thing. Made more sense than paying somebody else to do it—it's not like the whiskey needs someone singing it lullabies at night—but no, it wasn't what he wanted to do as a job."

Which gave her an opening to ask about the distillery. But she wasn't quite ready. Instead she quickened her pace for a few steps to cover up the fact she wasn't sure what to talk about next.

Will, being taller, kept pace pretty easily. The path was steeper now and she had to go ahead of him, but when they came up to the top of the rise—her cursing the pie and the week or so of rest that meant she was feeling out of breath—he moved to stand beside her again where she'd stopped to admire the view. And catch her breath.

"So did the drawing work out?" Will asked. "Is that the right word?"

The drawing. That she'd done of him before she kissed him. "It was okay. I'm out of practice with figures." She wasn't about to admit she'd drawn him more than once since then.

"Well, if you want a model again, I'm happy to step in." He tilted his head at her. "Unless you have other models in mind?"

She shook her head. Nope. No one else was making her fingers—and other parts of her—itch.

"Never had an artist ask to draw me before," he said. "Or kiss me for that matter."

She winced. "Sorry."

"Don't be." He paused. "Unless of course you're not planning on doing it again. Is that why you asked me out here? So you could give me a polite 'It's not you, it's me' speech without an audience?"

chapter ten

Will held his breath waiting for Mina to answer. The wind lifted her dark hair, blowing it across her eyes before she pushed it out of the way.

"That's . . . to be determined," she said.

Well, that wasn't a flat out yes.

He made himself breathe. "Anything I can do to help make up your mind?"

She slanted a glance at him and moved closer to the edge of the path, which was only two feet or so from the edge of the cliff they were walking along. He moved with her and peered down.

The island turned wild here. The water that churned against the rocks thirty feet below him was deep and, according to the locals, unforgiving. Today it was a cold dark blue where the rocks weren't churning it into white spray. In the failing afternoon light, it looked treacherous. A shiver ran down his spine before he could stop it, and he stepped back from the edge automatically.

"You don't like deep water, do you?" Mina asked.

"Nope," he admitted. "Never have."

"Which explains why you didn't want to go out on the boat."

"Guilty as charged." He didn't feel terribly guilty but he tried to look contrite. She was changing the subject, but he was willing to give her a little more time to think about it. Not that he wasn't going to try and make sure that she'd decide in his favor in the end.

"Yet you moved to an island where the major form of transportation between here and the mainland is a ferry?"

"Ferries are big," he said. And he could sit inside and not think too hard about the endless depths of ocean beneath him. "Besides, the island was Stefan's idea. He has theories."

"Theories?" Mina's head tilted at him.

"About the salt air and its effect on the . . ." he trailed off.

"The whiskey," Mina said. Her voice went a little quiet on the word, but it wasn't the same dull tone she'd used the last time they'd talked about Salt Devil. It made him want to smile at her, but he'd learned his lesson. Slowly. Slower than tectonic plates, perhaps. That was the only way this might work.

"Yeah," he said softly. "That. And apparently my big brother is good at talking me into things."

"Apparently," Mina agreed. Then, "What are you scared of? With the ocean, I mean?" She sounded genuinely curious.

Boatbuilder's wife, he reminded himself. *Island kid.* Probably breathed saltwater.

"Sharks. Big squidgy things with teeth and tentacles." Oblivion. Falling into the cold dark and becoming part of it, lost forever, never seeing light again. Not getting to do what he wanted to do in the world. But that was hardly something he could say to Mina. She knew too much about oblivion and the abrupt ending of things.

She looked amused. "You know that cows kill more people than sharks each year, right?"

"Yeah, well, you won't see me farming either," he said. Farmers had to get up way too early. Plus, whiskey seemed safer than living, breathing animals. Granted, a whiskey barrel could crush him to death if it somehow got free of its shelving, but it wasn't likely to actively try to kill him. He shrugged. "Give me a nice safe lake or a pool any day."

Mina laughed. "Don't lakes have monsters?"

"Never heard of Nessie eating anyone," he said.

"Yes, but this is America. I think our lake monsters might be a little more wild."

He shook his head. "My lake monsters are Nessie-like. Peaceful. Shy. Leaving poor humans alone. Blame the Scotsman in me." He studied her a moment. Dark hair, pale, pale skin. Big eyes the color of wild seas. His Scots ancestors would have thought her a selkie perhaps. Come on to land to tempt men into the kinds of things they damn well knew better than to do. "You should believe in Nessie too."

"Oh? Why's that?"

"You can't tell me there's not Irish or Scottish some-where in your past. Not with that skin." The words came out a little rougher than he'd intended as a sudden mem-ory of how that pale skin had warmed, turning nearly the same shade of pink as her lips, when she'd kissed him, flashed through his head.

The skin in question suddenly went the exact shade he remembered, and his breath caught. He stepped a little closer.

She didn't move away. "Why does pale skin have to equal Irish or Scottish? Maybe it's Scandinavian or Russian or . . ."

"Not with those eyes. Selkie eyes," he said. He reached out and ran his thumb along her cheek, forgetting all about slow as though he'd never even heard the word. "Mermaid eyes."

Mina stared up at him. Then she sighed. "Never any damn mistletoe when you need it," she said. Then dragged his head down to hers.

It was surprise he felt at first. Shock, maybe. That Mina was kissing him again. But shock gave way to delight and then to hunger. Damn.

He liked her mouth.

He liked all of her. He needed more. His fingers curled into the fabric of her coat and he pulled her closer. The kiss in her studio had been too fast and too out of the blue for him to do much more than stand there and take it, but this time he wanted more. Wanted to know how she felt against him.

Even through the layers of clothes between them, he could feel her curves. Feel where her body said female. She was lean and in good shape, and there were muscles under those curves, firm against his fingers, but there was no mistaking her for anything other than a woman.

His brain roared for more, his cock hardening, need

and heat and want coalescing in his brain and body, setting him alight. He moved his mouth harder over hers and her lips opened, the kiss going deeper as he tasted more of her.

Nothing but her and the clutch of her hand at the back of his neck and her body pressed against him and the oh-so-sexy noise she made when he pulled her even closer.

Mina.

Until suddenly she stepped back a little. Just enough to pull her mouth away from his, and it was over.

Damn it. He fought every instinct he had. The ones yelling at him to pull her back into him.

Slow. He was doing this slow. Slow and smart.

Fuck. Never had anything sounded less appealing as he fought to bring his breath back under control. Mina was breathing hard too, eyes greener now as she stared up at him, looking simultaneously startled and satisfied.

"Definitely a mermaid," he managed to say as the sound of his heart banged in his ears louder than the roar of the sea below them. He tried to think of something other than her. Something boring. Like the rock of the island and the tectonic plates below that had thrown it up out of the ocean. But that only made him think of lava. And heat. And how badly he wanted to kiss her again. Do more than kiss her. Have her naked beneath him with all that pale skin his to explore and delight. His hands were still twined in her coat, gripping the fabric hard so he wouldn't pick her up and throw her over his shoulder.

"Mermaid?" she said, sounding dazed. That much was good. Dazed, he liked. Though this was hardly the place for her to be dazed. This rocky headland wasn't exactly full of anywhere that two people could sneak off and . . . okay, perhaps not so much thinking about that.

"Temptation. That's what mermaids do." He closed his eyes a minute. Tried to remember they were standing out in the open. In broad daylight. On Thanksgiving. With her family all expecting them back at some point.

"Isn't that sirens?"

"Same thing."

She shook her head. "Pretty sure it's not. And if you'd ever heard me sing, you'd know I'm not a siren." She smiled up at him.

"Pretty sure you're wrong about that." He took a breath. "So? This kissing thing . . . is it a one-time deal?"

Her mouth curved. "Given it's not the first time it's happened, I don't think it can be."

It was an effort to loosen his grip. He didn't want to let go of her but he didn't want her to feel like she had to stay there. Not if she was regretting what just happened. "Seems to me like the question then becomes whether it might happen again?"

She looked down.

"Sorry," he said. "I said I wouldn't push. I won't. Tell me it's just a Christmas miracle and I'll back off."

She snorted. "It's not Christmas yet. So it's probably a little early for miracles. I think you drank too much of Faith's champagne."

He'd only had one glass. It was damn fine champagne but not as heady as the woman sitting across from him had been. He didn't need booze to feel good anyway.

And with Mina Harper running through his veins, that was especially true. But perhaps he was laying it on a little thick. "More like too much of Lou's turkey. That bird was a miracle even if it isn't Christmas."

"Now that I can agree on," Mina said. Which didn't answer his question at all. "Her gravy should probably be illegal."

"Agreed. I was watching Stefan when he tasted it. I thought he was going to keel over from culinary delight. I bet he's trying to get the recipe out of her as we speak."

"He'll be disappointed," Mina said. "She might deign to teach him how to make pies. She might even give him a cookie recipe or two. Lou shares a lot, but she doesn't tell anyone how to make her gravy." She looked back the way they'd come. "Speaking of gravy, we should head back. This mermaid wants some more pie."

Okay, that was clear enough. Moment over. For now. "I guess swimming around all day burns lots of calories?" he asked, stepping back from her.

"Damn straight," Mina said. "And all that luring men into temptation is a hell of a workout. Mermaids earn their pie."

He could think of far more enjoyable ways to burn calories, but he'd save that suggestion for another time. And Lou's pies were as good as her gravy. If he couldn't spend any more time kissing Mina today then pie might be a good distraction. "I'm sold," he said. That earned him a brilliant smile of approval.

"Pie it is," she said. "And Will?"

"Yes?"

"I don't think it was just a one-time thing. Or a two-time thing. But I still need time, okay?"

He nodded. "Mermaids get to call the shots." He wondered whether he should just go jump in the ocean to quench the heat that swept over him as he watched her turn to walk back toward the house and all those inconvenient other people who meant he wouldn't be kissing her again.

"So, I'm leaving with Ivy and Matt. We're hanging out at their house. You're invited, if you want."

Will looked around from the TV he'd been mostly ignoring to find Stefan standing beside him. It had been a couple of hours since he and Mina had come back from their walk. There'd been more pie, more conversation, and now there was music in some parts of the house and a movie playing in the background in the den where Will had ended up. Most people seemed to be settling in for the evening, though one or two had left already. And now it seemed, Stefan was going to bail as well.

Should he go? Mina hadn't sought him out again. She hadn't avoided him, they'd crossed paths during the course of the evening, but he didn't think she was going to be inviting him over or anything. Not unless there really was a Christmas miracle. Still, he didn't want to leave.

"Or stay," Stefan said. "Up to you." He tipped his chin toward the door. "Mina's still here."

"She kind of lives here."

"She lives in the lighthouse."

"You know what I mean, this is her family Thanksgiving."

"Still, she's here. Maybe you should stay."

"Maybe you should quit trying to give me advice about women and go."

Stefan laughed. "I take it that's a no to Matt and Ivy's then?"

"It's a no. Enjoy yourself." Running the bar didn't leave either of them with much time for just hanging out. Stefan deserved a night with friends.

"I will." Stefan saluted him with the beer he'd been holding and wandered off again, leaving Will alone with the movie he wasn't watching. The others in the room seemed to find it interesting though. So he should probably leave them to it.

He went back downstairs to join the party. But he couldn't help keeping part of his attention on Mina as she moved around the room. Or help noticing that she was sending the odd longing glance toward the front door. Did she want to leave? Go home and paint or whatever she did? Was her head okay?

Was she staying because he was? She had invited him after all and he was guessing that anyone raised by Lou Henry had been brought up to look after their guests.

So maybe he should call it a night. Take advantage of the bar being closed and go to bed early for once.

He made his way across the room to Mina. "I'm going to head out. Thank you for a great dinner."

She looked slightly surprised. "The party will kick on for a while."

"I know," he said. "But I don't get that many nights off. Thought I might take advantage and catch up on some sleep. Isn't a turkey coma the traditional way to end Thanksgiving?"

"Something like that," Mina said. "If you're sure, I'll walk you out."

"I'd like that."

It took another fifteen minutes or so to find his coat and say thank you to Faith and Caleb, but eventually he was alone in the dark with Mina, walking down to where Lulu was parked.

Mina ran a hand along the Mustang's roof and down to the hood. "This is a very pretty car."

"Thanks. I like to think so."

"Dad had a Mustang at one point. But not a convertible."

"He missed out."

"Oh, he had lots of convertibles. Just not one of these."

"He was a car guy, huh?"

"Yeah. Though he kept most of them off-island at the other houses."

Other houses. How many exactly? It was easy with Mina to forget how different her childhood must have been from his. How different her life was now, even. She didn't act like it, but she was rich.

"Yet you drive a Jeep. You never wanted a sports car or something?"

"I like sports cars," she said with a shrug. "But the Jeep makes more sense here on the island. Not like you can go for long drives around here to appreciate an expensive car."

"Some people leave the island occasionally," he pointed out. "You can take cars on the ferry and everything."

"So I've heard." She smiled at him. "Though it's more fun to rent something different on the other end." Her hand was still trailing over the hood.

"I'm a one-car-at-a-time kind of guy," he said. "I like to focus my attention."

Mina's hand stilled. "Is that so?"

Her voice had gone low and it made his gut tighten. Made him want to reach for her. He shoved his hands into his coat pockets so he wouldn't. He'd promised her time. "Yes. Always been that way."

He took a step closer, despite himself. "You know, I've been thinking."

"Oh?"

"You said this wasn't a Christmas miracle. But maybe it could be."

She lifted an eyebrow. But she didn't move away.

"I mean, I get it. You lost someone. You have no idea what you want. And you don't approve of what I do for a living. But maybe, just maybe, this time of year you can forget all about that and just go for what makes you happy."

"And you make me happy?"

He tilted his head. "I'm not entirely sure. You're hard to read, Mina Harper. But then again, you've kissed me twice now. And I don't think you're the type for angry kissing, so I'm leaning toward you at least liking me."

Her mouth curved up. "Angry kissing? You sound like Faith."

"Faith talks about angry kissing?" He was confused.

"No, seduction cookies," she said and then looked kind of horrified. "No, scratch that."

Oh no. He wasn't letting that one slide. "Seduction cookies? You mean those cookies you brought me at Salt Devil?"

"Those were thank-you cookies," she said firmly.

"Then who are you making seduction cookies for?"

"Nobody. Go back to angry kissing."

"I'm more a fan of I'm-really-hot-for-you-and-I-really-like-you kissing." Even in the moonlight he could tell she was blushing.

"I think this conversation has wandered off track a little."

He was trying to remember what he'd been talking about. Kissing. Christmas miracles. Right. Her liking him. Or not. If that blush was anything to go by, he figured he was safe with the premise that she did.

"Right. Back to the Christmas miracle part. What do you say . . . want to give into the holiday spirit and just have fun?"

"Define 'fun.'"

"Whatever you want," he said.

Her head tipped forward, bangs falling so he couldn't see her expression. Then it lifted again and her eyes looked huge, the moonlight turning them dark and mysterious. "And what happens after Christmas Day? When the time for Christmas miracles is done?"

"Then I guess we see where we are. If you want to walk away then so be it."

"You think that's a good idea?"

"You don't?"

"I think most people don't actually work like that. That once you throw sex into the mix, things get messy."

"If you're doing it right, sure." He was determined to keep this conversation light hearted. Not to scare her off. That was becoming more difficult because she'd casually tossed the word 'sex' into the conversation. Kind of made it hard to focus on anything else.

"That's not what I meant."

"I know," he said. He shoved his hands deeper into his pockets, looked up at the sky for a moment. He'd lived here five years and he still loved how bright the stars were over the island. All those thousands of tiny suns burning fiercely, so far away. But he wanted to do a little burning close up. And if that meant he was going to get his heart smashed, well, fuck it. That was a chance he was going to take. Because he wanted Mina more than he wanted safety or sense or sanity. "Like I said, after Christmas, your call. And I promise that I won't hold it against you if you give me my marching orders."

"This is a pretty small island."

He shrugged. "How many times in the last three years had our paths crossed? A handful. I think it's big enough for both of us."

"In my experience, it gets a lot smaller when you're trying to avoid someone," Mina said.

"Well, we won't have to avoid each other if it's a mutual agreement."

"Do you really believe that?"

He shrugged. "Why not? If it's a Christmas miracle, we can add in a little no-hard-feelings addendum."

"I'm really starting to worry about your theory of how Christmas works," she said.

"Hey, I was a choirboy until I was twelve. I am down with Christmas."

"You were a choirboy?" One brow arched, clearly disbelieving.

"Why is that so hard to believe?"

"I'm just trying to picture you in one of those robes with the frilly collars."

"That's Catholic choirboys," he said. "We were Episcopalian. No frilly collars."

"And what happened when you turned twelve?"

"My voice broke. I stopped singing. By the time my voice settled, the other side effects of puberty meant I'd developed interests other than choir."

"Will Fraser. Boy soprano. Who'd have thought?"

He batted his eyelashes at her. "I have hidden depths. You should discover some of them."

"Because of Christmas miracles."

"Something like that. So, what do you say? Wanna give it a whirl? Or do I have to stand here and sing carols at you until you give in?"

"I'm not sure that carols work as a seduction technique."

"That's because you haven't heard me sing."

She looked intrigued. "Go on then."

Right. She'd called his bluff. Not that it was a bluff. Though now he had to think of a carol that was vaguely . . . sexy. He tried to remember what was on the Christmas playlists that they had for the bar, then launched into "Blue Christmas," keeping the volume down. Mina he would sing for, but he didn't need everyone in the Harper house judging his performance. Not when half the people at Faith's party were involved in the music industry in some capacity.

He was hoping Mina would cut him off, but she let him get all the way through two verses and a chorus before she held up a hand. "All right, you can sing."

Coming from Grey Harper's daughter, he'd take that as a compliment. "Just one of my many charms."

"Along with modesty?"

"Modesty is overrated. Particularly when you're trying to dazzle a girl." He took another half step toward her. "Are you feeling dazzled yet?"

"I'm feeling . . . something," she said, tilting her head back to look up at him.

"Something good?"

"I think so."

He couldn't stop the grin that spread across his face. "Excellent. So is that a yes to Christmas miracles?"

"If I say yes, that doesn't mean you're coming home with me tonight."

"Never thought I would be," he said. Hoped, maybe, in the stupid foolish part of his heart, but the majority of his brain knew that Mina didn't need to be rushed. Even if she was only giving him a month or so, he had to let her set the pace.

"Good. But what does happen next if I say yes?"

"Well, there's this thing called dating. It involves meals and spending time together and doing stuff."

"I have to work," she said.

"So do I. But not twenty-four seven. We'll figure it out. And hey, there's all the Christmas Festival activities to look forward to."

Mina groaned. "Don't remind me."

"Think of it as keeping the spirit of Christmas on your side."

"All right," she said reluctantly. "But I'm not doing that thing with the fake sleighs."

One of Angie's bright ideas had been sleigh rides around the island. Only with the distinct lack of snow on Lansing, she'd been forced to improvise with wheeled carts with some decorations filling in for the sleighs. Which in Will's mind was just a carriage ride, but apparently they were sticking with calling them sleighs. So he had to agree with Mina that they sounded a bit lame.

"I am happy to avoid fake sleighs," he agreed. "I can think of more fun ways to see the island with you anyway."

"Such as?"

He shook his head. "I think you'll have to wait and see on that one. Hidden depths, remember?"

She smiled. Then shivered. Which brought him back to reality. They'd been standing out here too long. He needed to go. He didn't want to, but he needed to.

"You're cold. I'm going to go. Thanks for inviting me. The food was great. As were other things."

"You're trying to get me to kiss you again, aren't you?"

"Is it working?"

"Maybe." She considered him a moment, then stood on tiptoe and pressed her mouth over his. Just for a few seconds. Just long enough to heat his blood and fog his brain all over again. To make him want desperately to pull her close, then closer still. Resisting that impulse actually hurt.

Then she pulled away and it was no longer an option. "Good night, Will."

"See you tomorrow?"

"I'm working during the day. And you have the bar at night?"

"We can figure something out. I'll call you."

"I might answer," she said. And then she was gone, slipping like a selkie through the night back to the house and out of sight.

chapter eleven

Mina spent much of Friday locked in her studio, still trying to make up for lost time. There was less than a
month now before she had to send her paintings to the
gallery. She'd promised them thirty, and though she had
painted more than that already she still didn't have thirty
she was happy to put on show for the whole world to see.

She tried to lose herself in the paint and not think
about Will, but wasn't exactly successful. For one thing,
her fingers kept starting to idly move to shift the lines
of the ocean she was trying to capture into something
more like a face. Will's face.

But the gallery was expecting seascapes, not por-
traits. Will's face could wait. But even when she mas-
tered her fingers, she couldn't stop her brain from
straying. She tried some of her usual methods for distraction. Podcasts. No, she lost track of the story after a
few minutes. Radio. No. She switched that off when she
figured out they were doing a favorite Christmas song

request show. And that people had apparently requested "All I Want for Christmas Is You" three times in a row.

Though, thankfully one of them had asked for the Michael Bublé version rather than the original Mariah. More soothing. But apparently Christmas music wasn't going to distract her today.

After that she'd switched to one of the playlists of movie scores she used as background noise, but even that hadn't been enough to put her into the zone. By three p.m., the light was fading and she had two new paintings, neither of which she was happy with.

She'd just returned from taking Stewie for a walk to try and shake off the bad day when her phone buzzed to life in her pocket.

She put the phone on the counter and hit speaker while she tried to wrangle Stewie out of his harness. Never an easy task when he was more focused on trying to puppy-dog-eye her into a postwalk cookie than on cooperating.

"Hello?" she yelled in the general direction of the phone as Stewie tried to thread himself and the lead around her legs, treading on her toes in the process.

"Mina?" It was Will's voice. "Where are you?"

"At home. Sorry, you're on speaker, just a second." She managed to get Stewie to sit long enough to finish the job of extracting dog from harness and then sent him to his basket with a liver treat to hold him temporarily. "Okay." She picked up the phone. "I'm back."

"Everything okay?"

"Yes." Except for the way her pulse picked up at the sound of his voice. "Just got back from walking Stewie." Did she sound breathless? Lord, she hoped not. But if

she did, hopefully he'd think it was just because she'd
been exercising. "Er, how's your day been?"

"Quiet so far. But I'm heading into town to help with
some festival preparations. Painting a few Christmas
trees or something."

"Painting Christmas trees?" Mina realized she really
hadn't been paying attention in the meeting.

"Fake ones. Part of the decorations. Thought you
might like to join me. After all, you're the artist."

"Not as far as anyone on the island knows, I'm not,"
she pointed out.

"Ah. Right. I forgot. It's your secret identity. Well, it
doesn't have to be a paint job worthy of Michelangelo,
so no one will suspect you know what you're doing. I'm
working later and I'd like to see you. Seems like a suit-
ably Christmas-y activity to kick off our . . . project."

"Is that what we're calling it?"

"Got a better term?"

*Doomed fling? Really bad idea? Moment of rashly
giving into temptation? Month-long booty call?* None
of those were exactly festive. And no matter what she
thought about it, she couldn't deny that she was happy
he'd called her. That he wanted to see her and hadn't
decided after a night's reflection that the deal she was
offering him was a crock and he was better off just bailing on the whole thing. " 'Project' will do for now."

"So is that a yes? I can come pick you up?"

"My house is in the opposite direction to the town
from your place."

"It's not far. Nowhere on the island is far. Plus, you
get to ride in the Mustang if you let me come get you."

A ride in Lulu that she could remember and actually

appreciate had some appeal. As did the man offering it. "Okay, it's your gas bill."

"I'll be there in about twenty minutes. Wear something you don't mind getting paint on." The phone beeped as he cut off the call. Mina looked down at her ragged sweats. Something she didn't mind getting paint on? That described a good chunk of her wardrobe. Of course, she was used to working in watercolor, which was not quite as hard on the clothes as oil paint or house paint. What did you use to paint Christmas trees? She had no idea. But regardless of the answer, she decided that she could come up with a version of paint-friendly clothing that looked a bit better than her current outfit. Even in twenty minutes.

It was just as well that she'd convinced herself to settle for a compromise between vanity and practicality. Because what Will had sold as a "few trees" was in fact fifty twelve-foot plywood Christmas trees. Plus piles of three foot-tall candy canes. That was a lot of paint. The old but not completely trashed jeans she'd changed into were not likely to survive if her previous experiences painting large objects held true. Large objects meant big brushes and rollers. Those were drippy and messy. She just hoped the paint in the large tins stacked up beside the piles of candy canes wasn't oil-based. Oil was a pain to clean up and the smell of turpentine tended to turn her stomach. There was a reason she worked with watercolor.

Beside her, Will was taking in the trees and paint. He didn't look totally thrilled either. None of the seven volunteers standing in the chilly shed with them did. And

Will, at least, had an out because he would have to leave and go to the bar in a few hours. Hopefully she'd be able to bail at the same time because he was her ride. Though, knowing Lansing, if they weren't finished by then one of the others would volunteer to take her home so she could stay and help finish the job.

"So how are we going to tackle this?" Sam Unger asked.

Ryan, dressed in jeans that were way too nice for a painting session, looked at the notes on his phone. "Candy canes are red and white. Trees are green with brown trunks." He waved his hand at the cans of paint. "There are plenty of brushes and things."

"Well, the candy canes should be easy," Mina said. "Paint them with a coat or two of white—whatever it takes to get good coverage, then add the red stripes. The trees will be trickier if you want them to look good. I guess we can mix a few shades of green using some of the white paint. Add a bit of detail."

Was everyone looking at her weirdly? "I painted some scenery in high school," she said. "I'm just saying."

"My notes just say green." Ryan said, looking bored.

"How are they being displayed?" Will asked.

Ryan frowned. "Why does that matter?"

"If they're being put up against buildings, we don't have to paint the backs. If they're free standing, we do."

"Stands, they have stands. So you need to do both sides." Ryan tapped something on the screen. "So I'll just leave you to it?"

"You're not staying to help?" Sam asked.

Ryan shook his head. "Sorry, work to do."

Given most of the island took the day after Thanksgiving as a holiday, that seemed unlikely. But Ryan had never been Mina's favorite person—and these days he seemed to have adopted Angie's dislike of all things Harper—so it was fine by her if he was bailing.

So instead of arguing, she just started sorting through the tins of paint trying to see what they had to work with.

By the time the first ninety minutes had passed it was clear that they weren't going to get the job done in a day. The cool weather was making the paint dry slowly and everything was going to need two or more coats. Still, it wasn't so bad, hanging out with Will, trying to figure out the best way to wrangle the giant trees into position so they could be painted. And there was something therapeutic about sloshing thick paint onto something so big, with no pressure to really make it pretty.

Endless green was somehow soothing. Plus it was simple enough that it hid the fact that she was distracted. Not by the paintings waiting for her back in her studio or by any of the other general holiday season things she should be thinking. Buying presents for a start. No, she kept finding herself thoroughly distracted by Will's arms.

It was warm enough in the shed once they started moving around. The mayor had provided a couple of patio-style heaters and between that and wrestling with the trees, Mina had taken off her coat. So had Will. What's more, he'd rolled up the sleeves on his shirt.

She'd always had a weakness for forearms and hands. And his were good. Very good. Muscled and strong and tanned. She'd been too focused on his face when she'd drawn him to pay that much attention to his body and too caught up in the taste of him when they'd kissed. But standing here with green paint staining her hands and a roomful of people, she was having trouble not staring.

Or not touching.

Will obviously had wielded a paintbrush before. She'd painted the lighthouse with Adam's help when they'd first moved in. Adam, having grown up with a boat-builder dad, had spent plenty of time staining or painting wood. He'd taught her the tricks, but she'd never been able to keep up with him. Will moved with the same easy rhythm as he wielded a roller over the trees, leaving Mina to fill in the edges and any spots he missed. The long sure strokes were kind of mesmerizing.

Part of her wanted to capture the line of him on paper. Part of her wanted those hands doing something a little more personal.

She wasn't quite ready for either of those things, so she tried to keep her head down and just work, but apparently her eyes had a mind of their own. Try as she might, keeping her gaze away from Will was nearly impossible.

Which was mortifying. There'd been some intrigued looks on the faces of some of the other volunteers when she and Will had arrived together. If they caught her staring at him every ten seconds, then the island grapevine would swing into action.

It was nearly impossible to keep a secret in such a small town, but she'd prefer to keep her and Will quiet. Not secret, but she didn't want everyone in the town getting involved. Not when it was temporary. The less "Oh poor Mina, did you break up?" questions she had to face after Christmas, the better. She'd had enough poor-Mina questions to last a lifetime.

Maybe it would be sensible to back out now. She bit her lip, considering it. But then Will moved back into her line of vision, bending to dip the roller in the paint tray again, a move that tightened his jeans over his butt as well as giving her yet another glimpse of those forearms in action, and she wavered.

God. She'd forgotten how to do this. Or maybe she'd never learned. She'd only dated a couple of guys when she'd been in junior high before she met Adam and her one-night stands had never involved dating. With Adam she'd been all certainty that everything was going to be just fine. That they'd be together forever. That it was right.

None of this confusing tangle of *What the hell am I feeling?* and *What the hell do I do?*

"Everything okay?" Will asked.

Mina started. Damn. Had he noticed how distracted she was? "I'm good." But she flushed as she met his eyes and dropped her gaze back down to the tree. Never had anyone focused quite so hard on the inch-wide edge of a wooden Christmas tree.

"Okay," Will said from above her.

Was she imagining things or did his voice sound vaguely . . . satisfied?

Do not look up. The brush slipped on the edge of the tree as she tightened her fingers on the handle. But she didn't look up, just kept painting.

But laying on foot after foot of green paint was rapidly losing its appeal, not that it had had much to begin with.

After she'd made her way around two more trees, Will finally put down his roller and came back to where she was working. "I need to head back to the bar. You nearly finished?"

She glanced down at the row of trees. There was still a lot of work to be done but her back was aching and so was her shoulder. A ride home with Will was a lot more appealing than staying back here. Once Will left, she was pretty sure that everyone would be grilling her about why she'd arrived with him. So yes, she was ready to go.

"Absolutely," she said, straightening. "I'll just clean up my brush." Will followed her over to the sink and rinsed out his roller while she'd removed the worst of the paint from her brush. They hung up the tools and made their goodbyes without too much effort, though Sam extracted promises from them both to come back to keep working on the trees on Sunday.

Mina winced inwardly at the thought of losing more time but couldn't think of a polite way of refusing.

"You're quiet," Will said as they pulled back onto the road.

"Just thinking," she said. "Too much to do. Too little time."

"Bill working you too hard?"

"Something like that," she agreed.

"You should tell him to take it easy. It's still not that long since your accident," Will said, sounding grumpy about it.

Guilt pinged Mina's conscience. "Bill's fine. It's something else."

"Care to elaborate?"

Did she? She contemplated Will for a second. Should

she tell him about the gallery? She hadn't even told Faith yet, but she wanted to tell someone. Maybe Will was the easy first step. She didn't need to be nervous about his reaction. Not like Faith's. Part of her knew it was silly to be nervous about telling her sister. Faith would cheer her on, but somehow telling her or Lou would make it all real. Besides, if Will knew about the gallery then she had an extra excuse to slow things down between them if she needed it.

"I've been asked to show some paintings at a gallery in L.A. after New Year's," she blurted. "It's my first show. And I'm kind of behind. I have to finish everything and get it to L.A. by the twenty-fourth. That's not much time." Less than a month, she realized, and felt the anxiety start to tighten her stomach again.

"Hey, that's great," Will said. "The show part, not that being behind part." He steered Lulu through the final turn onto the road that wound around the island from Cloud Bay to her place. "Do you think you can get it done in time?"

"Yes," she said, hoping she sounded more convincing than she felt. "But it will be tight between work and the festival."

"You should ask Bill for some time off," Will said.

"Lots of people want time off for the holiday," Mina said. "They have kids and families to juggle. I don't want to make it harder."

"By which I'm guessing that you've done your share of covering during busy times," Will said. "Just because you don't have kids doesn't mean you don't get to put yourself first sometimes. And this gallery thing is a big deal, right? If the art is what you want to do."

"It is." Her heart started to beat faster at the thought, and she made herself relax.

"Then tell Bill that. He'll figure it out. Take a couple of shifts a week off if you don't want to leave them in the lurch."

"The festival starts next weekend. That means tourists. Tourists means we'll be busy."

"Not that busy. This is Cloud Bay, not Hawaii. Like you said, we're not exactly the number-one Christmas vacation destination in California."

"Tell that to Angie," Mina muttered.

Will laughed. "You don't like the mayor much, do you?"

Mina shrugged. "Angie's okay. But she doesn't like my family. Never has. And that hasn't been helped by Seth and Lou seeing each other. She made Faith jump through a lot of extra hoops this year for CloudFest. So, she doesn't always make it easy to like her."

"Huh," Will said. "I guess that's why there's no one from Harper on the festival committee. I thought that was weird. But we were talking about Bill, not Angie. About you asking for some time off. Which will not cause Cloud Bay to fall into the ocean. I'm almost one hundred percent certain of that."

"Almost?"

"Well, there's a chance that it might, I guess. Seems unlikely though. So if you need to get your paintings done, I think you need to be a little selfish. Besides, you'll paint better if you're not tired from working nights. Be able to get up and use all that good morning light."

"How do you know about morning light?"

"TV," he replied. "My mom likes art documentaries. They're always talking about light."

"There are other ways I could free up my time," Mina said. "Ditch the festival painting or—"

"Do not finish that sentence if you are about to try and back out of what we talked about yesterday," Will said. "You're not having second thoughts, are you?"

"I—" How to explain?

Before she could think of the words, let alone work out whether or not she was having second thoughts, Will pulled the car over with a screech of tires. He undid his seat belt and slid toward her. Then his mouth was on hers, kissing her breathless.

When they finally broke free of each other, both breathing fast, he just slid back over and pulled back onto the road as though nothing had happened. "No second thoughts."

chapter twelve

Maybe she wasn't having second thoughts, but she was definitely having thoughts.

The unsettling kind.

With one kiss, Will had set her alight.

Again.

He hadn't said much more as he'd driven her home. Simply walked her to her door and said good night. Then he'd made his view on the subject crystal clear with another of those shattering kisses.

Her knees were wobbling as she opened the door and stepped through it, wondering if she should just get it over and done with and ask him in.

Ask him to show her what came next.

Because it seemed inevitable that there would be a next.

It would be so easy to find out what that would be.

All she had to do was reach out.

Call him back.

But it wasn't that simple.

The door closed behind her and she stood where she was, fighting against the sensation. She took two steps, reached for the handle. Pulled her hand back.

God.

She wanted.

Yearned.

And that was crazy.

She pressed her hands against the door, the wood cool against skin that was suddenly so hot she was surprised she didn't leave scorch marks. She lowered her forehead to that same cool wood and closed her eyes.

Hoping for a moment that, like a child, if she couldn't see a thing, it wasn't really there.

But she wasn't a child. And that didn't work when the thing she didn't want to face was in her own head.

Escaping her head now, where she'd been trying to keep it locked up. Tied down with chains of guilt and grief and denial.

But apparently those chains weren't strong enough. Or else her hormones had burned straight through them.

She wanted Will Fraser.

The knowledge beat through her. Pounding in her pulse, firing her skin. Lighting each nerve she'd been repressing to sudden burning life.

She wanted him.

Wanted his hands on her, his mouth hard on hers. Wanted to know what he felt like inside her.

Lusted in fact.

Crazy.

She let her head thump gently against the door, still

not sure she wasn't going to fling it open and go running wildly into the night after him.

She wanted Will and sex.

The hot and fast and dirty kind.

The grown-up kind.

The *complicated* kind. That was what she didn't want to think about. This kind of want led to other things. Things that could break her all over again.

She was thinking about it anyway. And that was terrifying.

Adam had been her first. Sex with him had been great after they'd figured out what they'd been doing. She'd loved him and wanted him and they'd burned up the sheets like any horny teens, but she wasn't sure she remembered this.

This sense of standing on the edge of a cliff and being willing to throw herself off it if it meant getting what she wanted.

And she had no idea if she was going to be able to resist doing just that.

Saturday morning found Mina sitting at Faith's kitchen table watching Faith pull what seemed like enough Thanksgiving leftovers to feed a small army out of the refrigerator, with suspicion. Breakfast, which had started off healthily with egg white omelets courtesy of Caleb, seemed to be degenerating. "Breakfast doesn't come with dessert," Mina protested as Faith started slicing into pies and pastries.

"It does when we have all these pies to finish," Faith said.

"You could just throw them out."

Caleb made a small sound of protest. "Lou's pies are too good to waste."

"Lou will make you pie anytime," Mina said, patting his arm. "You don't have to do this." Caleb however was watching Faith with approval.

"It's the weekend. People eat pancakes and donuts and muffins and all sorts of crap for breakfast on the weekends," Faith said. She put a bowl down in front of Mina that was full of pastry and fruit.

"What's this?"

"I'm calling it Surprise Pie," Faith said with a grin. She put down a jug of cream as well.

Mina's stomach rumbled despite herself. She hadn't really tasted what she'd eaten at Thanksgiving, and the pie or pies smelled sweet and delicious.

She poured cream and decided after the first bite that Faith might be onto something after all. Breakfast dessert was pretty damn good. Health be damned. Fat and sugar were awesome.

"You know," Faith said, "I wasn't sure that you'd come over this morning."

"Why not?" Mina managed, mouth still half full of what was a surprisingly good mix of apple, strawberry, and lemon meringue.

"Sam Unger mentioned that you and Will were down helping out with the festival prep," Faith said.

"Okay, that's my cue to leave," Caleb said. He picked up his own bowl of Surprise Pie and bent to drop a kiss on Faith's cheek.

"Can I come with you?" Mina asked.

"That would only be delaying the inevitable," Caleb said with a grin before leaving her alone with her sister.

"So," Faith prompted. "Is it true?"

"Is it true that Will and I used paintbrushes in the same vicinity?" Mina said, trying for innocence. "Yes."

"Sam said you arrived together. And left together." Faith wagged her spoon at Mina. "That's statistically significant."

Mina sighed. Sometimes living in such a small community really sucked. Why couldn't she live in a lighthouse on a proper deserted island? Where no one would be sticking their noses into her business every second? Though deserted islands probably lacked pie. "Sam has a big mouth."

Faith grinned. "So it's true. I knew it."

"Knew what exactly?"

"That you liked Will. So, tell me all about it."

"Nothing much to tell," Mina said. "We hung out, is all."

"Well, that's something to tell."

"If the next words out of your mouth are going to be something like 'it's about time,' then don't," Mina said. "Do not get excited about this."

"I just want you to be happy," Faith said. "Will's a good guy."

"So you've told me. Several times."

Faith held up her hands in surrender. "Okay. Okay. I'll back off. But if you feel the need to talk, I'm here."

"Thank you," Mina said. "And actually, there is something else I wanted to tell you." Having told Will about the art show, she might as well break the news to Faith. And Lou. In case the Lansing grapevine somehow got hold of that news as well and beat her to it.

"There is?" Faith looked intrigued. "Go on—or actually no, can I tell you a few things first? Harper Inc. stuff." She pulled a face. "I know it's the weekend but you're here and the next few weeks are going to be really busy."

That was the understatement of the year. Mina thought about the number of paintings she needed to finish in the next four weeks and suddenly regretted eating so much Surprise Pie. "Sure, get your CEO on." Her news could wait a few minutes longer.

"Cool." Faith launched into a summary of figures and profits and schedules that Mina only half followed. She was more than happy to let Faith run Harper Inc. and deal with Grey's legacy. And the money. But Faith was scrupulous about involving her and Zach in any big decisions and in keeping them updated about what was going on.

When Faith wound down, Mina nodded. She'd gotten the general gist. Things were good. Faith would send her copies of the reports and she could look at them in more detail when she had some time. "And what about your foundation project? Have you found a test subject yet?"

"Yes." Faith wriggled in her chair, practically vibrating with enthusiasm. "A singer Danny saw playing in a little club in Seattle when he was there. She's going to come out in January and we'll talk. See what we can do." Excitement bubbled through Faith's voice. She was funding a program to support female artists to get a start in the music industry, an idea she'd come up with during CloudFest the previous year. "It's taken a while with Caleb moving here and everything else that's been going on but I can't wait."

"I'm sure it'll be great," Mina said. "Lucky girl, whoever she—"

"Nessa. Her name's Nessa Lewis. She has an amazing voice. Danny says she's great onstage as well." Faith grinned.

"Well, Danny knows talent when he sees it," Mina said. "And speaking of people just starting out in things, I got asked to do a gallery show. In L.A. Also in January."

"Oh my God!" Faith levitated from her chair to race around the table and envelop Mina in a hug. "That's amazing." She pulled back. "When did you find out?"

"A little while ago." Mina hedged.

"So this is what you want? To be an artist?"

"To see if I can be, yes," Mina said. "But I want to do it on my own merits. Which is why I'm keeping it quiet. And I'm using Emmy's name, not Harper. It'll come out eventually but I'd rather that wasn't until after this show. If the pieces sell there, then I'll know it's because of me, not Dad."

"If that's what you want," Faith said. "Have you told Lou yet? Or Zach?" Her voice cooled a little on the last word.

Mina hid a sigh. Faith and Zach had fought last year and it was a bump in their ever-rocky brother-sister relationship that she didn't seem to have gotten over yet. And Zach hadn't helped by announcing he wasn't coming home for Christmas because his band was touring. Faith hadn't said much about it at the time, but Mina knew when her sister was pissed. "I'm going to tell Lou next time I see her. But I'll leave Zach for awhile." She doubted Zach would show up even if she did invite him. "That will help with keeping things quiet."

Faith's lips pressed together briefly but then she nodded. "Your show, you get to do it your way," she said, walking back to her chair. She ate a few more bites of pie. "Oh, and the lawyers working on the archive want to talk to me next week. Guess they've finally sorted out whatever was in that extra storage unit in Jersey."

Mina nodded. "I'm surprised they haven't found another one by now."

Faith shrugged. "Maybe we've found them all. Or maybe we'll be finding bits and pieces of Grey for the next twenty years."

"Knowing Dad, that seems more likely." She didn't envy Lou and Faith the job of trying to sort out Grey's estate and set up an archive of his papers and the memorabilia of his thirty-odd year reign as one of the world's biggest rock stars. She was happy to leave them to it. It wasn't like they were going to unearth anything too crazy. Some fairly random things had been discovered. And some pretty cool ones too. But nothing that really impacted any of them.

Grey had actually taken the time after he'd gotten his cancer diagnosis to make sure the basics were taken care of. He'd transferred control of Harper Inc. to the three of them before he'd died. They'd each already had trust funds with more than enough money to live on for life. And a lot of the assets like the houses and boats and cars had been owned by various companies that Harper Inc. owned. As were the rights to Grey's own music and his shares of the Blacklight profits.

But cleaning up everything else was taking a long time. Grey had owned properties all over the world and had never been shy about acquiring art or other toys he liked. Some of it he shipped home to Lansing. But, as they'd found out after he'd died and the lawyers started to dig into the paperwork, he'd also had a habit of renting storage lockers wherever he happened to be and stashing stuff when he left a city. He hadn't been so good about coming back to collect it. "But I guess it wouldn't be Dad if it was straightforward."

"No," Faith agreed. "But that's enough business. Time for more pie and you can tell me all about your show."

Sunday night, Will watched the rain battering the windows of the bar and tried not to check the time on his phone. The bar was empty at nine thirty and he doubted anyone would give into a last minute whim for a drink at this hour.

He'd spent the last hour cleaning the bar and there wasn't anything left to clean.

Which left him with nothing much to do but think about Mina. He hadn't seen her yesterday. He'd wanted to give her time to paint, then by the time he'd called in the afternoon, she'd been at work. Unlike tonight, the bar had been packed and he'd crawled into bed after one a.m.

Tired as he'd been, sleep hadn't come quickly. Not with Mina filling his brain.

He wanted to see her.

Wanted to touch her.

He reached for the phone.

"Calling for pizza?" Stefan asked from the kitchen door.

"I don't need to call for pizza when I have you to make it for me," Will said.

"Tonight you'll have to settle for leftover chili. I made too much."

"You didn't make too much, we just didn't have the usual crowd. So, how about we call it quits for the night?"

Stefan lifted an eyebrow, wiping his hands on the dishcloth tucked into his belt. "You got somewhere better to be?"

"Maybe," Will admitted.

"Mina?"

"Maybe?"

"You're a terrible liar," Stefan said, but he was smiling. He nodded at the phone. "Call your girl. I'll put some chili in the freezer for you."

"She's not exactly my girl yet."

"That just means you have to try harder."

"Thanks for the advice." No point telling Stefan that he wasn't sure that things were going to end well no matter how hard he tried.

"Any time, little brother." Stefan smirked at him and wandered back into the kitchen. Will grabbed the phone and headed to the front door, switching the open sign to closed before he dialed. The last thing he needed was some last-minute customer ruining his plans. Not that he actually had plans yet.

"Hello?" Mina's voice came through the phone.

"Hey, it's me."

"Will?"

"Were you expecting someone else?"

That earned him a laugh. "No. Sorry. I've been painting. Wasn't expecting a call."

"Painting at night? What happened to good light?" He was starting to get the idea that Mina wasn't someone who understood the concept of taking things easy. She worked hard. Maybe too hard. She needed to learn to play a little.

He'd be more than happy to help her with that.

"Messing around with some ideas for tomorrow. And sometimes, it's fun to try and capture the night."

Didn't he know it. "We're closing early. The rain is keeping everyone at home. So I was wondering if maybe you wanted to hang out?"

"Hang out? Is that like Netflix and chill?"

"No. Not unless you want it to be." He tried not to picture Mina naked on a couch.

"Let's start with hanging out," Mina said. "Why don't you come over? I'll make you cocoa."

Cocoa? Never his favorite drink. Not unless it had a good splash of something alcoholic in it to jazz it up. But it was a start. "I love cocoa," he said and headed back to the bar to find his coat and keys.

chapter thirteen

Mina opened the door before Will could knock. She'd watched him pull up through her bedroom window, wondering what exactly she was doing inviting him over at this hour. Most guys would interpret that in only one way.

Though maybe Will wasn't most guys.

But to calm her nerves, she'd come up with an alternative plan. From the expression on Will's face when he registered she was wearing a hat and carrying a coat, he hadn't been expecting it.

"Are we going somewhere?" he asked.

She shrugged, ignored the little buzz of pleasure at the sight of him. "I've been cooped up inside most of the day. I thought maybe you could take me for a drive."

Will looked back over his shoulder toward Lulu. And at the rain currently drumming on her shiny blue roof. "It's not exactly good sightseeing weather."

"I know the sights, I just need to get out." She tilted

her head at him. "I'm sure a car like that can handle a little rain." She wasn't sure actually. Grey had let her drive one of his classic cars once after she'd gotten her learner's permit. Steering it had been like steering a whale. But she remembered the rumble and the thrill of putting her foot down and feeling the car respond.

She liked cars. Even after Adam, she liked cars. Only now she felt kind of guilty about liking them. But it had been the driver, not the car that had killed him.

And she didn't want to think about Adam. She didn't want to think much at all. She wanted the night and the road and the man standing in front of her. "Besides, the weather is heading out to sea. If we go around the other side of the island, it might have cleared up by now."

"If that's what you want." He stepped back to let her close the door and they ran through the rain together back to the Mustang.

She felt a little guilty about dripping on the gorgeous leather upholstery when she slid inside the car but Will didn't look worried. In fact, he was grinning. She found herself grinning back as they headed out into the night.

It was exactly what she needed. The thrum of Lulu's engine and the smell of Will surrounded her as they ate up the miles, and she found herself grinning harder.

There were hardly any other cars on the roads, and Will handled Lulu with an easy familiarity that let her relax and just enjoy the ride.

In the dark and the rain there was a strange sort of freedom. A feeling that, for once, no one was watching. No one keeping an eye on her. She could do what she wanted and to hell with it.

Will didn't say much but he stole glances at her as

they drove. Glances that held something hot and dark that mixed with the motion and the engine sound to make her feel reckless. Made her want to be fearless again.

When they reached the far side of the island, approaching the beach up past the marina, Will slowed the car.

The rain hadn't let up at all.

"I'm not sure your theory about the storm heading out to sea is right," he said.

"It's just going slow. It will ease up. Why don't you pull up near the lookout and we can wait and see if it does?"

Will steered Lulu into the small bank of parking spaces that curved along the cliff edge next to the lookout. In summer it would have been packed with tourists enjoying the view back across to the mainland lights or local teenagers wishing the tourists would leave so that they could park, but tonight they had it all to themselves. She released her seat belt and tossed her hat and coat into the back seat as Will parked. He left the engine running. Just as well, otherwise things would get chilly pretty fast.

"I don't think I've parked here since I was a teenager," she said, peering through the windshield. Not much to see outside. With the rain obscuring the view there wasn't even the faintest glimmer of the lights from the mainland.

"Teenage Will would be skeptical about what Lansing Island teenagers did for entertainment," Will said.

"Your teenage self didn't like surfing and great weather all year?" She twisted her neck to look at him.

"No," he said. His expression went strangely flat for a moment. "And this is not exactly great weather." But he smiled again as he said it and that heat was back in his eyes.

She sat back and twisted toward him. So little distance between them. A foot or two. All she'd have to do would be wriggle forward a little and . . .

"Nice view," he said, gaze locked on hers.

"Generations of Lansing teenagers have thought so."

"I wasn't looking out the window." His voice had gone low. Rough. Tight. Like he was trying to keep himself under control.

She caught her breath, not exactly certain how good a grip she had on hers either. "Neither were they." She shivered a little as need started to settle in her belly.

"Why don't you come over here and let me warm you up?"

She didn't need a second invitation. Her body moved without thought at the words and she swung herself around and into his lap with an ease that suggested that maybe she hadn't forgotten everything her teenage self had known.

His eyes went wide for a moment, startled, before his hands came to her waist, resting just firmly enough to let her know that he wanted her right where she was.

The car was toasty warm now. Too warm as she watched Will's eyes and the heat there seemed to leap from him to her. The sound of the rain on Lulu's roof and the fogged-up windows and the lack of light made her feel as though they were in another world entirely. One where anything might happen—if she was just brave enough to let it.

"Just as well you've already seen the sights," Will said, voice still tight. "That rain is getting worse, not better."

She could feel the tension in him. Knew he was keeping himself tightly leashed. Because he wanted her to be sure. He didn't have to say it. The hunger on his face was clear. But he was holding back. For her. It made her want to see what happened if she broke all that carefully controlled restraint.

"Maybe we'll just have to make our own entertainment then." She pushed a little closer.

Will swallowed. Hard. "Music? I have music."

"Pretty hard to hear it over this rain," she said. "And there are other things we could be doing."

His fingers tightened at that, flexing hard against her skin, and his hips moved under her. Another shiver ran through her.

"What exactly did you have in mind?"

"If I have to explain to you, then I'm going to form a very poor opinion of teenage Will," Mina said, trying to keep her voice steady.

"Teenage Will wasn't exactly the world's greatest ladies' man," Will said. "He was kind of lanky and into science."

"Hot geeks are in now," she said. She put her hand on his chest. Felt the muscle tense beneath. Slid it a little higher, to touch the skin of his neck.

He sucked in a breath. "Sadly a decade or so after teenage Will's prime."

"Well, maybe present-day Will can make it up to him."

His hands tightened. Oh, she liked the feel of his

hands on her. And the scent of him, male and warm and right there. So close.

"Present-day Will thinks that's a damn good idea."

"So does present-day Mina," she said. "So how about you make your move?"

Seemed as though Will didn't need to wait for second invitations either. Because then he was kissing her. But not the kisses she remembered. Not quite so hungry. No, right now, Will's mouth was soft on hers, taking his time. Exploring her. His hands had tightened into her shirt, the pressure on her skin a good kind of too much, but they didn't move. Didn't wander. Didn't go seeking her skin. Which very much wanted to be discovered.

The perfect first-date kiss. The kind you could sink into for a day or so. But right now, it wasn't enough. She pressed herself into his lap. He was hard, no mistaking that. But even with her wordless invitation, he didn't take things further.

He was still being careful, she realized. Letting her set the pace. It was sweet, but right now she didn't want sweet. She pulled away, reluctantly. Because his sweet was oh so sweet. But she wanted more. He tilted his head, as though asking if everything was okay.

"Teenage Mina would appreciate you being a gentleman," she said. "But just so we're straight, I'm not her."

His brows flew up. "I know that. I just—"

She stopped him with a finger on his lips.

"Don't worry," she said. "You're not the first guy I've slept with since Adam."

He blinked at that. "O-kay."

"Is that so surprising?"

He shook his head. "It isn't. I don't care about what happened in the past."

She wasn't sure she believed him. But his eyes were steady. Waiting for her answer. She ducked her head, then lifted it again. "I'm a widow. Some people have ideas about how widows should be. Rules."

"Widow rules?" His mouth quirked at that.

"Yeah." It sounded dumb. But she wasn't going to explain it to him. He wasn't the one who'd walked down the street with all those eyes on him. Hadn't seen the pity and assessment behind everyone's eyes for the first two years. The flashes of judgment when she and Lilah had closed Carter's Boats. And now there was pity *and* speculation. She wasn't sure which was worse.

"Well," Will said eventually. "I don't know about anyone else, but I've always figured that there's only one rule that really matters when it comes to life." He pulled her a little closer against him and the salty scent of his skin made her head reel. Through the window she could hear the wind like a whispering rush matching the surge in her blood. Urging her on.

"And what's that?" She twined her hands in his hair.

"Do what makes you happy as long as you don't hurt anybody else in the process."

That made her pause. "That sounds like my dad. He liked doing whatever the hell he wanted."

Will shook his head. "I didn't know your dad, but from what I've heard of him he didn't always pay attention to the second part."

"He hurt people." She closed her eyes. Even the people he loved.

"I'm not going to hurt you," Will said. There was an

urgent, hungry note in the words that rang true to her. "*Never.*"

"Is that so?"

"I'll going to do my damnedest to make it so."

God.

He was solid, this man. Solid like the earth. Miles deep. Maybe that was why he made her burn so hot. There was a molten heart to him like the earth. Catching hers alight.

She leaned into him and kissed him softly. "I think I like your rule."

"Damn straight. Anyone who tries to tell you anything else can go fuck themselves. Too many people in this world think they're the damn happiness police." He grinned at her. "So are we done talking about other guys now?" One hand had found the gap between her T-shirt and her skin, and his fingers spread across her back, thumb feathering gently back and forth. She shivered, wanting that touch in other less innocuous places.

"Yes."

"Good. Because the only man here with you now is me. And I intend to hold your attention."

She was straddled across his lap, his hands under her clothes, parked in a Mustang. He had her attention. "I'm not likely to forget where I am."

A wrinkle formed between his eyebrows.

"Or who I'm with," she added, in case he'd taken that the wrong way. "It's just you and me." She hoped that would be true. Will wasn't one of those swipe-right guys.

But neither of those guys—perfectly nice as they had been, for guys out for sex via an app—had been someone she knew. Someone she'd been thinking about. Someone who'd been keeping her up at night, thinking about. Wanting.

She wanted this to be right. Good. She needed good. She needed *Will* to make her feel good.

And that was flat out terrifying. The thought stole her breath, and she stilled.

"Hey," Will said gently. "We can stop if you want."

Damn it. He was killing her with kindness. Stealing under her defenses like sea mist drifting up the beach, seeping under her skin and into her bones. If she wasn't careful, then she'd be the one in trouble come Christmas.

But the only way to deal with a sea mist was to wait for the sun to come out. To let the heat burn it off.

She had a feeling that she and Will would do just fine in the generating heat department. All that remained to be seen was what happened after the fire.

"I don't want," she said and bent her head down to kiss him again. Seeking the heat and the hunger. Wanting it to carry her away.

Will tasted hot and dark and needy. The taste of him flooded her mouth and made everything go tight.

That was it.

The thing she wanted. She put her arms on his shoulders, trying to wriggle a little closer.

Will groaned, his hand sliding upward. She wanted his hands on her. Wanted skin and muscle and warmth against her. He moved slowly, fingers tracing her ribs. She made an impatient noise and reached to bring his hand up her breast where she needed it.

He made a soft sound of surprise or pleasure, and

then he pulled his hand away. But before she could protest, it was back, this time tugging at the shirt she wore.
Buttons melted away at Will's touch and then his hand
was on her again, sliding over the lace of her bra, the
combination of hand and fabric, catching her nipple and
setting her skin on fire. He wasn't holding back now,
teasing her and tangling his tongue in her mouth until
she had to hold on to his shoulders to anchor herself
against the sensations.

Her bra came undone and his mouth moved to join
his fingers, and her head spun with it. She wasn't entirely
sure what she was saying, urging Will on with little
pleased moans and words that might not have even been
words.

God. It felt good. She sank down against him, pressing into him, frustrated by the layers of fabric between
them.

She hadn't thought this through. Should've worn a
skirt, but that would have required admitting to herself
that this was what she had in mind when she'd asked
Will to come over.

"You know," Will said, voice vibrating against her
skin, "this might be easier in a bed. You know, nice flat
surface, lots of room."

He was right. It would be easier. But it would also require stopping. Which would let the thoughts come
back. She didn't want to think. She'd spent three years
thinking.

"Too far away," she said winding her hands into his
hand and tugging his head back. "Don't stop."

"Impatient, are you?"

"Yes." She almost growled the word. "I am. Is that a problem?"

"No," he said. "But if this is what you want, then you're going to help me a little. Starting with losing those jeans."

"I'll lose mine if you lose yours," she said. She wriggled free of him with a brief undignified twist. But she didn't care about dignity. Sex wasn't about looking good. It was about feeling good. And Will made her feel good.

She squirmed out of her jeans—thank the Lord for big old cars—and saved time by taking off her underwear too. When she looked up, Will was watching her. And he hadn't yet undressed. But he didn't really have to. Male anatomy was helpful that way. All she had to do was reach down and slide that zipper open and he'd be all hers.

"Whatever you're thinking," he said. "I vote you come back over here and show me."

"Me too," she said and slid back to him. She swung her leg to straddle him again and reached for the buttons on his shirt. Will's fingers slid between her legs, which made her forget what she was doing.

"God, that feels good," he muttered and swept his thumb over her clit with precision. Her hips bucked. He pressed again. "Does it feel good to you?"

She nodded, temporarily deprived of speech by the pleasure of it. He smiled then and went to work, one hand on her hip, holding her still where she was, the other doing wicked wonderful things.

She floated on the sensations, but good as they were, they weren't quite enough.

"More," she said.

"More this?" Will asked.

"More you. In me."

The sound that came out of his throat was mostly incoherent, but his hands dropped away. The rasp of his zipper was the best sound she'd heard all day. Followed by the crinkle of foil. She hadn't even thought about that. She closed her eyes. Good thing one of them was sensible. Though she didn't want sensible, she wanted Will.

Will, who was pulling her down against him. And now it was flesh and flesh, all that lovely hard man sliding against her.

"Is this what you want?"

"Yes."

That was all he needed. He spread his thighs, pushing her knees wider, and then she felt him nudging her before he slid into her. Or she slid down onto him. She wasn't sure which. Just knew that the feeling as he moved into her was perfect.

She didn't want it to stop.

Luckily, Will didn't seem inclined to hurry things. No, he just moved beneath slow and steady, holding her hips so she had to let him set the pace. Let him determine each slide and retreat and return. Each one seeming to drag her a little deeper into whatever magic he was working. Wrapping her closer in touch and taste and sound. He moved and she moved with him, their rhythm growing faster but never breaking. Never faltering. As though the two of them had done this many times before.

As if he knew how her body would react to each thing he did.

The sound of the rain and the sounds she was making filled her ears, and the darkness and the steamed-up windows blocked out anything else that wasn't Will or the pleasure throbbing through her and the pressure building.

Will's teeth scraped her neck then he did something that changed the angle slightly. A shudder ran through her. She didn't know what he'd done but it felt . . . so good. She dropped her head back, closing her eyes, hips still moving with his.

"Look at me," he said roughly. "I want to see you."

She couldn't deny the plea in his voice. Not when it was somehow edged with command. She locked her eyes on his, so dark and fierce in the night, and let all the need she saw there, all that want and hunger directed at her, carry her over the edge as he thrust one last time and she came.

It took a few minutes to come back to herself. To stop floating in the sensations and anchor herself back in reality. The first thing she noticed was the sound of her breath in her ears. Rasping. She sounded like she'd run a marathon. Will did too. His head where it rested on her shoulder was hot. She knew how he felt. She was tempted to lean over and roll down the fogged window in the driver's side door.

The sea air might cool them both down. Might also give them pneumonia.

Instead she focused on bringing her breathing under

control. Not easy when she was still hard up against
Will, her skin tingling, the smell of sex surrounding
them, his hands under her clothes. Apparently once
wasn't enough to burn this out of her system.

Which meant they were just going to have to do it
again. She smiled at the thought.

"What's so funny?" Will asked, and she realized he'd
lifted his head and was watching her, pupils still wide
and dark in the moonlight.

"Nothing. Just feeling "—she stopped, wriggled a
little—"good."

That brought a smile to *his* face. "I'm glad to hear
it." He shifted beneath her. "Which brings me to the obvious question."

"And what's that?"

"Well, as much as I am one hundred percent in favor
of what just happened, I'm thinking that for round two,
perhaps we could go somewhere with a little more scope
for creativity."

"I don't know," she said, feeling happy that he wanted
round two too. "That felt pretty creative to me."

"Sure. Though, kind of restrictive." He grinned up at
her. "Trust me, I can do good things with unrestrictive."

His hand had strayed up to her breast again. She
closed her eyes. "Not sure I can handle it if you get too
much better at this."

"Oh, you can take it."

"Maybe." She sucked in a breath as his fingers teased
a nipple that was still sensitive in the aftermath of her
orgasm. "Didn't you say something about an obvious
question?"

"Oh, that." He rolled his fingers, and she had to bite her lip.

"Yes. That." She didn't know if she was talking about his questions or exactly what his hands were doing to her.

"My question is . . . your place or mine?"

chapter fourteen

Round two turned into several rounds . . . Will hadn't been lying when he'd said he could get creative.

She wasn't sure that she'd be able to move again. Not when lying face down on her bed with the warmth of a well-satisfied man beside her felt this good.

"Do you want anything?" Will asked, rolling onto his side from his back. His breathing had slowed and so had hers finally.

It took too much energy to talk so she just made a soft happy noise that hopefully he would interpret as "I'm good."

"Water? Coffee? Snack?"

She opened her eyes. Did he want something? This was, after all, her house, not his. But getting out of bed sounded like a terrible idea. "Aren't guys meant to fall asleep after sex?"

Will laughed. "That's for mere mortals."

"Oh? And what are you? A sex god?"

"If you say so."

Luckily for him, smacking him with her pillow would take too much energy. "Sex gods should be quiet after their work is done. Let us lesser beings pass out."

A finger ran down her spine. "That sounds boring. We sex gods require constant worship, you know."

She twisted her head toward him to find him grinning at her. "You cannot possibly be ready to do that again."

He shrugged a shoulder. "Well, maybe not. But I am a night owl."

The sensible response to that might well have been to suggest he go on home and let her sleep. After all, she had to paint tomorrow. But kicking Will Fraser out of her bed was another thing that sounded like a terrible idea.

She rolled over to face him, trying to wake up from the fog of satisfaction. "Even night owls need to sleep."

"Not just yet. Talk to me awhile, Mina Harper."

"I think you killed my brain cells," she said. But she smiled at him. Because he looked too good, rumpled and naked in her bed, not to smile at. "Was there something in particular you wanted to talk about?"

"No. Just talk. I like listening to you. Tell me something about you."

"Such as?"

"I don't know. What you like for breakfast. What your favorite movie is. What your family has for Christmas dinner."

"You have food on the brain."

"We just burned off a lot of calories."

"Do you want something to eat?" She tried to think

what was in her refrigerator. Something that could be turned into a midnight snack, surely.

"Not enough to get out of bed. So, talk to me."

"About Christmas dinner?"

"I'm curious. I mean, that was quite the Thanksgiving spread. Does Christmas top that?"

She shrugged. "It's different."

"Humor me. I'm not going home for Christmas this year. I need some inspiration for Stefan."

Was he angling for an invite to Christmas dinner? That would be going against their agreement. And he'd said he needed inspiration for Stefan. Was it just going to be the two of them for Christmas? That seemed . . . kind of sad.

"Unless of course, the menu is a secret like Lou's pie recipe."

The menu? It wasn't secret but it was kind of hard to explain. The Harper Christmas dinner had evolved to be . . . eclectic . . . over the years. They'd often traveled for the holidays either because Grey had a whim to or because the band was touring, and over the years, dishes from a lot of places had been added to the feast.

Starting the day with champagne and pastries and tropical fruits from their memorably hot Christmas in Australia. Having seafood as a starter. She wasn't sure whether it had been exquisitely fresh sushi in Japan or Scottish smoked salmon or the fish with ginger and lemongrass and chili from Thailand that had first started that. They'd spent one Christmas in Italy when Mina had been too young to remember much about it other than the fact that lasagna had been part of the feast and the housekeeper at the house Grey had rented out had given her a whole giant jar of Nutella. Lasagna had become one of their Christmas traditions as well.

And then there was traditional British plum pudding and mince pies to go with the pies and cookies that Lou had always made.

"Let's just say you wouldn't starve at a Harper Christmas," Mina said.

"I've found that to be true of most Harper meals," Will said.

"Lou's influence," Mina said. "I think she got used to cooking for a lot of people when she and Dad were married. He used to bring home strays all the time, so she'd have to feed twenty people at the drop of a hat. Now she tends to err on the side of overcatering. Faith and I picked it up from her."

"What about your mom?"

"Emmy? Emmy is not really a cook. I mean, she *can* cook and when she bothers, it's always tasty, but she just isn't that interested in food. Not the way Lou is. But she's an expert at finding awesome restaurants. Whenever I'm going to a new city, she's the one I ask for recommendations."

"She travels a lot for her job?"

"Not quite as much as she used to. But yes. Have camera, will travel. Or something."

Will made a soft sort of "humph" and Mina shrugged at him. "It's okay. She left when I was really young. And I had Lou. Emmy and I have made our peace with it. She wasn't really built to be settled down and raising kids. Maybe if she'd found a guy who was willing to be the one to stay home and let her take off when she needed to, it might have worked. But she fell for the old

Grey Harper razzle-dazzle and then I came along. I don't blame her for bailing when she did. She knew I was going to be well looked after. I can't say in her position, I wouldn't make the same choice."

"You don't want kids?" Will asked.

"I don't know," Mina said. "Seems like I have plenty of time to figure that out."

"Sure," he said easily. But she could feel a tension in him that hadn't been there a few minutes ago. He was the settling down type, this man. She knew one when she saw one. After all, she'd married one. And she'd grown up with a father who definitely wasn't, so she knew that kind when she saw one as well.

A kinder person than her would cut him loose before they got too much further into this. He'd said he was fine with this just being until Christmas, but she didn't really think he would be. Though maybe it was already too late. Sex changed things whether you wanted it to or not.

And maybe she was as single-minded as her mother when it came to going after the thing that she wanted, because this first taste of Will had in no way satisfied the hunger and she just wasn't ready to give him up.

Green paint was officially going on her least favorite things list. Mina stirred the particular shade of green she'd just refilled her paint pot with a few more times and stared up at the tree before her. She had wanted to just add a touch of shading to the trees to make them look a little more real. She looked down at the line of trees. She'd finished about three quarters of them. And, she had to admit, they looked good. She was kind of looking forward to seeing them once they were all done and installed.

But she still had twelve trees to go and she was running out of time. It hadn't sounded like a big deal in her head. But she'd somehow managed to forget just how big the trees were and that fifty of anything was a lot.

But not even an ocean of green paint was enough to ruin the good mood she was in today. Apparently lots of orgasms were exactly what she'd needed. She smiled to herself, then shivered a little remembering just how good last night had been. Which immediately made her wonder when she could get Will alone again.

That wasn't going to get any trees painted.

"Focus on the task at hand," she told herself sternly, eyeing the ladder. Letting your mind wander when you were perched on top of a ladder was a recipe for disaster. In fact, Bill would probably yell at her for climbing the ladder alone if he could see her, but all the other tree painters would be working today and she'd figured she could manage a few hours by herself.

She was halfway up the ladder when she heard the shed door slide open, letting in a blast of cold air.

"Mina, what are you doing here?" Angie's voice sounded surprised. Though her face, when, Mina climbed back down, looked more annoyed than anything else—mouth pinched and brows drawn down as she inspected the rows of painted wood.

"Just finishing these off." Mina waved at the trees. They looked good. The shading she'd added brought them to life.

But Angie didn't exactly look impressed. She frowned

at the trees, wrapping her long gray coat a little more closely around her. "They're being installed tomorrow."

"I know, that's why I'm finishing them now." Mina tried to keep her voice pleasant but felt herself bristling. She should be home working on pieces for her show, not here trying to make fake trees look real. Angie needed to learn how to show some appreciation for volunteers. Or maybe it was just her that she was annoyed with.

"I just have a couple more and they'll be dry by morning. The candy canes are all done." Most of the canes, Sam had told her, were to be hung from the streetlights. Others would accompany the inflatable snowmen that Ryan had mentioned way back at the committee meeting. The snowmen and the trees would be promenading down Main Street, to the small square by the ferry dock where the town's tree traditionally stood. She had no idea what plans Angie had for the tree, she was just glad she didn't have to paint anything for it.

"Good. And those trees had better be dry," Angie said, in a tone that was just a bit too close to a snap.

Mina put down the paint can. Angie might be the mayor, but that didn't mean she got to treat everyone else like lackeys. "Okay. Do you have a specific problem with what I'm doing or do you just have a bug up your butt today?"

Angie's perfectly groomed eyebrows flew upward so fast, Mina was a little surprised they didn't fly right off her face. "Excuse me?"

"You heard me. You're talking to me like I'm your servant or something and I haven't done anything wrong that I'm aware of. So I thought I'd ask you if I'd missed something."

Angie drew herself up a little straighter. Which didn't help. Even in her heeled boots she was only about five foot six. Which gave Mina a couple of inches advantage. "Oh, Harpers are too good to take orders, is that it?"

Mina felt her own spine snap to attention. Oh no. Angie wasn't going to play that card. "Well, I think just about anybody deserves better than to be ordered around when they're doing something to help you out. But that has nothing to do with me being a Harper."

"I'm sure you'd like to think that." Angie stared at Mina, blue eyes bright with dislike.

"What I'd like is for you to tell me what exactly my family has ever done to yours? Yes, your dad is dating Lou, but that didn't happen while your mom was alive and really, they're both adults and what they do is none of your business. So what exactly is your problem?"

"You think you own the place," Angie snapped. "And yet, the second you get bored, you'll all pack up and leave. Zach already has. Most of the other Blacklight guys are hardly here anymore. Harpers aren't exactly stable. Look at your dad. He was perfectly happy to screw over whoever he wanted."

"Excuse me?" Mina said, hearing the snarl in her voice. Okay, apparently oceans of green paint couldn't ruin her good mood but Angie could. "My dad never did anything to hurt Cloud Bay. Plus he's, you know, dead, so I fail to see how anything he may have done is relevant to you now."

"Just that the apple doesn't often fall far from the tree."

Mina bit back the *Then why aren't you as nice as your father?* on the tip of her tongue. "I've lived here all my life, just like you. So has Faith." She was going to leave Zach out of it.

"When you weren't traveling the world with Grey."

"The fact that my dad had a job that involved travel is hardly my fault. And that was before we got to high school. Faith's still here, I'm still here."

"For now," Angie spat.

"What does that even mean?"

"Do you think Caleb White wants to live on Lansing Island? If Faith leaves, CloudFest will close down."

"Well, firstly, that's not true. Harper Inc. runs the festival but everyone from Blacklight gets a say. And secondly, as far as I can tell, the only thing Caleb wants is to be where Faith is. This is our home."

"It's my home," Angie said. "And it's my job to protect Cloud Bay's interests. You can't stand there and tell me that Harpers only care about the island. You were quick enough to close down Adam's business."

Mina gaped at her. "Because he died. Because his family didn't—" No. Wait. She didn't owe Angie Rigger an explanation for that particular decision. Not when everyone knew what the explanation was. Adam and his dad were dead. Hank Shepard, who'd worked in the business for most of his life, had been ready to retire. Adam's sister wasn't a boat designer nor were his mom or Mina, even though both of them had worked in the office over the years. How the hell were they supposed to keep a boatbuilding business running without designers or boatbuilders?

Her grip on her temper dissolved like paint in water. "You know what, I don't owe you an explanation for that. And I'm not going to stand here and explain to you why you're being an idiot. *I* have to finish these trees for *your* Christmas festival. Or I can leave, seeing as though I apparently don't give a crap about Cloud Bay. Is that what you want?" She glared at Angie, wondering how far the mayor would push this. Which did she want more . . . the festival or to get the upper hand with a Harper?

Angie glared back but eventually, as the silence stretched and Mina didn't look away, the other woman dropped her gaze. "Fine. But they better be ready tomorrow." She turned on her heel and stalked out of the building before Mina could come up with a reply.

So tempting to hurl one of the paintbrushes after her. But no. That would be childish. If Angie thought the Harpers weren't showing enough town spirit, then Mina knew exactly how to prove her wrong.

It was barely seven the next morning when Mina took her copy of the *Cloud Bay Gazette* over to the main house and thumped it down on the table in front of Faith who was still in her Wonder Woman pajamas, finishing breakfast, with her long hair piled messily on her head and monster feet slippers completing her outfit.

"Something on your mind?" Faith asked mildly, moving her coffee mug out of the way of the paper.

"The Christmas Festival schedule is in here," Mina said, flipping through the pages to hunt for it.

"So I hear," Faith agreed. "Has it done something to upset you?"

"No." Mina found the page she was looking for and tore it out of the paper. "Right." She bent over the listing of events and started marking them up with the highlighter she'd shoved in her pocket before leaving the cottage. Tree lighting ceremony, sleigh rides, town Secret Santa gift exchange ceremony, Santa's parade and presents for the kids, Christmas cookie competitions, sand snowman building competitions, carol singing, and every other event that Angie and Ryan had cooked up were all scrutinized and noted before she pushed the page toward Faith. "Okay. Anything highlighted I can't go to, so you and Caleb will have to."

Faith looked startled. "Well, we were going to do carol singing and the Secret Santa—Lou made me promise that one—but other than that, I figured staying out of Angie's way was the better plan." Surprise changed to a frown. "And I thought you felt the same way."

"I do. This festival is kind of crazy but we need to be there."

"Why, exactly?"

"Don't ask," Mina said. She wasn't sure she understood her sudden motivation to show Angie Rigger exactly who had more hometown spirit entirely, but she did know that Angie had pissed her off yesterday. And that she wasn't putting up with it anymore.

"That's not exactly an argument to convince me," Faith said.

"Because I'm your baby sister and you love me?" Mina said.

"Closer," Faith said. "But I feel like I'm missing half the story here."

"If I tell you it's a dumb story and likely to just piss you off, will you just go along with me? C'mon Faith, it's not like I ask you for favors all that often. And I have to paint some of the time."

Faith sighed then narrowed her eyes. "Okay. But you have to answer me one question."

Damn. Had the security guys told Faith that Will's car had been at Mina's place all night? She thought he'd left early enough to avoid Faith or Caleb noticing. But Faith was bound to notice sooner or later. Unless she started going to Will's place. Not that she really knew where Will's place was. Did he live over the bar? If so, then it wasn't really an option she wanted to explore. There were definitely downfalls to sharing a property with your family. Kind of cramped a girl's style for carrying on a secret sneaky . . . project. No wonder Faith had stuck to keeping her love life strictly off-island for so long.

So the question was, which was more important . . . delaying Faith finding out the inevitable or making Angie see that she was wrong about the Harpers.

It had to be the latter.

"Ask away," she said.

"Was that Will's Mustang I heard this morning?" Faith was clearly trying not to smile, but one of her dimples popped to life in her cheek.

There wasn't much point trying to deny it. Lulu had a distinctive sound and Faith, like Mina, had grown up with Grey's car habit. She probably knew just as much as Mina about classic cars. Plus she and Caleb went to Salt Devil quite often, so she probably knew Lulu quite well.

"Yes," she said.

Faith squealed and hugged her. Then let go and held up her hand for a high five. "Way to go, little sis." She waggled her fingers when Mina didn't immediately hit her hand. "C'mon, high five."

Reluctantly, Mina completed the gesture. "Don't get too attached," she warned. "It's just temporary."

"I am applauding the step, not who you're taking it with." Faith said. Then frowned. "Though, to be clear, I'm just fine with it being Will." Her expression turned approving. "Because he's pretty—"

"How about we don't finish that sentence," Mina said. "And just focus on the festival. We have a whole lot of Christmas to get through."

chapter fifteen

The next week passed in a blur for Will. Between the Christmas Festival and the bar and trying to sneak a few hours with Mina, he hadn't really had time to think. He and Mina had put those hours to good use . . . the memory of just how good was the only thing that filled his brain when he did get a minute to think. So good that a few hours here and there weren't nearly enough. But he couldn't push her. He had to give her space. And time to paint. No way was he going to be the reason she didn't get everything she needed for the show done in time. That would only make her resent him. Not the emotion he was going for.

But lack of time with Mina and a stupidly busy schedule aside, life was good. Even if today was starting far too early.

He hid a yawn as he helped Stefan wrestle a sack of grain into the storage shed.

"Something keeping you up at night?" Stefan asked when the grain was safely shelved.

Will watched his brother give the pile of grain sacks a proprietary pat and shook his head. "Nothing. Just looking forward to getting through Christmas and then putting these babies to work." He eyed the full storage shed. All being well, they'd get another batch of whiskey barreled in the new year. And then, come summer, it would finally be time to finish their very first batch, the one they'd laid down when they'd first moved to Lansing. It was a long game, whiskey, and he tried not to think too hard about all the money tied up in the rows of barrels from each year since then currently sitting in their rackhouse quietly ageing and hopefully turning into something that would sell.

They'd agreed on five years for the first batch. Longer could be better but they had to start selling at some point to know whether Stefan's theory of salt air and whiskey would pay off. They'd been tasting along the way of course, and so far they both liked what was happening. But that didn't mean anyone else would. Neither of them had talked about what would happen if Salt Devil whiskey flopped. The bar did well enough, but they'd set it up mostly as cash flow for the distillery. If they couldn't pull that part of the business off, then they'd just poured both their life savings down the drain. He shook off the thought. Worrying about it wouldn't help. "I'll admit, life would be easier without this Christmas Festival but from the figures Angie has put together on accommodation and ferry bookings over the next month, it's looking like it may pay off." Salt Devil had definitely been busier than usual for the time of year last night.

Stefan raised a bushy dark eyebrow at him, clearly not missing the obvious change of subject, but didn't comment. Will knew he wasn't fooling anybody, least of all Stefan. After all, his brother was the one picking up the slack at the bar the times Will negotiated some time off. Stefan wasn't dumb. He wouldn't be assuming Will was off doing Christmas Festival administration at eleven at night. But apparently Stefan wasn't going to give him grief.

They worked in easy silence a bit longer, getting the various grains sorted and stacked in place, and then locked up the storehouse, activating the climate control system. Temperature variations helped the ageing process for the whiskey in the rackhouse, but damp winter air wasn't a good thing when you were trying to keep grain dry. The island made transportation of bulky goods like grain a challenge and sometimes they had to wait for several orders over a few weeks to gather enough grain for a batch. Including sometimes taking deliveries on the weekend. Which was why they were both up earlier than usual on a Saturday, having met the goods ferry at the ungodly hour of seven a.m. down at the harbor in Cloud Bay. Not so easy when Will had finally crawled into bed around two after a busy night at the bar.

Today was going to require coffee. All the coffee. Or a nap. He was meeting Mina for one of the first Christmas Festival events he'd been able to fit into his schedule this week, a sand snowman sculpture competition down on the town's main beach. But that wasn't until two. That should leave time to hit the sack again and try to catch up on some sleep.

"So, seeing as we're up here, want to haul some barrels around?" Stefan asked.

Damn. He'd been hoping Stefan might have been keen to catch a few more hours of sleep too. But he should have known better. Once Stefan was up, he was up. The guy could run on four or five hours sleep for days at a time if he had to. Will sometimes suspected he mainlined espresso, but had never caught him at it. "Sure," he said, trying to sound enthusiastic. Full whiskey barrels were heavy bastards. And moving them around the rackhouse, even with the assistance of their forklift, often required more manual labor than Will preferred first thing in the morning.

Stefan grinned at him. "Look at it this way. Do it now and that's one less thing to do during the week. And, hey, only three weeks until Christmas as of today."

Will nodded, trying to look as though that was a good thing. Three weeks until Christmas meant only one thing this year. Three weeks until Mina intended cutting him loose and sending him on his merry way. Which left him with less than three weeks to figure out how to convince her not to.

Sand snowmen sort of sucked, Mina thought as she arched her back, trying to ease the kink forming at the base of her spine. Making one sounded like fun and the actual building of one was fun—kind of. It might have been completely fun in summer. But standing on a beach on a wintry day playing with wet sand and cold water sucked. She and Will had arrived at the beach a little after two and now it was closing in on four, and she was over the whole thing.

Luckily the sun was shining—though the shadow their creation was casting on the sand was rapidly lengthening. And the wind coming off the sea was starting to pick up. The combination of cold air and water and wind had somehow made the experience colder and more uncomfortable than making actual snowmen. At least with those, you got to keep your snow gloves on.

"Whose idea was this again?" she muttered to Will as they tried to get the shells they were using for buttons to stay where they wanted them. She didn't think their snowman was going to win any prizes. His head had fallen off three times during construction, and their last hurried attempt at replacing it wasn't exactly the smoothest sphere. In fact, he looked a bit more like Frankenstein than Frosty. But she had to admit it was fun watching Will trying to figure out how to hide that fact.

She was definitely going to make sure she was busy the remaining two Saturdays before Christmas though. Angie had scheduled a repeat of the sand snowman competition every weekend. Her theory being that there would be some turnover in the tourists from week to week.

Mina didn't know if that was true or not but she wasn't going to volunteer to be back on the beach to find out. She could handle painting fifty giant Christmas trees, but cold wet sand sculpture was not her thing.

By the time they were done, her fingers were throbbing from cold. She would have mugged a small child for a hand warmer of some sort. Shoving her hands into her pockets at every opportunity only resulted in sandy pockets and hands that were still frozen.

But despite the cold and the unpleasant conditions, she'd gotten to hang out with Will. And that had made her happy. The first fifteen minutes or so after they'd arrived she'd felt as though every local on the beach had been watching them, but then she'd relaxed. Scheduling time together this week had been like trying to do a particularly fiendish jigsaw puzzle in the dark. She didn't want to waste her time today feeling weird.

Even if she'd rather be home in her big bed with him doing all those inventive things to her body than standing on the beach, she was determined to enjoy herself. And she did.

Will, she was coming to realize, was easy to enjoy. He was solid, she knew that. He had depths. And some of them were playful depths. Grey would have been uber competitive at an event like this and, thinking about it, Adam probably would have too. Will, on the other hand, clearly cared about figuring out how to do the job well but didn't seem to care about winning.

He spent his time teasing some of the other teams, and he and Caleb had bucket-filling races, but he just laughed if he lost. And when she started get cranky as the cold set in, he turned his sense of play on her, making her laugh too as he goofed around with seaweed and sand and stole moments of touch in a subtle way that warmed her blood a little without the kind of obvious display of affection that would have made her feel like she was under the spotlight again.

Then there was that thing where he really wasn't hard

on the eyes. The easy way he moved and wielded the
various tools they'd been presented with reminded her
a little of Grey with a guitar in his hands. A man in his
element, sure of himself. Would he look the same way
behind a bar? Or doing whatever it was he and Stefan
did at the distillery?

Not that she was going to see him there.

As they lined up beside their lopsided creation for the
final judging, Mina heard a snort of laughter from Faith
and looked over to see her sister collapsing in giggles
against Caleb as their sandman started to crumble. Caleb looked resigned and then not at all bothered as Faith
stretched up to kiss him next to the wreckage.

"Well, I guess we're not coming dead last," Mina said
to Will as she turned back to regard their own creation,
trying not to laugh as well.

Will nodded. "I need a bit more practice. Snowmen
I can do but it's a long time since I made a sandcastle."
He tilted his head at the lopsided figure. "I thought your
islander skills might help."

"Sandcastles I can do," Mina said. "But sand sculpture is a whole other thing. Besides, in summer my dad
was usually touring. We didn't always spend a lot of
time on the island until the festival rolled around. At
which point the beaches get crowded and the pool was
more fun."

"Your beach is private, isn't it?" Will asked, dribbling
more water onto Frankensnow's head and smoothing the
sand. Then he straightened, looking over Mina's shoulder. She turned to see Angie and Ryan approaching.

The mayor was the judge of this particular contest,
which meant that they would have been well and truly

screwed even if they'd made the best damn sand snowman in the world.

"It is. Not that we stick to that rule. But during Cloud-
Fest, we have to keep the fans off it. Too close to the
house. Most fans are lovely but you never know when
someone might get . . . overenthusiastic."

"I guess so," Will said. "Was that weird, growing up
with security?"

"Not really. I didn't know any different. Frustrating
and annoying at times, yes. But mostly kind of comforting knowing they were there. Especially good when
you're trying to get in or out of a venue or hotel when the
band was touring. But as a kid, you want your dad to
be safe. Grey had a few encounters where things got
weird—I think all the Blacklight guys did. Still do. But
security was always there to get them out of it." She
stopped as Angie came up to them, forcing a polite smile
onto her face. She hadn't crossed paths with Angie since
their argument about the trees, having spent most of the
week madly painting in her studio, happily ignoring
anything that wasn't watercolor or Will. She'd gone to
the first round of the Christmas cookie-off—because,
cookies—but had stayed at the back of the town hall and
out of Angie's way.

The trees had obviously dried in time as they were
safely installed along Main Street. They looked good.

"Mayor Rigger, Ryan," she said, nodding to Ryan
as Angie studied their sculpture. Ryan flashed a tight
smile but didn't reply. His usual slick style was somewhat marred by the rubber boots he'd chosen as winter beach footwear and he looked distinctly out of his
element.

Angie didn't answer either, though she smiled at Will before she and Ryan moved on to Faith and Caleb.

"Is it just me or did the temperature just drop a few more degrees?" Faith said to Mina after Angie had moved on again. "I know Angie doesn't like me but she wasn't giving you any love either, sis. What's up?"

"Nothing," Mina lied. "Everything's cool."

"Literally," Faith said. She shivered theatrically. "I don't know about you two, but Caleb and I were thinking about grabbing a coffee and something to eat while we thaw out. Want to join us?"

"I have to be back at Salt Devil by five thirty," Will said. "But coffee sounds good." He turned toward her, eyebrows lifting in a "What do you think" expression.

There was no reason to say no. After all, half the town had seen them together today. But for some reason a double date with Faith and Caleb felt very . . . official. And this was supposed to be casual.

It *was* casual, she told herself firmly. So there was no reason not to eat cake and coffee with the man. Coffee was the definition of casual. And coffee meant another hour with Will today. Ignoring the small twinge of worry in her stomach, she smiled up at Will. "Lead me to the cake."

Will pushed aside his empty plate and tried to ignore the urge to order more cake. Jin's Diner was a Cloud Bay fixture, serving an odd mixture of burgers and Chinese food. And cake. Very good cake. Jin herself had retired, but now her daughter and son-in-law carried on the tradition. The coffee was pretty good too—not as good as his maybe—but it was hot and had done the job of thawing them all out. Mina had peeled off her coat and looked much happier than she had half the time on the beach. He had to admit, as much as he'd enjoyed figuring out how to build a sand sculpture, spending two hours wrist deep in wet sand or cold sea water wasn't the most pleasant experience. The weather hadn't been particularly cold for this time of year, but the beach was windy and the wind had found every damp patch on his clothes. He'd have to make sure that the committee came up with another idea if the Christmas Festival had a second year.

The kids at the contest had seemed to be having fun, but it wasn't going to do Cloud Bay any good if a tourist got hypothermia. Sand sculpture contests could be saved for summer.

Still, after two cups of coffee and a slab of chocolate cake that would have fed three people, he was mostly thawed out. And he wasn't going to complain about an afternoon spent with Mina. The only thing that could have improved the day would be if he managed to sneak Mina away for an hour of privacy at the end of the contest. But Faith had invited them for coffee and that had been the end of that hope.

Faith, who was sitting opposite him in the booth, sipping hot chocolate and talking about some singer he'd never heard of with Mina. From time to time he'd caught her watching him through those big gray-green eyes so like Mina's. He wasn't yet convinced Faith didn't have an ulterior motive for the coffee invite although he thought she knew him well enough that she shouldn't have wanted to play the old "vetted by the big sister" card. But maybe things had changed now that he was actually dating Mina—at least as far as Faith knew, that was what they were doing.

On Faith's side, Caleb sat, adding the odd comment to the conversation but mostly seemingly content to sit and watch Faith. Will wasn't sure when he'd ever seen a guy so clearly in love and not giving a crap who knew. It made him feel weirdly jealous. He was pretty sure if he shot Mina the kind of look Caleb gave Faith, she'd run a mile.

So he settled for resting his thigh against hers and making nice with her family while the weather turned nasty outside, rain hitting the diner window hard enough to make it rattle. That might put a cramp on the night's crowd at the bar. Rain made the tourists stay in. Maybe he'd get an early night after all. One with Mina.

He was just starting to think that he needed to make a move toward leaving when Mina suddenly started rummaging in her purse. She pulled out her phone, frowning at the number on the screen before she answered.

"Bill, hey," she said. "What's up?"

Her frown deepened as she listened to the answer and then slid out of the booth, walking quickly out of the dinner.

"Crap," Faith said. "That's not good."

"What's not good? I thought Mina was on leave this week," Will said, trying to ignore the twist in his gut that told him that Faith's assessment was right.

"Which means if Bill's calling her then there's something going on. An all-hands-on-deck type something."

Faith nudged at Caleb who eased out of the booth to let her out, but before she could go after her sister, Mina came back into the diner, moving fast.

"Sorry," she said. "I have to go. We have a call out."

"In this weather?" Will said. The rain moved from annoying weather quirk to alarming in his estimation.

"That's kind of what we do," Mina said, with a tight smile.

"What's wrong?" Faith said.

"Boat in distress," Mina said. "We're scrambling everyone."

Will didn't know exactly what that meant, but it didn't sound good. In fact, it sounded like Mina was about to get on a boat and deliberately head out into the storm brewing outside.

His gut twisted tighter. Crap. He'd never thought too closely about what Mina working for search and rescue really meant. She'd told him she worked the radio. But this didn't seem like that.

"I need a ride down to the station," Mina said as she reached for her bag.

Right. Her car was at the cottage. He'd have to do something about that, later. "I'll take you," he said. He slid out of the booth, grabbing the jacket he'd discarded over the back of the booth and fishing in the pocket for his wallet.

"Go." Caleb waved him off. "This one's on us."

Faith was nodding beside him. "We'll get Stewie when we go home. Go."

Mina apparently didn't need to wait to hear anything else. She was heading back toward the door as he was shrugging on his coat. He caught up to her as she reached Lulu.

"Sorry," she said. "I guess this wasn't quite what you had in mind for this afternoon."

"Nothing to be sorry about," he said as he unlocked the door for her. "This is your job. We got to hang out." He only waited long enough for Mina to fasten her seat belt before he backed Lulu out of the diner's lot and pointed her nose toward the road down to the harbor. The tires slid a little on the wet gravel at the side of the asphalt and he eased back slightly. Mina needed to get there in one piece. Unlike the last time she'd gone out in a storm. The light was fading rapidly now. Soon it would be as dark as the night of her accident. And she was heading out to sea. That felt far more dangerous than driving her car.

"Are you sure you're up to this?" he asked before he could think.

She'd been staring out the windshield, leaning a little forward as if urging the car to go faster. But that brought her head around. She was frowning again. "I'm fine."

"I'm sure no one would blame you if you said you weren't," Will said, glancing at her sideways. He needed to focus on the road in this weather but he wanted to see her face. Make sure she was telling the truth.

Her head tilted. "I'm fine," she said firmly. "This is what we train for, Will. I've done this before. It will be okay."

He clamped his mouth shut on the automatic "That's easy for you to say" that rose in his throat. Bringing up the fact that what she was about to do was dangerous

felt like tempting the gods somehow. And Mina knew
well enough how fate could turn on a dime.

So did he. So all he could do now was let her go do
her damn job.

And hope she made it back to him in one piece.

Because driving through the rain, fear chilling his
veins, he knew that he had no idea what he'd do if she
didn't.

chapter sixteen

Mina fought a battle with her eyelids as she steered the Jeep the last few hundred feet of her drive. Earlier, she'd been cold, wet and buzzed, buoyed by the excitement of a successful rescue. Now she was cold and exhausted, the adrenaline drop that had hit her halfway home leaving her longing for sleep. She'd turned down the Jeep's heating, hoping the cold air would keep her awake long enough to reach her bed. The rain hadn't really eased up since she'd left the diner and she had tried to be careful making the drive back around the island. Not easy when her body was fighting her.

Nearly there.

Shower. Bed. Sleep. The three words were a mantra in her head but they vanished as her headlights illuminated the unmistakable shape of Lulu parked outside her cottage.

Will? What was Will doing here?

Some of the fatigue lifted as another wave of adrenaline hit.

She wasn't sure if it was excitement or worry and didn't have time to make up her mind. Will was at the Jeep door before she'd even cut the engine.

"Are you okay?" he demanded, pulling the door open.

"What are you doing here?" she said, still surprised. Will was rapidly getting soaked and she shoved at him gently. "Let me out."

"Are you okay?" he repeated. But he stepped back to give her room.

She climbed out of the car. Will's arms came around her. Hard.

"Will, you're kind of squashing me," she said. "I'm okay, honest."

The pressure around her ribs eased. "Are you sure?"

"Yes, I'm fine. Things got a little hairy at one point but—" She stopped. It was kind of hard to tell in the rainy darkness, but Will looked suddenly pale. "I'm fine. Let's go inside."

She grabbed her purse off the backseat. Her backpack full of gear sitting in the back compartment could wait until she figured out what was going on with Will.

He didn't say anything as they made the short dash to the cottage and she let them in. By the time she'd turned on the lights, turned up the heat, and put the kettle on the stove to make tea, he still hadn't said anything. But he watched her every second, as though he was worried she might just vanish. His skin was definitely a couple of shades lighter than its usual healthy tan.

She pulled down mugs and peppermint tea. It didn't

seem as though caffeine was likely to help the situation. "Take off your coat, I'll get you a towel for your hair." He didn't even seem to have noticed he was soaked.

He had removed his coat by the time she returned and had moved to stand near the kettle, watching it instead of her.

"A watched kettle never boils," she quipped, passing him the towel.

As if to prove her wrong the kettle started to whistle as Will lifted the towel and rubbed it through his hair, leaving it spiked up in all directions.

"You want to tell me what's going on?" she asked as she poured the water into the mugs.

"I wanted to make sure you're okay."

"It's three in the morning."

"I couldn't sleep. So I came over."

That seemed like more than just wanting to know she was okay. She jiggled the tea bag in her mug. "You seem kind of freaked out."

"You were out on the ocean in a middle of a storm."

"With a highly trained team. Doing our *jobs*." she pointed out, keeping her voice gentle. He was clearly freaked out, even though she wasn't entirely sure why.

Will frowned. "Yeah, well, your job kind of sucks."

"Excuse me? Search and rescue sucks?"

"Putting yourself in danger sucks." Will shuddered and took a mouthful of tea. Then pulled a face and put it down.

The shiver brought back an image of him staring down at the ocean from the cliffs near Shane's house at Thanksgiving. O-kay. So he hadn't been kidding about the not liking water part.

"I wasn't in danger," she said softly. "But we saved three people tonight who were."

"If they were in danger, weren't you in danger?" he said hotly.

"No. We were in boats that hadn't broken down. We had the ability to call for backup. There are risks involved in what we do but they're well-controlled risks. This isn't even particularly bad weather." She'd seen much worse. Not often, and tonight had been nasty enough, but she wasn't going to tell Will that. "So do you want to tell me what's going on?"

"No," he said and pulled her to him and kissed her. A kiss part anger, part fear, part hunger. A kiss that chased the last of the chill from her bones and instead lit a fire that sent a glow straight through her. For a minute or so she gave into it, gave him what he wanted. Proved to him she was still right there. And then she broke away.

"Yeah, that's not going to work," she said, moving around the counter.

"Felt like it worked just fine to me," Will said. He wasn't pale now and his eyes had turned the darker green she was coming to know so well.

"I liked it too. But I'd also like to know what's going on with you."

"Maybe I'm just not used to dat—*projecting with*—someone with a risky job."

It was possible. But she didn't think that was exactly the problem here. "I've been around boats and the ocean my whole life. I know what I'm doing. So for the duration of our . . . project, you're going to have to be okay with it. You know, I could take you down to the station tomorrow, show you how it all works. Even take you out on the—"

"No!" The denial came too quickly to have come from anywhere but deep in his gut.

"Will, talk to me," she said. "You told me at Thanksgiving that you didn't like the water. You didn't tell me why."

"The first time I ever went on a boat, my best friend died," he said. "I was twelve. So was he. We went to stay for a week with his grandparents in Maine and we went out on a boat and"—he took a shuddering breath—"there was a storm. He got swept away."

"Oh, Will."

He looked haunted. She knew how he felt. Losses grew easier over time perhaps but they didn't leave you. "That must have been horrible for you."

"It was," he said. "For a long time, I felt like it was my fault."

"Why?"

"I thought he made his grandpa take us out to show off to me." He shook himself, like he was trying to cast off the memory.

"But that wasn't true, right? And it wouldn't have been your fault even if it was."

"No. Doesn't mean it didn't feel true. People think all sorts of odd things when they're grieving." He leaned his hands on the counter, slumping slightly.

Was that aimed at her? She hesitated, trying to read him. His voice had sounded almost absent, so maybe not. "So let me guess, you haven't really been sailing since then?"

"My rule is nothing smaller than a ferry." He glanced down at his hands.

"Which once again forces me to wonder what you're doing living on an island?"

He looked up. "Because there's no point letting fear run your life. Then it wins."

Once again she felt like he was talking about something more than just tonight. But if he was, they were wading into an area she wasn't ready to discuss.

"But in that case, you shouldn't have been so worried."

"I said I didn't let fear run my life. That doesn't mean I don't feel it sometimes." One side of his mouth lifted. "So do you want to come back over to this side of the counter? See what we can do to take my mind off it?"

"Oh, so I'm good for a distraction, am I?" She tried to sound indignant, but it was hard to resist the man.

"You're good for more than that," he said. "Much more. But right now, a distraction is what I need. And I can't think of anything better than losing myself in you." He crooked his finger, beckoning her toward him. Toward temptation.

She'd always thought she was pretty good at resisting temptation. Grey's friends—even Grey himself— had been a lesson in what happened if you gave into it too often. But apparently Will was the Achilles' heel she hadn't known she had. Her feet moved of their own volition, finding their way back to him like a compass seeking north.

Will's hands found her with the same certainty, pulling her into him. This time the kiss was just hunger, reigniting what they'd started earlier with a speed that was startling. She tried to get closer to him, hooking a leg around his thigh, and in response he lifted her onto the counter, settling between her legs, one hand curving around her thigh to coax up around his hip. God.

That felt good. When she arched into him, felt the warmth and hardness meet her, all she wanted was more. More Will. More everything.

More everything required less clothes. She fisted her hands into the back of his shirt, yanking it upward. Will got the message fast and started working on her sweater, pulling it up and over her head. The layers of shirts and thermals she wore beneath it vanished in rapid succession. Her bra was one of the boring black ones she kept in her gear bag, but that didn't seem to bother Will. No, he looked at her like she was decked out in silk and lace and then simply tugged the cup down and fastened his mouth over her nipple.

She'd thought she'd warmed up, but his mouth was hot on her skin, seeking and teasing, the sensation on the edge of pain. She found his left hand, brought it to her other breast then used the last few fleeting seconds of brain power before she went mindless to undo the bra so it could fall away. After that, she couldn't think of anything but Will. She braced herself on arms that felt distinctly wobbly and let her head fall back, giving into the sensations. Will didn't let her catch her breath, his hands and lips working her into a rapidly melting puddle of delighted woman.

"Lie back, baby," he urged. She didn't hesitate to obey. After all, he was doing such a good job that it seemed stupid to do anything else. She lifted her hips as he undid her jeans, wriggling a little to help him ease them free.

Part of her was dimly aware that she was lying naked on her counter, that her curtains were open. But this was private property and Faith and Caleb, who were the two closest human beings, would be tucked up in bed. And really, right at this moment, as Will eased her legs open, she wasn't sure she would have been able to bring herself to make him stop even if there was an audience.

"So pretty," Will murmured, his thumb pressing into her clit, making her hips buck toward him. Apparently that was an invitation, because the next moment his thumb was gone and instead his tongue moved slowly across her. This time she moaned. Then she might have begged as he did it again. The man had skills. How did he know her body so well already?

How did she know his? Even with her eyes closed, she could picture him as her hands slid over muscle and skin, finding the lines of his body. Knew that she could reach for a pencil and draw those lines as easily as she could write her name. Like the shape of him had slid under her skin and into her memories. Burned there with heat and pleasure. Every time he touched her, it only deepened the effect.

Right now, his mouth was making her mindless. She wasn't sure she would remember her own name, but she was certain she wouldn't forget his.

"Will," she said, half breath, half plea.

"Not yet." His voice was muffled but certain. The sound vibrated over very sensitive skin, making her forget what she was asking for.

"I want you like this first. Want to feel you come apart."

God. She wanted that too. Her body took over, rising to meet each stroke of his tongue.

"That's it," he said fiercely. His hands pushed her

legs wider and then his tongue was joined by fingers, sliding into her, stroking her, the doubled sensation wonderful and terrible. She wanted to hold on and let go. Afraid to do either. Not entirely sure if she let go at this point that there'd be anything left of her to come back.

But what a way to go.

And Will, it seemed, was determined to make sure she got there. He kept up the torment, pushing her closer to the edge. Until she was teetering there, feeling the orgasm waiting for her, endless and deep, waiting for her to drop into it, as easily as diving into the ocean. But she didn't want to give up the pleasure for the release. Not just yet. Even knowing what waited for her on the other side, she hesitated, like a diver curling her toes onto the edge of the board, letting the anticipation build. Until finally the urge to fall was just too strong and she had to let go, had to give in to what he wanted and let herself come, knowing that he was waiting there, strong and sure to catch her on the other side.

Will had done more than catch her. He'd picked her up, carried her off to bed and made love to her twice more. Adrenaline. Will might have come up with her new favorite way to work it off.

Still, now he was still asleep—understandably when it had been after five when they'd finally fallen asleep and it was only half past seven—and she was awake. Awake and still unable to get his reaction out of her head.

Lying here worrying about it, however, wasn't going to help. If Will was more involved than he should be, there was nothing she could do about it. At least, nothing right now. But she couldn't just lie here. Sleep didn't seem to be an option—she'd been trying for thirty minutes to fall back asleep.

If Stewie had been here rather than at Faith's, she'd take him for a walk and come back before Will woke.

Actually, that wasn't such a bad idea. It was Sunday, so Faith didn't have to go to work, but there was no need for her or Caleb to have to get up early to walk Stewie if Mina could get there first and bring him home.

Either the walk would wake her up properly or distract her enough that she'd be able to sleep again when she got back.

It didn't take long to slip out of bed, find clothes, and creep out of the room. Will was sleeping the sleep of the well-satisfied male and barely stirred. She closed the door behind her and headed outside.

The storm had finally cleared and the sky was a sharp winter blue, the sun bright even at this early hour. It wasn't nearly as cold as the previous day either. Typical. The day she wasn't going to spend several hours playing with wet sand was the one with the nice weather.

But the morning was so pretty, the sun making all the surfaces newly washed by the rain shine and sparkle, that she decided to walk along the beach and cut back up to the main house farther up rather than go through the gardens. It was the longer way but that would give her time to clear her head.

She took the fork in the path toward the beach, letting her mind wander.

Maybe she could raid Faith's fridge for breakfast supplies. She wasn't entirely sure what was in hers. Having spent all her free time during the week painting, she'd been eating thrown-together meals made from whatever had been in the fridge and pantry without paying much attention and really couldn't have said what might still be left. She'd been planning a grocery store run after the snowman competition, but that hadn't happened.

Faith however, was bound to have something she could steal to cook for Will. Eggs. Bacon. Bread for toast. Frozen waffles. She'd take what she could get.

Her stomach growled agreement and she quickened her pace. Will wasn't the only one who'd worked up an appetite.

But when she came around the headland, a happy bark startled her and she looked up to see Faith and Stewie playing fetch a few hundred feet down the beach.

Stewie must have caught her scent or something because he came barreling along the sand toward her, doggie smile stretched awkwardly by the tennis ball held in his mouth.

He danced around her when he reached her, spitting out the ball so he could try to lick her face. She bent down to hug him. Big goofus.

"Someone missed you," Faith said as she came jogging up behind him. She reached down and picked up the ball. When she threw it back in the direction they'd come from, Stewie left off harassing Mina, apparently satisfied that she hadn't abandoned him forever, and charged after it.

"Sorry," Mina said. "Was he a pain?"

"No," Faith said. "He whined a bit when it started getting dark but he settled down. He always does." She smiled then frowned. "I didn't expect to see you for hours. What time did you get home?"

"Around three," Mina said.

"Shouldn't you be sleeping?"

"I woke up. Thought I'd come grab Stewie so you and Caleb could get on with your day. I can sleep later." Not too much later though. She still had painting to do.

Faith nodded and looked back over her shoulder at Stewie. Who was digging at something in the sand and didn't seem like he'd be bringing the tennis ball back anytime soon. She turned back to Mina. "Will still asleep?"

Mina blinked. "How did you know Will was at my place?"

"The security guys buzzed to see if it was okay to let him in last night. They knew you weren't home."

"What time was that?"

"About one?" Faith said.

Two hours? He'd waited for her for two hours last night. She hid the wince. "Sorry."

"We weren't asleep," Faith said. "I wanted to know you were home too."

This time she did wince. "Sorry. In that case, you should still be in bed too."

"I will be heading back there soon,' Faith said. "But Stewie needed out." She paused, twisted a length of hair that had come free of her messy bun around her finger. "Was Will . . . okay?"

"Why wouldn't he be?"

"He seemed pretty worried last night. He came back to the diner after he'd dropped you off. Borrowed my spare key to your Jeep so he could bring it up to the station for you."

"Will did that?" She'd assumed it had been Faith or Caleb who had brought the Jeep into town for her.

They'd done it before when she'd been called out from somewhere and hadn't had her car with her.

Faith nodded. "Yep. He insisted. He's a good guy, that one."

Yes. He was. That was the problem. "I know."

"Are you two—"

Mina held up a hand, cutting Faith off. "It's temporary. We agreed."

"Agreed?" Faith was wearing sunglasses, but Mina was fairly sure she was rolling her eyes. "Whose dumb idea was that?"

"It's not a dumb idea," Mina said. "Will's a good guy, he's just not—"

"Is this because he runs a bar?" Faith said. "You know that's kind of idiotic, right?" She sounded cranky. But then she smiled, shaking her head at herself.

"It's my life, Faith."

"I know," Faith said, shaking her head again. "You know, I always seem to end up having heart-to-hearts on the beach. Maybe we should build a little stand here. Like in Peanuts. Make a little 'the doctor is in' sign for these chats."

"Last time I checked, you weren't a doctor," Mina said.

"No, but I am an expert in dumb relationship rules. After all, mine almost cost me Caleb."

"Caleb's different."

"Only because I was smart enough to realize I couldn't let him get away," Faith said. "Will obviously cares about you. Don't you think you should at least give him a chance? Entertain the possibility that maybe he's the one you shouldn't let get away?"

"I already had that guy," Mina said. This conversation was so not the one she wanted to be having on two hours of sleep.

"Adam wouldn't have wanted you to be alone forever. God, Mina, you're only twenty-three."

"Which means I have plenty of time to find another guy. One who doesn't make his living from selling booze."

"That's ridiculous," Faith said, frowning at her. "I drink. Caleb drinks. Even Lou drinks. Ninety-nine percent of the people you know probably drink. You haven't cut any of us out of your life."

"Consuming alcohol is different from having your whole life be about it," Mina said.

Faith's expression softened. "Oh honey. Will's not Dad. And he's not the guy who hit Adam. That guy wasn't even drinking at Salt Devil."

"Trust me, I'm well acquainted with the facts of the accident that killed my husband," Mina snapped. She looked past Faith, hoping to catch Stewie's eye. She needed to leave. But Stewie was paddling in the water, not even looking in her direction.

"Then you need to start accepting it was an accident. That guy was over the limit, yes. But it was raining too. And late. He made a stupid decision. He paid for it. Adam paid for it. Don't make Will pay for it too. Not if that means that the one who's really paying for it is you."

"Well, that's my decision, isn't it?" Mina said, digging her fingers into the sand against the urge to just get up and walk away.

Faith held up her hands. "Yes, yes it is. And I won't keep bugging you about it. But you need to think about this. God knows, Grey wasn't the world's best male role model when we were growing up, and most of his friends weren't either. And yes, he was an alcoholic. But I've never seen Will drunk, and he and Stefan are fierce about cutting people off at the bar if they think they've had enough. He likes whiskey, yes. But he's not trying to ruin anybody's life."

No. Maybe not. But Mina was getting the feeling that he was going to ruin her heart.

chapter seventeen

Will hesitated at the door to the town hall, feeling weirdly nervous. Which was dumb. There was nothing about a Secret Santa exchange that should make a grown man feel nervous. Except he'd managed to draw Lou as his giftee. Which had added a whole new layer of pressure to the thing. What did you buy for the woman who was, for all intents and purposes, the mother of the woman you were hung up on but who didn't know that? It didn't feel right to go the gag gift route or to give Lou a boring box of chocolates or bottle of red.

It had taken him nearly a week of trying to come up with ideas as well as trying to subtly pick Faith's and Mina's brains before he'd finally bought his gift the previous day. Which was cutting it kind of fine, but part of his usual Monday errands included picking up the bar's grocery and meat orders for the first part of the week from Cloud Bay, so he'd managed to deliver his gift to the collection point at the mayor's office just before the midday cut-off time.

But now he was second-guessing his final choice. He'd been planning to get her a cookbook but when he'd dropped into To Be Read, Cloud Bay's sole bookstore, and confessed the reason for his visit to Patty Bleecker, she'd told him that she had the latest murder mystery by Lou's favorite author out back, waiting for the release day on Tuesday. She'd let him have a copy and told him she'd put Lou off if she came looking for it before then. So he'd left with that and a bag of the chocolate sea salt caramels that Patty's wife, Evie, had made and that was that.

It was a good gift. The right gift. What better gift for a woman who taught English than a book by her favorite author? But somehow, he was wondering if he should have gone for something simpler. Not because Lou wouldn't like the book but because, if he was honest, he was worried that Mina would think he'd gone to a lot of effort to figure out the gift. It had been a week since she'd been called out during that stupid storm and even though she hadn't raised the subject with him again, he knew she'd been . . . well, "alarmed" wasn't quite the right word but "surprised," at least, by his reaction. Or overreaction.

Not his finest moment ever. Here he was trying to play it casual and see if he could win Mina over slowly, and then he'd screwed it up.

Mina had been . . . different since. He'd thought they'd been moving in the same direction, and now she'd drifted a little. She hadn't refused to see him, though she was still working furiously to complete her paintings, and she hadn't kicked him out of her bed. But there was something about her that made him feel like she was floating just a little out of his reach. And he had absolutely no idea how to pull her back to him. She liked him, he knew that. They managed to talk for hours when they weren't tearing each other's clothes off. But he got the feeling that getting her to admit she liked him . . . maybe more than liked him . . . was going to be difficult.

Still, he'd agreed to their deal. Hell, he'd proposed it in the first place. So he was going to have to suck it up if Mina actually stuck to it. But he'd have paid a million dollars—not that he had a million dollars—to find a way to make sure she didn't.

He moved through the room, looking for her. The town hall was large and echo-y, and between the Christmas carols being piped through the speakers and everyone talking, the noise was nearly deafening, so it wasn't likely he'd be able to hear where she was. A smarter man would have arranged to meet in a certain spot, but he hadn't been that smart lately. Plus he'd been trying to keep things light. There were plenty of faces he recognized, and he paused to speak to several people while he tried to circle the room, but so far Mina hadn't appeared. So, maybe she was running late.

Should he have offered to pick her up?

He hadn't—again, because he was trying to be casual, but maybe that had been dumb.

Stefan had agreed to open the bar late tonight, Will having convinced him that ninety percent of the locals would be at the Secret Santa anyway, so it wasn't as though they'd been losing money by staying closed a couple of extra hours. And, looking at the size of the crowd gathering, that had been the right call.

Angie had been smart to schedule this particular event for Monday night. Monday meant most of the weekend tourists would have left and, because it was still nearly two weeks out from Christmas, the tourists who might be coming for longer stays hadn't yet arrived. So most locals were free to attend.

Which was kind of nice. There were things about living on an island—other than being surrounded by the ocean—that were frustrating sometimes, but he had to admit that he did like the sense of community. His mom had been too busy working after his dad had passed away to take them to too many events like this. And the neighborhood they'd been able to afford hadn't really been the kind of place that held them. His mom had been more focused on him and Stefan getting good grades so they could go to college and get out of there than getting to know the neighbors.

Which they'd done. And now he and Stefan were here, in the middle of the ocean, trying to make whiskey and screwing up their love lives. At least, he was screwing up his. Stefan seemed to have given up on the idea altogether. Probably not what his mom had in mind.

She'd be happier if they'd settled down and produced grandchildren rather than barrels of whiskey. He caught a glimpse of a dark head through the crowd and felt the quick tug in his gut that told him it was Mina.

He straightened his shoulders. His mom hadn't raised

him to be a quitter. So he wasn't going to give up on being able to tell her that he'd found someone just yet.

Mina saw Will making his way across the room and felt the now familiar wave of happiness and guilt sweep through her when he smiled, looking delighted to see her. She smiled back, hoping the expression didn't give her away, and turned her attention back to the small stage at the end of the room where Angie was standing at a wooden lectern, dressed in a gorgeous red suit. Ryan stood beside her dressed as an elf. He looked like he wanted to be anywhere else, barely hiding his annoyance at having to wear a dorky costume with what Mina could only imagine was a major effort of will. But at least he was trying to hide it. Angie, on the other hand, looked irritated whenever she looked over to where Mina and Faith were standing with Caleb.

"What's up with the mayor?" Will asked as he joined them. "Did one of you steal a reindeer or something?" He grinned at Faith and Caleb as he slid an arm around Mina's shoulders.

"No, we were just born Harpers," Mina said, shaking her head at him.

"What?" Will said.

"In case you haven't noticed, the mayor is not a fan of our family," Faith said. "Though usually she hides it a little better than tonight. Not sure what we've done in particular right this minute."

"At a guess, showed too much Christmas spirit," Mina said.

"Isn't the whole point of having a Christmas Festival

to let people enjoy the holiday?" Caleb asked, sounding baffled.

"Yes. But by turning up we're ruining Angie's perfect theory of how the Harpers are out to destroy Cloud Bay."

"We're what?" Faith said, her voice rising in volume. Her eyes narrowed at Mina. "Does this have anything to do with you insisting we cover all the festival events?"

"It's not really the time to discuss it," Mina said. Crap. She hadn't meant to let that slip out. The last thing she needed was for Faith to decide to confront Angie here in front of practically the entire population of the island. Which her sister was more than capable of doing. Crowds and public scenes didn't exactly faze Faith.

"I think it's the perfect time—" Faith said.

But just then Angie tapped the microphone and the room went quiet.

"You're going to tell me exactly what's going on after this is done," Faith hissed at Mina. She stepped back to stand beside Caleb, pasting a smile onto her face that probably looked genuine to anyone who didn't know her well. Faith's eyes had deepened to the stormy green that meant trouble. Or maybe that was just the reflection of the green dress she was wearing. The dress, the color of the fresh tips of pine needles, looked perfectly simple, hugging Faith from neck to knee, but somehow—teamed with the tiny diamond snowflakes winking in Faith's ears and around her neck—perfectly evoked Christmas and managed to make Angie's red suit look boring in comparison. Mina, on the other hand, had stuck to black trousers and a crimson cashmere sweater that suddenly felt way too warm in the crowded room.

"Everything okay?" Will whispered as Angie made a show of inviting Santa aka Bill up on the stage and Ryan started to call out names to come up and get their gifts. They started with the kids—who ranged from wide-eyed, tiny adorable to teenage-hiding-their-pleasure-under-embarrassment-and-coolness and all of them cute enough to make her smile—and then did the adults in alphabetical order, so there was plenty of time before it would be Mina's turn. She'd drawn Leah for her Secret Santa recipient, which had made life easier. She'd just had to buy her a box of her favorite mint candies and a terrible zombie movie and could relax knowing that Leah would love them. Nice to get someone she knew well for once. The previous year she'd had one of the assistants who worked at the back office at the ferry company. Someone Mina didn't think she'd ever even spoken to, though she knew who she was.

"Everything's fine," she said to Will. "But if Faith tries anything with Angie later on, I might need you to run interference."

"Sure," Will said. "But you're going to have to tell me what this is all about."

"Later," Mina said. Angie was watching them again, and Mina didn't like her expression. She had a feeling the mayor was up to something.

The parade of gift giving rolled on. By the time Faith's name was called, Mina was very glad she'd worn flat shoes and that she had Will to lean on. Next year, if they were going to have this many people attending, they were going to have to change the format. At least set out chairs. She watched as Faith climbed the stairs to the stage, accepted her gift from Santa, and then came back down without saying anything to Angie at all. Mina let out a breath of relief as Ryan then called her name.

She moved quickly to the stage, wanting to get the whole thing over and done with as soon as possible. But as she took the gift from Bill in his Santa suit and dropped a kiss on one of the few inches of skin left bare by his impressive Santa beard, Angie stepped up to the microphone. Instead of announcing the next name on the list—Lizzie Hermann if Mina was remembering correctly—Angie said, "I'm sure everyone will want to join me in congratulating Mina, who's going to be having an art show at the DeVitt Gallery in L.A. in January." Smiling poisonously at Mina, Angie started clapping. "Such a coup for one of Lansing's favorite daughters."

Mina, still wondering if she was hearing things—how the fuck had Angie found out about her show?—tried to find a smile. The room broke into a round of applause and Bill leaned over to say "Congratulations, kiddo" as Mina fought the urge to drag Angie off the stage and into a back room where she could tear her a new one.

Somehow she made it off the stage and back to Will.

Faith, standing next to him, was smiling but her eyes gave her away. She was pissed. She grabbed Mina and made a show of hugging her.

"I thought your art show was a secret," Faith hissed into her ear.

"So did I," Mina hissed back.

"Then how the hell did Angie find out about it?"

"I have no idea." Mina said. God. Angie had just killed any chance of her doing this under the radar. A whole island couldn't keep a secret. The news would be out in no time at all. "Fuck," she muttered. "Don't make a scene," she added as she pulled back from Faith.

"Oh, I won't. Not yet," Faith said but she didn't go back to stand next to Caleb. Instead, she reached out and pulled Caleb over to stand next to the three of them. A united front, Mina assumed. Meant to send Angie a message.

It should have made her feel better, but she really just wanted to get out of there. But she wasn't going to give Angie the satisfaction of making her retreat. So she set her teeth and pretended to pay attention to the rest of the gift exchange. It seemed to take an eternity but it eventually ended. Though any hopes Mina had of making a speedy getaway after that were dashed when people started coming over to congratulate her.

It should have been fun. A moment of victory when the town learned about her good news. Instead Angie had turned it into torture. Lou and Seth made their way over and joined the wall of Harper unity as Mina smiled endlessly and said thank you to each well-wisher, operating on autopilot. At least she'd had practice with having to deal with crowds and being polite when she wasn't in the mood. Grey had taught them the importance of maintaining a good front and how to work a room when they needed to. Mina had never expected to have to use that lesson here in her hometown, but she was glad she had learned it.

But as the hall finally emptied out, leaving just the six of them and Angie and Ryan, she couldn't quite manage to keep up the act.

"What the hell was that?" she demanded as Angie

walked over to join them, looking smug. Idiot woman. Did she really think Mina was going to take this lying down?

"What?" Angie said, her voice sounding genuinely puzzled. She'd missed her calling. She could have won an Oscar for her little innocent act. Though politicians must need to be good actors too. So maybe she'd found the right job after all. After all, this way she could act *and* connive. "I thought you'd want to share your good news with the town?"

"If I'd wanted to share my good news, I would have shared it already," Mina said. "A fact you must understand, given that if you know about the show, you know I'm using my mom's name, not Harper. How the hell did you find out anyway?" Her voice was loud in her ears and she was vaguely aware that Will had moved to stand beside her.

"You Harpers aren't the only one with friends in L.A.," Angie said.

"Oh, for fuck's sake," Mina said. "Is that what this is about?"

"What do you mean?" Angie said.

"Yes, Mina, what do you mean?" Faith asked, moving to her other side. Her sister's voice was low but it held a note that Mina recognized. She'd never realized just how much Faith sounded like Grey when she was pissed, but the resemblance was plain. And from Angie's expression, it was clear that Angie had never had the experience of dealing with Grey in a rage.

"Maybe Angie should explain," Mina said sweetly. "Angie, do you want to tell Faith what you told me the other day?"

"I don't know what you're talking about," Angie said. Her expression was turning slightly nervous.

Mina wasn't sure whether Angie had finally noticed Seth standing with Lou or whether she'd worked out that she was about to deal with two pissed off Harpers . . . not to mention Lou. Angie had gone to school in Cloud Bay. And no student of Lou's—past or present—should be dumb enough to risk getting into her bad books. Students called Lou "the Terminator" when she was on a tear, because she didn't let anyone get away with shit in her classroom or anywhere else. But apparently Angie hadn't learned that lesson. Maybe it was time she did.

"Yes, you do," Mina said. "You remember. You explained to me so nicely how you thought we Harpers were no good for Lansing and how we didn't give a crap about the island and that we were all going to just leave one day and leave the economy in ruins. You do remember that, don't you?"

"She said what?" Faith said at the same time as Seth Rigger said, "Oh, honey. No."

"You heard me," Mina said, turning to Faith. She smiled at her sister. "Looks like Angie's found out our diabolical plan."

Faith's eyes were fastened on Angie. "Angie, I always thought you were kind of mean but I never knew you were stupid too."

"Faith," Lou started.

Faith held up a hand. "No, Mom. Sorry, but this is between Angie and Mina and me. So Angie, is Mina right? Is that why you thought you could just spill my sister's business, because she's a Harper and we're all just heartless monsters?"

"I—" Angie said. "I was doing what's best for Cloud Bay."

"I fail to see how my sister's exhibition has anything to do with Cloud Bay," Faith said. "But I can tell you what does. And that's the financial contribution my father and his friends have made and continue to make to this community. We've been here for nearly thirty years, so I really fail to see how that counts as lack of commitment on our part. Do you want me to remind you how much money CloudFest brings to the island?"

"That doesn't mean you get to do whatever the hell you like," Angie said, anger twisting her face.

"I would like you to tell me how we're doing that?" Faith asked. "Harper Inc. pays taxes here on Lansing. We pay all your permit fees. We've complied with all the red tape and regulations we've been asked to comply with. And you've made sure that's been plenty over the last few years. So tell me, Ms. Mayor, what exactly I or my family or my dead father who's buried in the same cemetery as your mom, have done to piss you off?"

"I—" Angie said.

"Nothing," Mina interrupted. "We've done *nothing* wrong. Other than Lou dating Seth. And Angie's a grown-ass woman, so I'm really hoping this doesn't all boil down to her sulking about her dad being happy."

"Honey?" Seth said. He didn't sound happy at this very moment. "Do you want to tell me what this is all about? I don't understand. Mina says her show was a secret, so why did you tell everybody? That wasn't the way I raised you."

"Not to mention," Will said suddenly as Angie stayed

silent, "that if you were really worried about the Harpers pulling out of Cloud Bay, the smart thing to do as mayor would be to do your best to keep them here, not piss them off."

Mina grinned at him. "An excellent point," she agreed. "But I think that maybe Angie and Seth need to have a little chat. So perhaps the rest of us should leave them alone."

Will shook his head. "Not before she apologizes to you. She can't fix what she's done, but she can do that much."

Angie looked like she wanted to punch him.

Seth cleared his throat. "I agree. We need to fix this." He turned back to his daughter. "Angie?"

"What?" Angie said. "Don't tell me you're taking their side now. Just because you're sleeping with—"

"Angela Victoria Rigger, you will apologize to Mina right now," Seth roared. For a moment, Mina thought Angie was going to cry as she stared at her father. But she didn't, even though she looked like she'd wanted a hole to open up beneath her and swallow her. Or maybe a teleport to appear so she could get the hell out of there. "And then, Mina's right. You and I need to have a talk." He turned to Faith. "Faith, do you mind taking your mom home for me please?"

"Not at all," Faith said sweetly. "Right after Angie says sorry."

"Angela," Seth said, returning his attention to Angie. "I'm waiting."

Angie stuck out her chin. She faced Mina. "I'm sorry," she said.

It wasn't exactly the most sincere apology Mina had

ever heard. But for now it would do. She didn't want to deal with Angie any more tonight. She'd leave that to Seth. She nodded in Angie's direction.

"Mina," Lou said. "Tell Angie you accept her apology."

"I'm thinking about it," Mina said.

"Mina, it's Christmas."

"Something Angie seems to have forgotten," Mina said. "So, sorry, Lou, but it's going to take me a little while to find my Christmas spirit. I said I'm thinking about it. And that's going to have to do for now."

"Well, that wasn't exactly how I imagined tonight going," Will said when they reached Lulu. Mina had marched out of the town hall and through the parking lot like a woman on mission. Will just wished he knew what that mission was. She was pissed, that much was clear. He couldn't blame her. The stunt the mayor had pulled had been bullshit. "Are you okay?"

The lights in the parking lot were yellowish, but he thought she looked kind of pale.

"I have no idea," Mina said.

She was looking past Lulu. The town hall was up on one of the high parts of the town, where the land sloped up from the harbor. The parking lot looked down to the marina. All the boats were decked out in lights for Christmas, a sea of winking colors, swaying on the water. Pretty. Soothing in a weird way, as long as Will didn't think too hard about the fact they were all boats.

Mina turned back to him, wrapping her arms around herself. "That was . . ."

"Bullshit," he offered, and she managed a smile. He

didn't know how to make it better. He didn't know if anyone *could* make it better. Mina had wanted to do this on her own, and Angie had just taken that away. Seth had mentioned fixing the situation, but how was that possible? There'd be people already looking up the De-Vitt Gallery website. Presumably her name would be there. Or the name she was using. Someone was going to blab that Mina Logan was really Mina Harper.

"It really was bullshit," he said again. "Angie shouldn't have done it. And all this is about Seth dating Lou?"

Mina nodded. "That's my best guess. She's never really been friendly to us. I mean, she's a year older than Faith and a year younger than Zach. She was done with high school before I got there but from what Faith told me, Angie was a pain even then. She's always been a bit of a queen bee."

"And Faith's not?" Will said, teasing.

He won half a smile. "Faith will take charge if she needs to. She's had to. Zach pretty much bailed on her and I was still too young to help much when Grey got his diagnosis. And she'll get the job done. She's always been good with people, but until Grey got sick, she wanted to be a musician, not a CEO. She does a good job at it because it turned out she likes it, but she doesn't spend her time trying to get more power. And she doesn't have that 'my way or the highway' thing going on like Angie does." Mina bit her lip, glancing back at the hall.

For a moment Will thought she might just march back inside and deck Angie. "What can I do?" he said. "What do you need?"

"Right now, I don't want to think about it," Mina said. She looked up at him, moving a little closer. "You think you can help me not think for awhile?"

"Absolutely," he said and bent to kiss her.

chapter eighteen

This week really needed to end, Mina thought as she looked at her bleary-eyed reflection and winced. Will was picking her up in thirty minutes for yet another Christmas Festival event, and she looked like she'd been hit by a truck. A big truck. With lots of spiky bits.

Though, really, who could blame her? It had been a crappy week. Tuesday morning she'd rung the gallery and told them who she really was. Seth had made Angie agree to contact everyone in the town to ask them to keep Mina's secret, but Mina figured the cat was out of the bag. Better to confess and let the gallery be prepared. They'd been delighted to hear she was Grey Harper's daughter. Had started babbling about publicity and platform. They'd been less delighted when she said she still wanted to exhibit as Mina Logan. The compromise position was that Grey would be mentioned in her bio but that the gallery wouldn't make that public until the show opened. Which might give her a tiny shot at seeing whether she could sell on her own.

She stepped into the shower, turned the water on hard. As it pounded on her head, the knots in her shoulders started to ease. She had nine days left before she had to get everything to her framer. She'd sent off a batch of finished work earlier today, but she was still six paintings short. Finishing six more by her deadline was doable, but she would have to be on her game all next week to get there.

Not necessarily easy when there were still a few more festival events to attend. Faith had told her to skip them, but she wasn't going to give Angie the satisfaction of staying away. That would let the mayor avoid having to face what she'd done. It might be Christmas but Mina wasn't letting her off that lightly.

Nope. Angie was definitely on the naughty list.

Besides, she had to admit, she was starting to enjoy herself, doing crazy Christmas events with Will. Will was definitely on the nice list. He'd been doing everything he could to make her life easier this week. He'd brought her food so she didn't have to interrupt her painting time to cook. He'd sent her flowers on Wednesday and even brought her a batch of Stefan's cookies yesterday. And he'd been there after he closed the bar each night, perfectly happy to distract her with as many glorious orgasms as she'd wanted.

She knew she shouldn't be letting herself get used to him, but it was getting harder to resist. But resist she would. Soon. Nine more days and it would be Christmas Eve. Then Christmas Day. And then, their project would be over and she could go back to being safe, sane

Mina. Focused on her show. Focused on what came after her show. Not that she had any idea what that might be just now.

And she didn't have time to figure it out right now. She shook herself out of her fog with a blast of cold water then jumped out of the shower, shivering and cursing the impulse. It had worked though. She was now wide awake and managed to dress and throw on a little makeup in record time. By the time Will knocked on the door, she'd been ready and waiting for five minutes.

"Do you wanna go on a sleigh ride?" Will said when she opened the door. He handed her a peppermint candy cane that looked big enough to club an elf to death with.

"Why, Mr. Fraser. Are you trying to lure me into your sleigh with candy?" she said as she took the cane.

"Of course." He grinned at her, waggling his eyebrows theatrically. "Is it working? Or do I need to add more incentive?"

"Such as?"

"Telling you all the things I'm going to do to you after the sleigh ride?"

She laughed at that. "Sold. Though I'm not sure Santa approves of talking dirty during sleigh rides."

"Only because he's stuck in a sleigh alone with a bunch of reindeer for company," Will said. "Talking dirty to reindeer would just be weird. But I'm sure he'd sing a different tune if he had Mrs. Claus along for the ride." He held out a hand to her. "C'mon, we're going to be late."

"Now I have a mental image of Santa making out with Mrs. Claus," Mina said as she climbed into Lulu. "And that's just wrong."

"Hey, old people like sex too," Will said.

"Is Santa old?" Mina asked. "I mean he looks old but he doesn't get any older. And he's magic. So he might be young."

"Old, young, does it really matter? He works hard, let him enjoy a little nookie with his wife."

"This conversation has gone to a very weird place," Mina said, trying not to dissolve into laughter.

"Well, I can change the subject. Start talking dirty to you right now," Will said, sounding hopeful. "Stefan gave me the night off, so I don't want to waste it."

Mina peered out at the darkness. There were more than the usual number of cars on the road for this time of day, most of them heading into Cloud Bay. Angie might be a bitch on wheels at times but she'd obviously struck a chord with the Christmas Festival. "I think you'd better focus on just getting us to the sleigh ride to start with," she said. "Wait until someone else is driving for you to get back to working your evil wiles on me."

"My wiles are awesome, not evil."

Yeah, they kind of were. Not that she was going to tell him that. She just rolled her eyes at him and pointed at the road.

Will laughed at her but set his eyes on the road ahead. He took her hand as they stood in line for the sleigh rides. Mina had to admit that the sleighs—which were really horse-drawn carts that had been altered to look like sleighs with some niftily painted plywood attached to their sides and a generous helping of fairy lights and bells—looked pretty in the darkness. Maybe she could be Team Sleigh after all.

And when Will pulled her close and closed his teeth

gently over her ear after they'd settled into place in the back of their allotted sleigh, it warmed her right down to her toes. Definitely Team Sleigh, if she got to ride in one with Will. But she pushed him away.

"Not right here in front of everybody," she whispered as the driver clucked to the horse and the sleigh lurched into motion.

"I think everyone knows that we're seeing each other by now," Will said.

"Yes, but that doesn't mean we have to prove Angie right by scarring the kids for life by making out in the middle of Main Street."

Will grinned at her. "It's educational."

"Someone else can educate them. You can just wait until we get out of town." If she'd understood the route correctly, the sleigh rides headed out of Cloud Bay and went up around the back of the town. They came back along the coast before returning to the town square. It was the same route that the carts took tourists for scenic rides in summer. But then the horses weren't decked out in bells and Christmas baubles, and the drivers wore caps and sunglasses not Santa hats. Still, given Lansing didn't have the snow for real sleighs, it was a clever idea. And the proceeds were all going to the clinic, to search and rescue, and to a few of the other local volunteer operations.

She leaned into Will, letting the rhythm of the cart soothe her as they made their way down Main Street. It didn't escape her that she and Will were receiving approving nods and smiles from some of the locals they passed.

Which made her feel guilty all over again. Everyone

was so happy to see her dating again, and so many people had sent her e-mails or messages offering congratulations on her show and promising to keep her secret that it seemed mean to disappoint them.

But she couldn't keep dating Will because the town liked him and wanted her to be happy. That was hardly a sensible basis for a relationship.

As the cart turned onto the road that would take them around the edge of town, Will leaned over and whispered, "How about now?"

He pressed a kiss into her neck while he waited for her answer. And, hell, it felt so good, that what else could she possible say but "Yes"?

By the time the sleigh ride had ended, Will's skills at dirty talk had her ready to jump him. She didn't really care who was watching. Will had some serious game. Maybe they could just go back home and she could see if he could actually do half the things he'd been promising her?

Her knees actually wobbled when he took her hand to help her out of the cart. That was kind of embarrassing. A family of three were waiting in line to take their place in the sleigh and the woman was eyeing Will with a very appreciative look on her face. Rude. Not to mention greedy when she was standing right there with her husband.

Mina looked around the crowded square. She really didn't want to deal with hordes of people right now. Fresh air. That was what she needed. A breather before she lost her head completely and decked the next woman who ogled Will.

She tugged at his hand. "Wanna go for a walk?"

"Now?"

"Do you have somewhere better to be?"

"No, but I was thinking we could—"

"Walk first. C'mon, just down around the marina. It'll be nice."

Will looked unconvinced but didn't protest. They slipped out through the crowd. The noise receded into the distance as they moved away from the town square, letting the more familiar noises of the waves slapping against the jetty and the creak of the boats as they rocked on the water take over. Up close, the lights decorating the masts and sheets and railings of each craft turned the normally black water into a rainbow dazzle of light.

"Pretty," Will said, as Mina paused to take in the sight.

"The water or the boats?" she asked.

"Both, I guess."

"Which boat do you like best?"

"Mina, I don't really know anything about boats," he said.

"You're going to have to learn eventually if you're staying on Lansing."

"Don't see why. Plenty of people live near mountains and never go rock climbing."

"Maybe not, but they still know what mountains are called."

"That's pretty easy, there's only one kind of mountain, isn't there?"

She shook her head at him and headed farther down the marina. Stopped again near the mooring for Grey's yacht. It was decked out in Christmas lights, just like

the others. Once upon a time, she would have been responsible for those but it hadn't crossed her mind this
year. Faith must have done it without her. "What about
this one?"

Will studied the yacht a moment. "It's very . . . boaty.
Floats very well."

She nudged him. "Be serious."

"I am serious. Other than I'm guessing it's a sailboat
because it has that big-ass mast, I'm not much good to
you. Nice lights though." He gazed up at the rows of red,
orange, and pink twinkle lights wrapped around the mast.
Definitely Faith's work. Mina wouldn't have used pink.

"Want to go aboard?" she asked.

"Wait . . . what?" he asked. "Whose boat is this?"

"It was my dad's. So it kind of belongs to me and
Faith and Zach. We're neglecting her though. Ziggy—
do you know Ziggy?"

"Everyone knows Ziggy," Will said. "He comes to
Salt Devil now and then."

"Well, Ziggy takes her out sometimes when he's on
the island. Dad taught him to sail. Or he taught Dad. I've
never really been sure which."

Will was looking at her oddly. Had she freaked him
out showing him the yacht? She wasn't even sure why
she had. Maybe trying to prove to herself why he was a
bad idea. She didn't have much time to sail right now
but she wasn't going to give it up for the rest of her life.
"So, do you want to see?"

"It's kind of dark. Why don't you bring me down here
another time? When it's daylight."

"If it was daylight, I'd want to take her out." It was a
challenge.

"If it was daylight, maybe I'd let you," he said.

"Really?" She hadn't expected him to say that.

He hitched a shoulder, peering down into the water. "Maybe. I guess it's not good to stay scared forever." He glanced up at her. "What do they say, feel the fear and do it anyway? Or something like that, I guess."

"Maybe," she said. She'd never thought of herself as particularly fearful. She wasn't balls-to-the-wall run-at-the-world like Faith and Zach could be, but she wasn't a coward. Or she hadn't been, rather. Because, standing here, watching Will in the moonlight, all the colors of the boat lights playing across his face, she realized just how much she wanted him. And that how much she wanted him was maybe the scariest thing she'd faced in a long time.

She waited for him to say something else but he just stood, watching her.

From over the water came the blare of the ferry's warning horn. This time of year the last ferry arrived at nine.

"Getting late," Will said softly.

"Yes."

"So I have an alternative proposition for you. I'll come back and admire your dad's boat in daylight if you come home with me tonight."

"To your place?"

"Well, I wasn't planning on taking you to Stefan's apartment, that's for sure."

His place was on the grounds of the distillery as far as she knew. She wasn't quite sure how she knew but she did. Maybe Faith had told her at some point.

The distillery. The supposed root of all her objections

to the man standing in front of her. Seemed he wasn't above issuing a challenge of his own.

"How about it?" Will said. "Just this once. If you're going to break my heart on Christmas Day, seems like you could spend one night with me in my bed. Leave me some memories."

God. She didn't know what to say to that. So instead, she just nodded and let him lead her back toward the town and his car and whatever came next.

She called Faith to ask her to go over and take Stewie for the night as Will drove them back out of town. Her fingers, as she tapped the screen to end the call, were shaking. Just a little. But enough that she noticed. She folded her arms, tucking her hands in so she couldn't see them trembling.

It was dumb to feel nervous. It was just a place after all. Just an apartment and some other buildings. Will and Stefan had bought what had been farmland somewhere near the bar and set up their operation there. Or was the bar on the land as well? She'd never stopped to think about it. She knew where the bar was, of course. But the distillery wasn't open to visitors and Adam had never been a whiskey drinker anyway, so she'd never needed to know exactly where it was.

So she paid attention to the route Will took, heading about a quarter mile past Salt Devil and then turning right to head inland. He hadn't driven far before he pulled into a driveway and stopped Lulu. "Got to open the gate," he said before climbing out.

"Low tech around here," he said wryly when he got

back in and started easing Lulu through the gate before stopping again to shut it behind them. Mina tried to see what lay beyond the puddles of light cast by Lulu's head-lights but all she saw was more gravel road. But it was only a short drive again before Will parked. The move-ment of the Mustang must have triggered a bank of secu-rity lights because it was suddenly very bright outside her window.

"Home sweet home," Will said. When she got out of the car, he was waiting by her door. "So, this is the main building. This is where we'll have our cellar door and do tastings and that kind of thing when we're up and running." He pointed past the building. "Grain storage and the malting room over there. Then the stills. The rackhouse is up on the hill."

"Rackhouse?"

"Where we store the whiskey once it's barreled."

The land rose steeply from what she could make out. "Isn't that a little inconvenient?"

"It catches the breeze up there. Stefan wants it to get what he calls "all that good sea air." Should make the whiskey unique. Plus having the rackhouse up there means most of the smell blows away."

"What smell?"

"Part of the alcohol evaporates out of the barrel while the whiskey ages. Sometimes the smell can be pretty strong. So if you smell whiskey or anything else, don't freak out. That will be it. We're fairly lucky here. We're a small operation and like I said, the sea winds disperse any fumes quickly, so it's rarely a problem."

"O-kay."

"And that's enough about whiskey," Will said. He

pointed down the hill. "That's the bar down there. And the cottage where Stefan lives."

She squinted where he was pointing. The bar was actually a lot closer than she'd thought. She'd never noticed all this up on the hill behind it, but then she'd never had reason to look too closely. The cottage—which looked more like one of those weird tiny houses she'd seen on TV than anything she'd have called a cottage— was tucked away on the other side of the bar out back. She had seen that building before. She'd just never realized it was a house rather than a storage shed.

"And that's the ten-cent tour." Will unlocked the door to the building he'd parked beside. They stepped inside and almost immediately headed up a set of wooden stairs. "Not much to see down there, yet," Will said. "We'll set that up last." There was a door at the top of the stairs, painted a very boring shade of brown. He unlocked that, ushered her in, and took her coat and hat. She put her purse down on a table just inside the door and looked around curiously as Will flicked on lights. It wasn't big. One largish room with a living/dining area taking up most of the space and a small kitchen tucked into one corner. Will probably ate at the bar most days. At the far end of the room there were two more doors, which she deduced led to a bedroom and a bathroom, but that seemed to be it.

It smelled like Will though. And looked like him somehow too. The furniture was dark wood, the big squishy sofa and a matching recliner upholstered in a heathery green wool. The walls were white and dotted with pictures of mountains she thought were Scottish and photos of people she didn't know other than a couple that had Stefan in them. There was a bookcase stuffed with books and a sort of basic level of lived-in messiness that reminded her of her own cottage.

Comfortable, not showy.

Not that she'd expected showy from Will.

"Drink?" Will asked from the kitchen. "Coffee? Hot chocolate?"

"Hot chocolate sounds great," she said. While he made it, she took the opportunity to look a little more closely at the pictures. "Are these Scotland?"

"Yes. I spent a summer working at a distillery up near Inverness when I was in college. Gorgeous place. I'm going to go back one day. Those are by one of the guys I worked with."

"He's good," she said. The paintings were atmospheric and realistic. "Was your grandfather from around there?"

"No, further down south. A wee village near Oban, as he would have put it," Will said, doing a remarkably good Scottish accent. "I went to see it one weekend. Not much there now. It was busier apparently in his day when there were a few of the smaller distilleries operating in the area. But it's just a general store and a pub and not much else these days. Makes Cloud Bay seem positively huge in comparison," he said with a smile as he brought a mug of hot chocolate over to her.

She took it and let him guide her over to the sofa. Let him pull her in against his side, where she could feel him, warm and strong and comforting against her. He hit a remote and soft music started playing from speakers she couldn't spot.

God.

What was wrong with her?

It should have been the perfect evening. It *was* the perfect evening. For somebody else. Someone who could take everything that Will was so clearly offering her. But at she sat on his sofa sipping the hot chocolate he'd made her and listening to someone croon about missing somebody at Christmas, she knew she couldn't.

It wasn't the distillery. It wasn't the alcohol. Faith had been right about that much. But what was becoming clearer with every heartbeat was that she just couldn't go through it. She couldn't lose someone all over like she'd lost Adam. Like she'd lost Grey. Couldn't have her heart burned to ash a third time.

She wouldn't survive it. So she had to do the sensible thing. The wise thing. She had to give him up before it got to the point where it was already too late.

The sensible thing—the smart thing—would be to do it tonight, now. While she still could. But every time she tried to open her mouth and make the words come out, she just couldn't. Not tonight. Not when he was so clearly flat out delighted that she was here with him.

Just a little longer. She could do that. She could have him a little longer and still be able to let him go. She just had to remember what she had to do. Be careful. Use her head.

She finished the hot chocolate. Put the mug down on the low table in front of Will's overstuffed sofa. Maybe she had to use her head, but right now she didn't want to think. No, she wanted to use her body instead, and let him make her forget everything for maybe the last time.

"Will?"

"Yes?"

"Wanna show me the bedroom?"

"Hell, yes."

They were laughing and tearing at each other's clothes as they half-fell through the bedroom door. She was expecting Will to show her something wild and wicked, but when he had her naked, he picked her up and carried her over to the bed. Laid her down on the quilt in the moonlight and then proceeded to take everything very slowly. Slow and sure and sweet. So sweet and hot she thought she was going to drown in him. Turning every part of her to molten delight, like her veins were filled with honey. Golden and perfect.

She couldn't resist him like this. Could feel her heart cracking as he held her close and filled her up and set her alight. And, at the end, as she came apart in his arms, she couldn't entirely remember what she'd been guarding against as she fell down into pleasure and then into the sleep that followed.

chapter nineteen

Will woke with the warmth of Mina curled against him. For a moment he couldn't figure out what had woken him. But as he yawned, the smell of smoke filled his nose and he swore.

"Mina, wake up." He shook her.

"What?"

"I smell smoke. Get dressed. Quick." He switched on a lamp, started searching for his clothes, trying to think. The fire couldn't be in this building or the smoke alarms would be going. Ditto if it was any of the distillery buildings. They all had separate alarm systems and the main control panel was downstairs. Alarms going off there would also trigger alarms here. So that was a relief. A fire in the distillery or the rackhouse would be a nightmare. Alcohol exploded rather than burned. In fact, they might never know anything about it before it all just went up and took them with it. He shoved his feet into boots and crossed the room in two strides to pull the curtains open. His room looked down the hill toward the bar.

"Fuck."

Mina joined him by the window. "The bar's on fire," she said, sounding puzzled. Then she seemed to snap fully awake. "Will, the bar's on fire!"

"I know." He was already running for the door. Stefan. Stefan would be down there. Might be inside. He had no idea what time it was. "Call the fire department."

He didn't wait to see if she did as instructed. Just ran downstairs and out into the night, charging down the path toward Salt Devil. As he got closer, the stink of burning wood and oil and plastic billowed up to him, the wind blowing it his way.

Shit. Not good. But he couldn't stop to think about the direction of the wind. Not when Stefan might be inside.

"Will!" He heard Mina shout from behind him. "Will, wait. The fire department is already on its way."

Good. That was good. But it would still take time for them to reach this side of the island. The fire station was in Cloud Bay. The smoke stung his lungs as he reached the fence line between the distillery and the bar and vaulted over it, vaguely registering that part of the fence was on fire too. The path down from the distillery had a wooden railing. If that went up . . . could the fire travel back up the hill that way?

Nothing to do about it if it did.

"Will, wait," Mina called again. "Stop."

He didn't stop. Stefan was nowhere in sight in the back lot behind the bar. The windows in his cottage were dark, but the roof was burning. Where the fuck was he? Bar or cottage?

The worst of the fire seemed to be coming from Salt Devil. Kitchen fire maybe. In which case, maybe Stefan would be trying to get to the fire hose around the side of the bar. See what he could do to stop it.

"Stefan," he roared. "Are you here?"

No answer. Fuck. He couldn't hear sirens. And he wasn't going to wait. He had to find his brother.

"Will." Mina's hand closed around his arm. "Will, they'll be here soon."

He shook her off. "Go around the front. Get out of range. This place is full of alcohol and cooking oil and all sorts of shit. Go around the front and wait for the firemen."

"What are you going to do?" Her eyes were huge in her face.

"I'm going to find my brother."

"No. You can't." Her hand grabbed at him.

"Mina, go." He shoved her toward the alley. The fire didn't seem bad on that side. "Go now." She started to move. "*Go!*" he yelled again before heading in the other direction.

Stefan wasn't at the fire hose. Which didn't leave many options. He was either inside, out front, or somewhere else entirely. Options two or three meant he was safe. Option one meant Will needed to go in and find him.

It wasn't exactly a choice. He turned on the hose enough to drench himself and then used the axe that hung beside it to smash the nearest window and climb inside.

The smoke was choking, the heat nearly unbearable. He couldn't see anything. The kitchen was billowing flames. Anyone in there was dead already.

He couldn't think about that. Wouldn't think about it. Keeping hold of the axe, he made his way toward the front of the bar, pausing to cough and yell for Stefan, moving as slowly as he could, trying to see through the smoke, keeping low and trying to feel around him with his feet and hands in case Stefan was lying on the floor.

He didn't find him. And by the time he'd reached the front door, his head was reeling from the smoke and the heat and the deafening roar of the flames, which grew louder with every passing second.

No way he could go back and look again. Not if he wanted to make it out alive. Make it out to Mina. He offered up a short prayer to whatever god might be listening and lifted the axe, intending to smash through the window beside the front door rather than try and work the deadlock. Only to stumble back as the door flew open and two firemen stood blinking at him. One of them reached for him and pulled him out through the door.

Where he stood blinking and coughing while the firemen streamed past him, wrestling hoses into position. Someone yanked him out of the way and pushed him in the direction of the road. As his eyes cleared, he realized that Mina was waiting for him. She looked terrified. And beside her, smoke smeared and stony faced, stood Stefan.

Will stumbled across the road toward them—needing to know that Stefan was okay—when Mina loomed up in front of him.

"What the hell were you doing?" she yelled. "Are you crazy?"

"I—"

She didn't wait for him to explain. Didn't give him a chance. Just started yelling at him, telling him he'd been more than stupid in about seven different ways before she burst into tears and collapsed against his chest, sobbing.

For a moment he stared over her head at Stefan, still not entirely sure he wasn't imagining his brother standing there. Then Stefan jerked his head in a nod and pointed further down the road away from the confusion of trucks and vans and police. Will nodded back and herded Mina off in that direction, wondering how the hell to calm her down.

He wasn't exactly feeling calm himself. Half his face felt raw, the skin stinging and throbbing, and his throat hurt like hell. The wind was blowing strongly, the air a weird combination of soothing cold and salt that only made his face feel worse.

Eventually Mina stopped crying. Pulled away from him. "You could have died," she said, sounding broken.

"I didn't." He tried to sound soothing, but it came out more like a rasp. "I'm okay."

She didn't really seem to hear him, shaking her head. "It's not okay."

"It is," he said. "I'm fine. Stefan's fine. We have insurance. We can rebuild."

She froze. "You what?"

"We can rebuild the bar," he said absently. The wind gusted again and he shook his head trying to clear it. There was something about the wind he should be thinking of. But he couldn't remember.

"The bar that almost killed you?" she said incredulously. "Why the hell would you want to do that?"

"Because it's what I do," he said. "It's my dream."

"I'll give you a million dollars to do something else. Give the bar to Stefan. Take up professional surfing. Or knitting. Or golf. I don't care."

"I—what?" He couldn't think. Money? She was offering him money. "You think I'd take your money and walk away from something I've wanted to do my whole life?"

"Yes," she said, expression deadly serious. "You should."

"This from the woman who told me there was no way she'd give up search and rescue? Would you stop painting for a million dollars? If you didn't already have the money," he added, half a snarl. Because she did have the money. Had it and a lot more if she could offer it to him so thoughtlessly.

"It's not the same. Painting is art . . . this is . . ." She waved a wild hand at the bar, scowling.

"What? Just booze. Filthy alcohol?"

"Yes," she yelled. "It is. It kills people. It could have killed you and Stefan tonight. Why do you have to go back to that?"

She'd never really had to work for something, he realized with a start. Not in the put-every-penny-in, risk-it-all kind of way. "Because it's my life. And my life savings. Stefan's too. It's in my blood."

"I said I'd give you the money."

"I don't want your damn money." He stared at her, anger churning through him. She glared back.

"So you won't give it up?"

"No," he said.

"Then, I'm sorry," she said. "And this . . . project is over."

What the hell? "What are you talking about? Mina . . ." He reached for her and she jerked back.

"No. This was a bad idea from the start. Let's just cut our losses."

"Cut our losses? You just want to walk away. Now?"

"Seems like a pretty good time to me."

"You were just in hysterics because you thought I could've been hurt. And now you're going to stand there and tell me you don't care about me? That you can walk away? You're going to keep up this bullshit about not liking alcohol and use that as an excuse to run?"

"It's not an excuse. I'm just reversing a bad decision."

Maybe he'd passed out in the smoke and was having a nightmare. "Two hours ago you were in my bed."

"Things change." She lifted her chin. "We had an agreement."

He wasn't going to change her mind. He could see that. He could get down on his knees in the dirt and the smoke and the wreckage of his life and tell her he loved her, and she'd still walk away. So maybe it was best to let her go. He stepped back. Straightened shoulders that were starting to throb too, now the adrenaline was fading. "Fine," he said. "Have a great life."

He didn't stay to watch her walk away. Wasn't sure he would run after her and make an idiot out of himself trying one last time to win a heart that wasn't his to win if he did. Instead he turned and trudged back to Stefan.

Who was staring past the flames dying under the on-slaught of the fire hoses and up into the night sky. Will followed his gaze. Saw the plume of the oily black smoke whose bitter taste was coating his throat. Saw it writhe and twist and saw the same wind that was slapping at his back carrying it up the hill toward the distillery. Toward the rackhouse directly in its path. Toward all the whiskey sitting in those barrels, just waiting to soak up whatever flavors the air carried to them.

"Fuck," he rasped. "That's not good."

Stefan just looked at him. "No," he agreed.

Will bit back the rest of the curses burning in his throat. They were already too late if the smoke was strong enough to taint the whiskey. Insurance money could rebuild the bar. It could even replace the barrels and buy fresh grain to start more whiskey. But it couldn't give them back the five years of hard work that they might have to pour down the drain if the whiskey was ruined. Couldn't give them back time. Couldn't necessarily keep them afloat another five years while they tried to start over either.

So he'd managed to lose Mina and maybe his life's work in one night. Merry fucking Christmas.

If there was any justice in the world, Christmas would be canceled, Mina decided when her phone woke her way too early on Christmas Eve. She'd finally finished her paintings and had couriered them to the framer the night before. She wanted to sleep for days. Throwing herself into her work had apparently been distracting her from how much she missed Will.

She'd managed not to think about him by spending every waking hour painting. She'd blocked his number from her phone, turned off her e-mail, and pretended

Will Fraser didn't exist. She'd even stonewalled Lou, who'd turned up on Saturday morning, having heard about the fire. She'd refused to listen when Lou had tried to get her to reconsider. Not even when Lou told her that the smoke might have ruined the entire stock of the Frasers' whiskey. She didn't care. She wouldn't care.

She couldn't love Will Fraser.

Because it would ruin her.

She'd finished the portrait she'd started of him. She hadn't been able to stop herself. Maybe it had been an attempt to exorcise him from her brain. It hadn't worked. The painting was brilliant. Too good. The sight of him staring out at her from the paper had made her want to cry. She'd stopped herself, but only barely. She'd almost put it in the pile of pictures to go to the show. But then she'd changed her mind and put it carefully away in a drawer, telling herself it was because it would be wrong to show a portrait of him without his permission—and no way in hell was she going to call and ask him for that—and not because she didn't want to give up this last tiny piece of him she still had.

She'd locked the drawer and then picked up her brush and painted the ocean again.

When she'd crawled into bed the night before, she'd expected to pass out after working so hard for a week. But instead, she'd burst into tears and hadn't been able to stop crying until sometime near two a.m. So much for not caring.

Stewie, who'd climbed up beside her on the bed and tried to cheer her up by licking her face, had had a very soggy patch on his coat by the time she'd finally managed to sleep.

He made a grumpy whuffling noise at her now as she stretched across him to reach for the phone, clearly sharing her view that there had not yet been enough sleep.

"Hello?" she croaked into the phone.

"It's me," Faith said. "I'm calling a family meeting. Can you come up to the Harper office about nine?"

Mina blinked, trying to make her brain work. "It's Christmas Eve, can't it wait?"

"No," Faith said.

Well, crap. That couldn't be good. "What time is it now?"

"Just after seven. You sound terrible. Did you celebrate finishing your paintings by going on an ice-cream bender or something?"

"Something like that," Mina muttered. Better that Faith think she had a self-inflicted stomachache from too much Chunky Monkey than a self-inflicted broken heart. "Nine. Fine. See you then." She hung up before Faith could interrogate her any further.

Christmas was definitely canceled. She would do this meeting and then maybe she'd pretend she had stomach flu. It wouldn't be a total lie. The thought of trying to smile through Christmas Day was making her feel distinctly sick.

She made it to the Harper offices about ten minutes before Faith's deadline after showering and pulling on ratty sweatpants and an old Blacklight hoodie. The place was deserted—because sensible people didn't work on Christmas Eve—and she let herself in. Faith and Lou were sitting at the big table that doubled as staff lunch area and conference table in the break room. Faith had her laptop open in front of her and a stack of file folders piled beside it.

Ominous.

"Morning," Mina managed. "Coffee?"

"Wow. You look terrible," Faith said.

"Are you okay, honey?" Lou said, coming over and reaching out to touch her forehead.

"I'm fine. Just sleep deprived. I was painting all hours this week."

"Are you sure? You look like—"

"Like she idiotically dumped a perfectly great guy nine days before Christmas?" Faith suggested.

Mina glared at her. "Will is not a topic that's up for discussion. Subject closed."

"The subject might be closed if you actually looked happier," Faith said. "But as you look wrecked, I'm going to invoke the big-sister amendment and keep nagging you until you see the light."

"I hate you," Mina muttered. "I hate Christmas. I hate everyone. Except you," she said to Lou as Lou handed her a mug full of coffee. "You, I still like."

"You might not when I tell you I think Faith is right," Lou said. "But I'll wait until after you've had your coffee for that."

"If this family meeting is some kind of Will-related intervention, I'm leaving," Mina said, gulping coffee. "I mean it."

"As fun as that sounds, nope, we have other stuff to talk about," Faith said.

"So talk." Mina took a seat next to Lou. "Is this about

the archive stuff?" Just what she needed. Estate talk. Because dealing with your dead dad's shit was always so festive.

"Something like that. And I wish I could say that I had news that would cheer you up, but I can't," Faith said.

"Look at it this way, I don't think I can feel much crappier," Mina said. She blew out a breath and tried to pull herself into some semblance of together. "So what is it?"

"Hang on. I have to dial Zach in." Faith hit a few keys on her keyboard and then swung the laptop around to face Mina and Lou as the call connected.

Zach's face appeared. Mina felt herself smile, despite herself. She hadn't seen her brother in months. She didn't think Faith had even talked to him in months. And even though she thought it was kind of crappy that he seemed to be doing his best to avoid coming home, and yes, he'd pulled a hell of a stunt on Faith at Cloud-Fest by canceling his appearance at the last minute, she still missed the big lug. But she kept that mostly to herself. Zach was hardly Faith's favorite person right now. "Hey, Zach," she said, figuring Faith wasn't going to be the first to say hello.

"Hey yourself," Zach said. He studied her through the screen. "You look tired."

Mina rolled her eyes. "Have you looked in a mirror lately?" Unshaven and bleary eyed, Zach wasn't looking his best either.

"Sorry." He hid a yawn with his hand. "We had a gig last night then flew here to Atlanta. I haven't actually been to bed yet. But Faith"—he slanted a wary glance toward their sister—"insisted that we had to do this today."

"Because it's important," Faith said tartly. "You are still part of this family. At least on paper."

"Faith," Lou said quietly from beside Mina. "Be nice."

Faith pressed her lips together looking down at the stack of papers in front of her.

Mina bit back the sigh of exasperation. Zach had let Faith down last summer and Faith was holding a grudge. Mina wasn't sure she wasn't right to, but Faith being so mad at Zach wasn't making it any more likely that he'd decide to come home and try to work things out.

"So," she said brightly. "Atlanta, huh? Must be pretty there at this time of year. Not so damn hot." She'd only ever been there in summer when Blacklight had played. She remembered sweet tea, peach pie, and the unrelenting sticky heat as soon as you stepped outside.

"There were decorations at the airport," Zach said. "That and this hotel room are about all I've seen so far. So, I'll get back to you." He leaned back in whatever chair he was sitting in, giving Mina a better glimpse of the hotel room behind him. It looked like your standard beige hotel decor. Not exactly the luxury that they'd traveled in with Grey. Did it bother Zach that he wasn't doing as well as Grey had at the same age? Probably. But it was hardly the time to ask.

She'd been thinking about success lately, as her show grew closer. What happened if she was a hit? Would it change her life? Would she have to get used to leaving Lansing behind more often? Of doing exactly what Angie had said the Harpers would do? She'd always been content here.

Unlike Zach. Who'd always burned to leave Lansing

from the time he'd first picked up a guitar. But even he seemed to find the demands of his career a struggle.

"So, shall we get on with it?" Faith said.

"Sure," Zach replied. He lifted a cup that Mina hoped held coffee. "This isn't going to keep me awake too much longer, is it?"

"Wouldn't want to keep you from your beauty sleep." Faith picked up a document. "So, I had an e-mail from the lawyers today."

"About the New Jersey storage unit?" Lou asked.

Faith nodded. "They've sorted out the papers finally."

"Anything interesting?" Zach said, looking bored.

"Mostly just bits and pieces. Nothing significant in the actual stuff in the unit, so they're sending it here for us to sort through." She looked at Lou, her expression a little apologetic. "No sign of any missing masters."

Many moons ago Grey had made a solo album but never released it. He claimed he'd pitched the masters into the ocean. Destroyed them. For some reason, Lou, who was usually the most practical one in the family, had never believed his story. But if she was right, then Grey had hidden the damn masters somewhere no one had managed to discover yet.

Lou nodded, lips pressed together.

Faith turned back to the laptop. "They mentioned a couple of guitar cases, Zach, so I'll let you know what's in them when they get here."

Zach perked up slightly at that. "Cool."

None of the guitars that Grey had used regularly in his career were unaccounted for, but their dad had bought guitars like other people bought T-shirts. Some

of the ones that had been found in Grey's stashes around
the world had been worth a fortune.

"The only other thing they found that's significant
was a bank deposit box key. It took them a little while
to find the deposit box. But they have now."

Mina found herself leaning forward in her chair.
Spare guitars and artwork and other bits and pieces were
nothing out of the ordinary for Grey. But the estate
lawyers had thought they'd found all the bank accounts
several years ago. "What was in the box?"

"Details for a Swiss account."

"Another account?" Zach said. "Are we suddenly
even richer?"

Faith shook her head. "They've managed to access
the account. And it was only ever used for one transac-
tion. Seems like Grey deposited five hundred thousand
dollars in cash about six months before he died. And two
days later, he transferred it out again."

Zach let out a low whistle. "Half a million? That's a
reasonable chunk of cash."

"Yeah," Faith said.

"Do we know who the payment went to?" Lou asked.
Her voice sounded unusually subdued. Mina twisted to
look at her. Lou looked worried.

Faith shook her head. "They're still working on it. It
wasn't to any account they know about it and they've run
up against a wall trying to trace it back to Grey himself. So it seems most likely he gave the money to someone else."

"Half a million dollars?" Zach said. "Why would he
be paying out half a mill not long before he died? We

know he didn't buy any new houses or anything then, don't we?"

"Not that we've ever found any record of," Faith agreed. "He traveled around a lot in that last year, you know that."

Grey's farewell tour, he'd called it. Once the doctors had said his cancer would get him in the end, he'd insisted on saying goodbye to his friends in person. Faith and Lou and Mina had all tried to get him to rest and stay on Lansing, let the friends come to him, but he'd been determined to do things his way, as always.

"What do you think, Lou?" Mina said. "Any ideas?"

"He never told me anything about it," Lou said, looking unhappy. "But if I had to guess, I'd say it was probably a woman."

"A lover?" Zach said. "He wasn't seeing anyone seriously then, was he?"

Lou shrugged. "Not that we knew about. But that much money, even for Grey, is meaningful."

Faith was biting her lip. "A woman. Or there's another possibility."

Mina had no idea what she was talking about. She didn't care about the money. They all had more money than they could spend in their lifetimes. But the thought that Grey had hidden someone important to him in those last months made her want to cry.

"What possibility?" Zach said.

Faith hitched her shoulder. "Another kid. That much money, it could be a pay-off."

Mina's mouth fell open. "You think Dad had another kid? That he never told us about? Even after he got sick?" She looked at Lou, hoping for a denial, but Lou still looked troubled, twisting the band of sapphires she wore on her right hand. The last thing Grey had given her before he died.

"I don't know," Faith said. "But you can't deny that with Dad, anything is possible."

"Well, we need to find out," Mina said, feeling sick.

"The lawyers are working on the bank that received the money. It's in Switzerland. It's going to take some time. But I thought we all needed to know. I've talked to Danny and Billy and Shane and they're all claiming to know nothing. They don't have any reason to lie, so I guess we're just going to have to wait."

"I don't see why he'd keep it a secret," Mina said. "Not when he didn't have long to live. Wouldn't he just tell us?"

Lou put a hand on her knee. "No point speculating until we know what's going on. You'll just drive yourself crazy trying to figure your father out."

That was true. That had always been true. But that didn't make it any easier. God. Mina wanted to talk to someone. And she realized with a sinking heart that the person she really wanted to talk to was Will. Which wasn't going to be happening any time soon. She stood, pushing back her chair. "I'm going for a walk."

chapter twenty

She walked back to the cottage, still in a terrible mood. Grey had had another kid? Or a lover? Someone he hadn't told them about?

Someone he'd never been able to share with them? Someone who hadn't been there when he'd died?

Fuck. She didn't want to think about it. It made her heart hurt.

It made her want to cry all over again, and she wasn't sure she had any tears left.

As she got nearer to the cottage, she could hear Stewie barking. He didn't usually make much of a fuss when she left him for a short time. Was someone there? She broke into a jog only to pull up short when she came around the corner from the garden path to see Stefan Fraser standing just outside her front gate.

Perfect.

Why shouldn't her crappy day get worse?

"Stefan," she said warily as she walked over to the

big man. He wore his usual plaid shirt, jeans, and boots. Along with an expression that was distinctly unfriendly. "Can I help you?"

He held out an envelope. "This came for Will."

"Shouldn't you be giving Will's mail to Will?"

"Not sure he needs this mail." He thrust the envelope closer. "Take it."

She obeyed, not seeing many other options. She could, of course, call security to get Stefan to leave but that seemed like overkill. But without extra manpower or something like a forklift, she had no chance of making Stefan move an inch if he didn't want to. Will was tall and solid, but up this close, Stefan seemed suddenly gigantic in comparison.

The envelope was slightly wrinkled and smelled faintly of beer. Today was Sunday so there wouldn't have been any mail unless the guys at the post office had decided to make a late run to deliver any last-minute Christmas parcels and mail. But the envelope was plain white, though the paper was heavy and expensive. She flipped it over. The DeVitt Gallery was printed in a familiar logo across the left hand corner.

"That's the place you're having your art show, isn't it?" Stefan asked.

She nodded. "Yes, though I'm not sure why they're writing to Will."

"Because he asked for an invitation to your opening night," Stefan said. "He was planning this whole surprise for you in the new year."

He was? But why? They were meant to have been broken up by Christmas . . . unless. . . . "Oh," she said, eyes blurring suddenly. Will had been hoping to convince her not to end it. He'd been planning on still being with her.

"Yeah," Stefan said. "So I'm thinking you can probably put that to better use now. No point him having it." He stared down at her, dark eyes unhappy. "Unless, there's a reason he might still need it."

"I—"

"You know," Stefan said. "I've seen him hurt before. Seen him grieving. Not sure I've ever seen him heartbroken."

"I didn't mean to—I mean, we agreed it was just casual."

"Well, that hardly ever works," Stefan said. "Not when one of the two people involved was already mostly in love with the other."

"What?" Mina said. "I hardly knew Will. How could he have been in love with me?"

"From where I'm standing, I'm not entirely sure. Bad luck, I'm guessing. But he's had a thing for you from the first time he saw you. Never did anything about it because you were married and then you were widowed. Will was never going to let himself mess anything up for you. But then you gave him an opening and I guess he just couldn't resist. Maybe he thought he could win you over. Which is also his bad luck, it seems, because it turns out he couldn't. And now he's the one who's messed up."

Mina stared up at Stefan. She wasn't sure she'd ever heard him talk so much at one stretch. Not even back in the day when she and Adam had gone to parties at Salt Devil. He'd always been the quiet observer in the back of the room. But here he was doing his version of reading her the riot act as far as she could tell. She stroked the envelope with a finger.

"How is he?" she asked.

"How do you think he is?" Stefan said, scowling.

She flushed. "It's not that I don't . . . care about him."

"Then what is it? Because I have to say that you look just as bad as he does."

"I just . . . can't. I lost Adam. I can't go through that again."

"So you're just going to be alone for the next sixty or seventy years?" Stefan said.

"Have you been talking to Faith?" Mina asked, suddenly suspicious. This speech was awfully familiar.

"Nope. But if we're all saying the same thing to you, maybe you should listen. Because that's a long time to be alone. I mean Will, he'll move on eventually. He wants a family. Wants to build something with someone. Which means it'll be just you in this lighthouse. Is that what you want?"

Put like that, it didn't sound great. Not when she added in the mental image of maybe having to watch Will get married to someone else. Her dad had given half a million dollars to someone he hadn't been able to be with just before he died. He'd obviously had regrets over something. Is that how she wanted to end up?

Stefan was watching her. He looked less mad and more . . . concerned, maybe. "You know, Will's not the kind of guy who leaves. He stands by people. Hell, he moved to this island so I could make whiskey the way I wanted to even though he hates the ocean."

That made her smile. "He said you were very persuasive."

"I didn't have to try too hard. I'm his brother and he wanted to make me happy. You saw him, he's the guy who runs into a fire for you. I'm guessing if you gave him a shot then the only way you're likely to ever have to say goodbye to him is . . . well, something out of his control. And even then, I reckon that if heaven exists, he'd be the first person you'd see waiting for you."

Her eyes did blur at that. More than blur. Tears splashed onto the envelope she still clutched because she knew that Stefan was right. Will wouldn't leave. She might still lose him but he wouldn't leave her. So the question was whether she was willing to risk paying that price again for a chance of letting him prove that to her.

"Oh crap, don't cry," Stefan said. "I'll take the damn envelope back."

She hugged the envelope to her chest, shaking her head and trying to smile at him through the tears. "No. No. I'll give it to him myself."

Will looked up as Stefan came into the office, feet thudding on the floorboards.

"Something up?" He braced himself, not sure he could take one more thing going wrong.

"You about done with that?" Stefan asked, nodding at the computer.

"Nearly." Will studied the spreadsheet in front of him, eyes threatening to blur. He and Stefan had spent the week dealing with the aftermath of the fire. Cleaning out what could be salvaged at the bar—which wasn't much—then moving everything that wasn't smoke contaminated or ruined from Stefan's cottage to the empty rooms downstairs from Will's as temporary living quarters.

Then the really nerve-wracking part—going through the rackhouse to test the whiskey. The news wasn't as bad as it could have been. It wasn't all good either. He was just about done cataloguing that and readying the samples they were sending to be tested in case there was something in the whiskey that he and Stefan couldn't taste in the barrels they'd decided were okay.

In a twisted kind of way, he'd been glad to have something so all consuming to focus on during the days. It had kept the worst of his feelings about Mina at bay. Stopped him thinking about how stupid he'd been to give his heart to someone who clearly hadn't wanted it. Or how the hell he was going to survive without her. But all of those feelings came back during the long, long nights. He was exhausted.

"I thought we should go to the carol service," Stefan said.

Will felt his mouth drop open. "What?"

"You need to get out of the house. You look terrible."

"It hasn't been the greatest week of my life," he pointed out, hearing the defensiveness in his voice.

"I know. And you've had some time to wallow. But you have to go out sometime."

"And you thought carols might cheer me up?"

"You're the one who was a choirboy," Stefan pointed out with a smirk.

"*'Was'* being the relevant part of that sentence."

"You're on the festival committee. This is the last event."

"I've been to more than my share of events." He scowled at Stefan, who'd been pretty steadfast on avoiding most of the Christmas Festival. Not a big joiner, his brother. So why the sudden change of heart?

"Yes. So you should see it through."

Huh. That argument he could understand, coming from Stefan. His brother was big on keeping promises. On finishing what you started. But his brother should also understand how Will felt. After all, Stefan still hadn't climbed back on the horse after Lizzie had dumped him. Or maybe he did understand. Maybe this was him trying to make Will feel better somehow. Might have been easier to say it by bringing an expensive bottle of Scotch and drinking with him, but then again, whiskey was kind of a sore subject this week.

But still, if Stefan had decided to embark on a "get Will out of the house" campaign, Will knew from experience it would be easier to just go along with it. Only question was, would Mina be there? He hoped not. At least most of him hoped not. But there was a secret masochistic part that just wanted to see her face. And maybe that part just needed the band-aid ripped off before the wounds had any hope of healing over. He took a breath. Nodded at Stefan. "I need to finish this up. About another hour."

"The carol service starts at five."

That gave him ninety minutes. Might be cutting it fine. He definitely needed a shower before he could appear in public. "I'll meet you there."

"Good," Stefan said. His expression was odd, but Will was too tired to try to figure it out. "Make sure you do. Or I'll be coming to find you."

She was hovering. She'd never really understood what "hovering outside" something meant before. But, as she waited outside the gate murmuring apologies to people trying to make their way into the Methodist church—whose turn it was to host the Christmas Eve carol service this year—feeling conspicuous and anxious, "hovering" seemed to fit.

Where the hell was Will?

Probably just as well she wasn't standing on church grounds while she was thinking that. After the way she'd behaved with Will, she was fairly certain she'd made Santa's naughty list this year. No point risking getting struck by lightning for swearing on church land or something.

Maybe Will wasn't coming? She should have asked Stefan if they were planning on coming tonight. But he might have said something to Will. Well, it wasn't a big island. She could hunt down Will Fraser if she had to.

Unless he'd gone home for Christmas. Though he'd said something about his mom being overseas. But he had other family.

Crap.

She really should have asked Stefan. If Will didn't show, she'd just wasted several hours of planning.

"Everything okay?" Faith asked from behind her. "We're saving you a seat."

She wasn't going to turn around. She knew Faith would be looking amused. Lou and Seth were already inside, along with anyone else Mina considered a friend on the island. It didn't exactly take Sherlock levels of deduction to figure out who she might be waiting for.

"I'll be in soon, I'm fine." That was a lie. And if things went how she planned, she wouldn't be in at all. She was kind of sad about that. She liked carols. Had been hoping that this year, they might be easier to listen to. That maybe she was getting Christmas back. But then again, that was before she'd been an idiot and broken up with Will.

"If you say so," Faith said. Mina heaved a relieved sigh when she heard the tapping of her sister's boot heels retreating back down the path to the church.

The number of people still arriving had slowed to a trickle. Still no sign of Will. Damn it. He wasn't going to show up.

But just as she was about to turn and leave, she heard a very familiar engine rumble coming down the road.

Her heart started pounding as Lulu came into view. Will pulled into one of the few parking spots open and shut off the engine. Maybe he hadn't seen her?

But when he didn't emerge immediately from the Mustang, she figured he had. And that he was probably sitting there wondering whether or not to start the engine again and drive away.

Not going to happen. She jogged over to the car, wondering if anyone else could hear the blood roaring in her ears. Probably not. She bent and knocked on the window. Her leather gloves turned the sound to a dull tap, but apparently it worked. Will rolled down the window.

"Mina," he said warily.

She stared at him for a moment, drinking him in. He looked tired, shadows dulling his eyes. Well, she knew how he felt. She'd spent several hours with every lotion and potion in her bathroom trying to make herself look a little less like a total wreck. She wasn't entirely sure she'd been successful.

"I was wondering if you might like to take a walk with me," she said in a rush before she lost her nerve.

"I'm meeting Stefan at the carol service," he said. His tone was cool. Very cool.

She ignored him. "That church is packed already. You'll never get a seat." She was babbling. She couldn't help it. She took a breath. "Please, Will?"

His lips pressed together. Oh God. He was going to say no. Or maybe not. Her heart felt like it was going to burst through her chest, it was beating so fast. He climbed out of the car slowly. He stood by Lulu, studying her, his face very serious. She tried to remember how to breathe as she waited for him to say something, all her attention on him. He was wearing a suit. A very nice navy suit. Which did very nice things for his body.

Please.

She waited while he pulled a coat over his suit and locked the car. "So. Let's walk," he said, shoving his keys deep into his pocket.

Mina nodded, trying to ignore the relief that made her legs suddenly shaky, and set off. The church was a few blocks back from the harbor. Not too far. The carol service was held early so no one had to keep their kids up too late and people could do whatever else they wanted to do with their families on Christmas Eve. The sun was starting to set as they walked, sending long fingers of golden light across the town.

Will didn't say anything. Just walked beside her, keeping a distance between them.

"Is your whiskey okay?" she asked tentatively. Anything to break the silence that was ratcheting her nerves up to the breaking point.

His brows flew up. "Who told you about the whiskey?"

"Lou. She said something about how the smoke might ruin it."

He nodded. "We've lost about half the barrels of our most recent batch. Those were stored on the wall of the rackhouse that faces the fire. Luckily for us, the wind changed before the smoke could taint all of it. Our oldest batch is fine as far as we can tell. We're doing some last tests, but it looks like we'll be able to launch next year, like we planned."

"That's good," she said. Relief managed to wash some of the nerves away for a few seconds.

"It is?" He sounded puzzled.

"It's what you want to do, right?" she said. She turned onto the harbor road, heading out along the marina path.

"Yes. But I didn't think that was something you were a fan of."

She didn't answer that. Not yet. "Let's walk." Will nodded. He was starting to look a bit more cheerful. Almost smiling, she decided as she took a sideways peek at him. Hopefully that was a good sign.

The shadows were lengthening fast. December sunsets didn't last long.

But she knew the way even in the dark. And before long they were standing by Grey's yacht again. All the lights were on. She'd made sure of that. In fact, she'd spent several hours putting up even more. There wasn't a spare inch that wasn't twinkling gently in all the colors of the rainbow. She'd even wound lights around the mooring lines—at considerable risk of falling into the harbor. And she'd left the gangplank down.

"Mina?" Will said. "What are we doing here?"

"We had a deal," she said. "You said you'd come on Dad's yacht if I came to your place." She was trying to sound calm. She didn't feel calm. She had to shove her hands into her pockets to hide the fact they were shaking.

"I thought that any deals were off when it came to you and me," Will said slowly.

"Well, I thought that maybe you could come aboard and we could talk about that." She took a step back toward the yacht. Maybe the lights would dazzle him into going along with her plan.

Will didn't move. "You made it pretty clear we didn't have anything to talk about."

"Yeah. About that. I'd plead shock, but to be honest, I was being an asshole. If I promise to behave better this time, will you please get on the boat?" She stepped to one side of the gangplank, gesturing for him to go ahead. She didn't let her eyes move away from his face.

"Define 'better,' " Will said. But then he stepped forward and put his hand on the gangplank railing. Which swayed slightly. He froze. "You know, I said I'd do this in daylight."

"Sunset. Christmas lights enough to blind you. Close enough." She moved behind him to block any retreat. "I'm right behind you."

Will went up the gangplank. Stepped onto the boat. Stopped when he saw the mistletoe she'd hung from the string of lights right overhead.

"Mistletoe?" he said, turning back to her.

"It's traditional this time of year."

"Only if you're intending to kiss somebody. Are you planning on kissing somebody?"

She couldn't be certain, but she thought he was trying not to smile. Which made her slightly less nervous. But only slightly. "That kind of depends."

"On what?"

"On whether you'll accept my apology."

"For being an asshole?" he said.

"For that. And for being an idiot. I—" Her throat had gone dry. She swallowed hard, tried again. "I got scared."

"Because of the fire."

"Partly. But I was scared before then. Too scared to see what was in front of me."

"And what was that?"

"You," she said simply. "A man who I hope might be in love with me. I had one of those once before. Adam . . . Adam was a good man. And I loved him. And I lost him. Losing him broke me in so many ways that I didn't realize when I'd managed to put myself back together again. Didn't see that I was ready to fall in love a second time. All I saw was the risk that I might get broken all over again."

"And that scared you," Will said softly.

"Yes."

"Does it still scare you?"

"A little. But a very smart guy told me that you should feel the fear and do it anyway."

"I see." His hand had found her hand, somehow, fingers tangling in hers. "Do you think you'd be less scared if you knew for sure that I was in love with you?"

"Maybe," she said. "Though I'm not sure why you would be when you know what a mess I am."

"Because you're my kind of mess," he said. "Because

the first time I saw you, I thought you were one of the most beautiful things I'd ever seen. I didn't know you then. I know you now. And now I know you're better than beautiful. You're brave and funny and yes, sometimes, a bit of an idiot. A gorgeous mess."

She was crying again. Why was she crying?

"Don't cry," he said. "I'm about to tell you I love you."

"I think you just did," she managed. She swiped at her eyes with the end of her scarf.

"I love you, Mina Harper," he said. "I know that I don't much like water and you don't much like whiskey but maybe we can meet somewhere in the middle?"

"I guess whiskey's not so bad. Just don't expect me to drink it."

"I can live with that. As long as you don't expect to turn me into a sailor. Deal?"

"Deal." She smiled at him. "You said we could be a Christmas miracle. Maybe we can just be a Christmas mess instead?"

"What exactly is a Christmas mess?"

"Something shiny and real and hopeful? Something that lasts." She didn't know if she was making any sense at all. But he was smiling at her now.

"That sounds perfect to me," he said. "So, Mina Harper, do you want to be my Christmas mess?"

"Yes," she said, before he could take it back. "And I think you should stop wasting my perfectly good mistletoe." Then she reached up to kiss the man she loved.